LIAR'S BEACH

ALSO BY KATIE COTUGNO

Birds of California

Rules for Being a Girl

You Say It First

9 Days and 9 Nights

Top Ten

Fireworks

99 Days

How to Love

KATIE COTUGNO

EMBER

Produced by Alloy Entertainment

Text copyright © 2023 by Katie Cotugno and Alloy Entertainment
Cover photograph copyright 2024 © by Paul Tessier/Stocksy

All rights reserved. Published in the United States by Ember, an imprint of Random House Children's Books, a division of Penguin Random House LLC, New York. Originally published in hardcover in the United States by Delacorte Press, an imprint of Random House Children's Books, a division of Penguin Random House LLC, New York, in 2023.

Ember and the E colophon are registered trademarks of Penguin Random House LLC.

GetUnderlined.com

Educators and librarians, for a variety of teaching tools,
visit us at RHTeachersLibrarians.com

Library of Congress Cataloging-in-Publication Data is available upon request.
ISBN 978-0-593-43328-7 (trade) — ISBN 978-0-593-43330-0 (ebook) —
ISBN 978-0-593-43331-7 (pbk.)

Printed in the United States of America
1st Printing
First Ember Edition 2024

FOR CHARLES JUDE, MY FAVORITE MYSTERY

1

TEN DAYS BEFORE THE POLICE CARS CRUISED SILENTLY down the driveway at August House and we all became a national news story, Jasper picked me up at the ferry in Vineyard Haven.

"There he is," Jasper called, slouching elegantly against the driver's side door of the Mercedes in sunglasses and a crisp white button-down rolled to the elbows. He looked like a magazine ad for a cologne called Entitlement. "What's up, Linden?" He grabbed my duffel, tossing it carelessly into the back of the forest-green coupe. "I thought you were coming in last night."

The buttery leather of the passenger seat was cool through my T-shirt as I slid into the car. "Ferry was full," I lied. In fact, one of the other checkers at the grocery where I'd been working since June needed a shift covered, and even though I was technically done for the summer—the dorms at Bartley opened in two weeks—I wasn't in any position to be turning down the cash. It wasn't the first money-related fib I'd told Jasper, or any of our friends from boarding school in Northampton. And, in all likelihood, it wouldn't be the last.

Jasper shrugged, incurious. "Well, I'm glad you're here, anyway. How's your foot?"

I wiggled my pale, skinny-looking ankle, just recently liberated from its fiberglass boot. "Still attached." Then, not particularly wanting to talk about it, I raised my eyebrows. "What about you? Summer as dire as you thought it would be?"

"Total fucking snoozer," Jasper said, peeling out of the parking lot. "Every day I think about committing a murder just to spice things up." He glanced at me out of the corner of his eye. "I'll try to control myself now that you're here, I guess."

"Gentlemanly of you."

"Yeah, well, I'm a gentleman."

We cruised through Vineyard Haven, passing mom-and-pop clam shacks nestled between luxury boutiques and Michelin-star restaurants. I'd been to Martha's Vineyard once before, as a little kid; some guy my mom was dating at the time had a summer rental in Edgartown and invited us out for the weekend. I think he was auditioning to be my new dad and spent forty-eight hours calling me *bud* and trying to convince me to toss a Frisbee around with him. In retaliation I accidentally-on-purpose stepped on a jellyfish and spent most of the weekend reading waterlogged mysteries under an umbrella, scowling as hard as I possibly could.

"How was the internship?" Jasper asked now, turning down the volume on the radio. The Mercedes was glamorously vintage enough that it didn't have Bluetooth, static crackling intermittently as we reached the outskirts of town. It was more rural here than I remembered, dense woods out one window and long stretches of beach out the other, the haunted Gatsby green of summer exploding all around us.

"What?" I blinked. "Oh, it was fine. Also extremely fucking boring." That was an invention too, an internship at a law firm in Post Office Square back at home. It was a stupid lie, the kind of thing that was easily fact-checked, but back at the beginning of the summer, Jasper kept making noise about coming to visit me in Boston, and it helped to have an excuse about why I was too busy.

We pulled off the main road and cruised for another ten minutes down a winding dirt lane, the occasional flare of sunlight sneaking through the dense, leafy canopy overhead. Every once in a while we passed what I assumed were private driveways, but for the most part the effect was more *remote wilderness* than *island paradise.* I was just starting to wonder if maybe I'd misunderstood what he'd said about his parents' place being at the beach when all at once the landscape opened up and there it was, standing tall and grand and enormous against the shocking blue sky.

"So," Jasper said, "this is August House."

"Uh." I cleared my throat. "Sweet." Over the last few years I'd gotten pretty good at not acting impressed by other people's giant houses, but I had to work to keep a straight face as he pulled into the circular drive, crushed seashells crunching under the wheels of the convertible. August House was a massive old white-shingled situation with a wide wraparound porch and a second-floor balcony and an actual, honest-to-god turret, plus a widow's walk up on the roof. Hydrangeas lined the walkway in an explosion of pink and blue and purple. An American flag flapped cheerily in the breeze.

I tried not to gape as I climbed out of the passenger seat, Jasper killing the engine and tucking the keys up under the visor. "Leave that," he said when I reached for my duffel. "Dean will bring it up."

I had no idea who Dean was, but I slung the bag over my shoulder anyway and followed Jasper through a white wooden gate and past a meticulously tended vegetable garden off to the side of the house. Out in the backyard was a giant bean-shaped pool flanked by a neat row of wooden lounge chairs and a covered patio housing a table with seating for twelve at least. A gap in the tall green hedges led to a staircase directly down to the beach: I could hear the waves crashing, smell the sharp brine of the ocean.

"Linden is here," Jasper announced, opening a second gate onto the pool deck.

Wells saluted from the water, where he was floating on an enormous inflatable raft shaped like a unicorn, his pale skin gone summer tan. "Hey, bro," he called, "what's up?"

"Not much." I grinned. Jasper's brother had graduated from Bartley two years earlier, back when we were freshmen. He was a business major at Harvard now, though according to Jasper, he spent most of his time getting drunk at the Owl Clubhouse on Holyoke Street. "Nice ride."

"Thinking about entering her in the Head of the Charles this year," he replied, then nodded at a guy sprawled on a lounge chair in a pair of lime-green swim trunks. "That's Doc; he lives down the beach. Doc, Linden; Linden, Doc. Linden's first name isn't Linden. Doc's first name isn't Doc."

I looked across the patio in not-entirely-pleasant surprise. "We . . . actually know each other," I confessed.

"I mean, not formally." Doc extended a smooth brown hand in my direction. "What's up, dude?"

"Oh shit," Jasper said before I could answer, "that's right, you guys are both lax nerds." He grinned. "There's definitely a joke in there about like, sticks and balls or some fucking thing, so just pretend it was funny, okay?"

"We always pretend you're funny," Doc reminded him, but his dark eyes were on me as we shook. "You still starting for Bartley this fall?" he asked. "I heard you busted your ankle back in the spring."

"Oh yeah," I managed with what I hoped was a casual shake of my head, "for sure." Doc was a star attackman for Ashcroft, a boarding school down in Rhode Island; he'd basically crushed us in last year's championship game, and that was when I'd been in the best physical condition of my entire life. The thought of facing him on the field after a summer spent hobbling back and forth to physical therapy made me feel slightly queasy. "It was no big deal. All good now."

Jasper nodded at his twin sister, Eliza, who was sitting at the patio table along with a redhead I didn't recognize, a hand of gin rummy laid out between them. "You guys know each other too, right?" he asked.

Eliza waved from across the yard. "Oh," she called, "Linden and I go way back."

"Old friends," I agreed. In fact, we'd only met a couple of

times before—once when the Kendricks had come to Bartley for Wells's graduation, and another time when she'd taken the train out to stay with some friend of hers in the girls' dorm and tagged along with us to a party. She lived at home with her parents in Connecticut, I knew, and was some kind of northeast horseback-riding champion. Last year Jasper had a photo pinned to his bulletin board of his whole family at one of her meets, Eliza in the full outfit with the breeches and helmet and everything like she was a nineteenth-century British archduke, but right now she was wearing sunglasses and a gingham bikini, her dark blond hair just skimming her shoulders. I glanced at her, then back at the others. Glanced at her again.

"I'm Meredith," the redhead volunteered pointedly.

Jasper smirked. "And that's Meredith," he admitted, and I waved. "Come on," he continued, "I'll give you the tour."

I followed him across the patio, past an outdoor kitchen with a built-in grill and through the sliding glass door into the cool, quiet house. "Meredith's parents used to have a place nearby, but they sold it last year," he informed me, "which means she's been at our house, like. All. Fucking. Summer."

"Uh-oh," I said with a laugh. His voice suggested either a decades-long blood feud or a vacation hookup gone bad. "Did you guys, like . . . ?"

"Oh, *fuck* no," Jasper said, like the very thought of it had his dick shriveling up in horror. "She's had a boyfriend since the Stone Age. And they're both idiots." He shrugged, reaching down to pet the golden retriever snoozing in a monogrammed bed near the mudroom. "This is Whimsy," he told me. "Come on, this way."

I'd had it in my head that beach houses were sort of scruffy, full of cast-off furniture and yellowing sci-fi paperbacks, but the Kendricks' looked freshly renovated, with huge picture windows framing a view of the ocean and an open kitchen that would have made my mom weep with pleasure. Right away I was worried about spilling something, even though I wasn't holding anything I could possibly spill.

Jas led me through the dining room and into the living room, past an actual library with built-in bookcases lining the three walls that didn't look out over the garden. And it all just kept going: we passed a study and a sunroom and a den with a projector screen, the sectional so wide and deep I had to physically stop myself from face-planting directly onto it and passing out until school started. August House was the kind of place where any number of people could stay for an indefinite length of time without anyone noticing—not like the apartment I shared with my mom back in East Boston, where my aunt Rosie had come to visit over Christmas and left her bras draped over the shower-curtain rod for days on end, the scent of her perfume hanging thickly in the air.

We traipsed up a flight of steps and down a long hallway, then turned and climbed another staircase that doubled back on itself until finally we got to a bedroom with walls that curved gently on two sides—the turret room, I realized, the one I'd seen from outside.

"Sorry it's so small," Jasper said, though it was bigger than both my room at home and the one we'd shared freshman year at Bartley, when we'd first been roommates. "Meredith is hogging the good guest room, since, you know, she lives with us now."

I shook my head. "Dude, it's fine." The bed was an intricately carved four-poster, the duvet cover a cheery blue-and-white stripe. A quartet of framed botanical prints hung on the far wall.

"They're poisonous," Jas said when he saw me looking at them.

"Huh?"

"The plants," he explained, gesturing with his chin. "Foxglove, hogweed, hemlock, stinging nettle. Those drawings are all over the house. My mom bought this whole collection of them from some botanist's estate sale in Newport, then got them home and some friend of hers was like, *Hey, dumbass, you realize the unifying theme of those flowers is that every single one of them is extremely fucking lethal.* But by then she'd already paid her decorator to come and hang them." He shrugged. "Anyway, your bathroom is around the corner. Just be careful because you have to hold the flusher down an extra minute if you take a shit."

I nodded. "Thanks for the tip."

"No problem. Meet you down at the pool." He shut the door behind him, his footsteps thundering down the narrow staircase. "Glad you're here, dude!"

Once he was gone, I looked at the plants for a moment longer, telling myself there was no reason to feel the tiniest bit creeped out by their graceful leaves and delicate, dangerous flowers. Then I changed into my bathing suit and headed downstairs.

2

JASPER'S PARENTS TOOK US ALL INTO TOWN FOR DIN-
ner that night. "Last one into the car is buying lobsters!" Mr. Kendrick called, putting one foot up on a kitchen chair and bending
to tie the laces on his boat shoes. I liked the Kendricks: They had
a matched-set quality to them that made me think of the lovebirds
our downstairs neighbor, Mrs. Le, kept in a cage in her dining
room. They even sort of looked alike, tall and thin with the kind
of casual tans you get from morning tennis and the occasional afternoon drive with the top down. Both of them looked extremely
hale.

We were tromping out to the cars when Mrs. Kendrick put a
hand on my arm, pulling me back into the tidy mudroom away
from the others. "Linden, honey," she said, "I just wanted to tell
you how glad we are that you could come stay. And to thank you
for being such a good friend to Jasper."

"Oh yeah, of course," I said quickly. "He's a good friend to
me too."

Mrs. Kendrick nodded. "He went through a lot this year," she continued. "I mean, we all did, obviously, but—" She broke off, letting go and waving her hand like she was batting something away. "Anyway. I'm being maudlin. We're happy you're here." She patted my shoulder. "Let's go eat fried fish."

"Okay," I said, a little confused. I knew there'd been some drama at the Kendricks' last year—Jasper's dad had gotten sued, I was pretty sure, though I wasn't sure why or for what and hadn't wanted to ask too much about it, even though obviously I wondered. But as a general rule, I tried not to ask my friends from Bartley too many questions, in the hope that they would take the hint and return the favor. "Yeah. Thanks for having me."

Dinner was at a seafood shack called Red's that Mrs. Kendrick had been going to since she was a little kid—the kind of dive that rich people on vacation can't get enough of, with colorful Christmas lights hung on the wall behind the bar and the smell of cornmeal batter thick in the air. They didn't take reservations, so we sat on a bench outside for half an hour while Wells napped with his head back against the faded red shingles and Jasper and Eliza complained about the wait. Meredith was texting furiously, her red hair like a theater curtain around her face. The sight of her thumbs flying over the screen reminded me I'd forgotten to let my mom know I wasn't dead at the bottom of the Atlantic Ocean, and I was pulling my own phone out of my pocket when Eliza looked at me suddenly, like she'd just remembered I was there. "So, Linden," she said, "you're from Boston?"

I nodded, knowing she'd assume Beacon Hill or Comm Ave, or maybe someplace like Brookline or Arlington that wasn't actually Boston at all. "Born and raised," I admitted.

"Are you obsessed with Tom Brady?"

"Fuck Tom Brady," I said without thinking, then whipped around to look guiltily at Mr. and Mrs. Kendrick. "Um. I mean—"

But Mrs. Kendrick only smiled. "Fuck Tom Brady," she echoed primly, and everybody burst out laughing; after a moment, I started laughing too.

They were easy to be around, the Kendricks. Don't get me wrong, my own mom was great—it's not like I was Harry Potter, living alone under a staircase and waiting for Bartley's answer to the Weasleys to come rescue me—but I'd always kind of wanted to be part of a big family, especially one as golden and unencumbered as this. It was easy to imagine the five of them rolling matching luggage across the tarmac en route to a family vacation in Mallorca or sitting around the tree drinking fancy champagne on Christmas morning. Gliding sleekly through life like a fleet of tidy sailboats, no drag on any of them at all.

"So what's the prognosis, Linden?" Mr. Kendrick asked once we'd finally been seated and ordered our dinners. It was loud in here, the dull roar of voices and laughter and clanking beer bottles echoing off the wooden-plank walls and sharply pitched ceiling. The Doobie Brothers crooned over the speakers behind the bar. "Are we going to see you tearing it up out there in the fall?"

"Dad," Jasper said, shaking his head. "He doesn't want to talk about—"

"No, it's okay." I nodded. Six months ago I'd been hooking up with a senior from Bartley named Greer, who had a crooked incisor tooth and the softest hair I'd ever felt on a human person. One Friday night in March we'd driven into town to see a movie at the second-run theater, and on the way back a deer jumped into the road. Greer swerved and hit a tree instead, and I came to in the passenger seat a couple minutes later with a motherfucker of a concussion and a right ankle smashed to what could politely be called smithereens.

At least, that was what we'd told everyone had happened.

"Prognosis is good," I said now, smiling gamely: another lie. The prognosis was middling at best, but that wasn't the kind of thing that people want to hear when they ask you about a sports injury, and it definitely wasn't something I wanted to announce. I hadn't talked to anybody about it—not even Jasper knew—but I was at Bartley on a full scholarship, the terms of which dictated that I maintain a 3.5 grade point average and play two-season lacrosse every fall and spring. To put it more bluntly: no lacrosse, no scholarship. Not to mention the glaring fact that if I had any hope of being scouted by colleges, I needed to be back on the field in September, just a few weeks away, not hobbling through my workouts and wincing in agony at every drill. Thinking about it was the kind of thing that had me waking up in the middle of the night, sweating through my sheets, so mostly I tried not to think about it at all.

"Well," Mr. Kendrick said now, "I'm glad to hear it. God knows we need you if we're going to finally beat Andover this year."

"I'm working on it," I promised cheerfully. Mr. Kendrick grinned.

Our food came just then, a mountain of shrimp and scallops and oysters, whole lobsters with little ramekins of butter for dunking and plastic bibs to wear over your shirt. I went to work on a paper boat of fish and chips while Jasper told a long and convoluted story about a kid we knew from school who'd sunk his entire trust fund into a hydroponic weed operation, and I tried not to notice the same thing I'd noticed about a lot of my friends from school, which was that they could be total douchebags to service staff. Meredith in particular was doing that thing people do when they've never had a job waiting tables, asking for one thing at a time so the waitress had to make a million separate trips to get them for her: first tartar sauce, then lemons, then a stack of extra napkins. It reminded me of that picture book my mom used to read to me, about the mouse who gets a cookie and then wants a glass of milk.

"Could I get some more seltzer?" she asked now, rattling the ice in her mostly full cup. Then, once she had it: "Whoops. A slice of lime for it too?"

"Sure," the waitress said, smiling tightly. She was about our age, with curly blond hair pulled back into a complicated, tricky-looking braid. Her uniform tank top was made to look like a jersey, with *Red's* scrawled in looping script across the back. "Anything else?"

Meredith smiled an airy smile. "That's it for now," she said, "but I'm sure I'll think of something."

"I'm sure you will," the waitress agreed. "Just shout."

Once she was gone, Jasper shot Meredith a look across the table. "Was that really necessary?" he asked. He looked personally affronted, though I suspected it had significantly less to do with the demands themselves than with how cute the waitress was. Jasper had always liked blondes.

"What?" Meredith looked at him blankly, then glanced down at her French fries and frowned, waving her hand to get the waitress's attention one more time. "Sorry!" she called out, though she sounded the opposite of remorseful; for the first time, it occurred to me that she might be doing this—whatever it was she was doing—on purpose, and not just because she was an oblivious princess. "Ketchup!"

This time, though, the waitress shook her head. "Sorry," she echoed, somehow managing to mimic Meredith's tone of voice exactly. "We're all out."

Meredith looked at her dubiously. "All out of *ketchup*?" she asked.

The waitress shrugged. "Wouldn't you know it," she said, "somebody else just got the last bottle."

I blinked at the waitress, quietly impressed. I'd worked in restaurants every summer before this one—you can't wait tables in a fiberglass boot—and I knew that feeling intimately, the deep and abiding urge to tell another person to go fuck themselves. I'd never actually had the balls to do it, and technically, this girl wasn't doing it either; still, she was a hell of a lot closer than I'd ever been. There was no way whatever was happening between them wasn't at least a little bit personal. "Dude," I muttered to Jasper, "why do I get the feeling this conversation isn't actually about condiments?"

Jasper rolled his eyes, then turned and smiled crookedly at the waitress. "Don't ask."

"Here," Eliza said once the waitress was gone, then turned to the table behind ours, touching a stocky retiree gently on his sloping shoulder. "Sorry," she said sweetly. "Would you mind if we borrowed your ketchup?"

The man looked surprised for a moment, then smiled at her, his jowly face openly appreciative. "Honey," he said, handing over the bright red squeeze bottle, "you can have whatever you like."

3

"YOU GUYS UP FOR ICE CREAM?" MRS. KENDRICK ASKED as we headed out into the muggy parking lot of the restaurant. I felt myself perk up like a little kid at the offer—the shop was only a few doors down, and I could smell the cold vanilla sugar from here—but Jasper shook his head.

"We're going to go meet up with some people on the beach," he replied, which was news to me. "We'll see you guys at home."

We stopped back at August House to drop the car, then trouped out through the yard and down the sand about half a mile or so to where a group was already gathered around the orange glow of a bonfire. It was a pretty night, the setting sun streaking the sky in purple and pink and navy. The brackish smell of the ocean mixed with the sharp, woodsy scent of the smoke.

"There they are!" Doc called when he saw us. He'd swapped his neon bathing suit out for a hoodie, though it was still pretty warm even at nine o'clock. "Was wondering if you all were going to show up or what."

"Obviously," Eliza said, popping up on her toes to give him

a hug. I rubbed idly at the back of my neck, swallowing down a sudden flicker of jealousy. "We like to make an entrance, is all."

"He's just hoping we brought more booze," Jasper said, dropping a scratchy-looking wool blanket onto the sand.

"I mean," Doc said with a lopsided grin, "that too."

We settled in. Wells unzipped the nylon cooler he'd carried down from the house, passing out beers like a tall, skinny Santa Claus. Jasper introduced me to a bunch of his Vineyard friends. The whole thing was a little too sprawling and relaxed to qualify as an actual party: people coming and going, groups spreading out and breaking up before wandering back together again. We ran into a couple of underclassmen from Bartley whose parents had a place in Chilmark; a girl Meredith and Eliza knew from their yoga studio stopped by with a bottle of fancy tequila. The fire spat and crackled, glowing sparks flying up into the air.

"You're quiet," Eliza observed, strolling up beside me with a beer bottle dangling from her fingertips, clinking the neck of it softly against mine.

I shook my head. "Just taking it all in."

"You are, aren't you?" She raised her eyebrows. "Better watch what I say."

"Why," I asked with a grin, "were you planning on confessing to something?"

"Maybe." Eliza winked.

Maybe. She was a beautiful girl, Eliza. I was just trying to work up the stones to ask if she wanted to go for a walk when I heard a familiar voice behind me: "Michael?" it called, and I whirled right the fuck around. Nobody but my mom called me by my first name—nobody, that is, except one person, and there she was, coming out of the darkness like an apparition from an entirely different world.

"Holiday," I said, feeling deeply and immediately like I'd been caught doing something I wasn't supposed to be doing. My mom had worked for Holiday's parents since we were both little kids, cooking their meals and cleaning their bathrooms and accepting their deliveries at their enormous Victorian house in Cambridge. My first memory was of Holiday accidentally slamming my fingers in the door of their linen closet, both of us screaming bloody murder. The ring finger of my right hand was still kind of weird and crooked at the tip. "Um, hey."

"Hey yourself." She wrapped me in a tight, unselfconscious hug that smelled like farmer's market bar soap and a little bit like weed. "What are you doing here?" she asked, letting me go and smiling over my shoulder at the group.

"Just, uh, staying with some friends from school," I said, motioning vaguely behind me at Eliza and Jasper and Meredith, who were looking at us curiously. Holiday barely had time to offer them a friendly little wave before I ushered her down the beach, lest she expect me to do anything insane like introduce her. "You?"

"My folks have a place here," she explained. The breeze was blowing her dark, curly hair all around, and she gathered it up in one hand for a moment, like she was trying to see me better, before letting it go again. "I'm surprised your mom didn't mention it, actually."

My mom *had* mentioned it, I remembered suddenly: "You

should text Holiday," she'd said when I told her I was coming to stay with the Kendricks; then, when I hadn't answered: "Michael? Are you listening to me?" I'd grunted a noise of acknowledgment and then immediately forgotten, the way you don't bother to store information that has no bearing on your actual life.

"Yeah," I said now. "I'm surprised she didn't too."

Holiday nodded. She looked older, which I guessed made sense since I hadn't seen her at all in the three years since I'd started at Bartley. She was also a full click prettier than I remembered, but it made me feel weird and honestly kind of perverted to notice that, like trying to get a secret look at your cousin in her underwear at your grandparents' house over Thanksgiving break. Not that Holiday was walking along the beach in her underwear. She wasn't even wearing a bathing suit. She was dressed in a loose-fitting black overalls–type situation made out of linen or something—the kind of getup our art teacher, Ms. Singh, would have worn to teach us about Dadaism in an overly enthusiastic tone of voice. Her lipstick was very, very red.

Neither one of us said anything for another moment, a pause that went on just slightly too long not to be weird. I racked my brain for a non-douchey way to bail out. It wasn't that I wasn't glad to see her, exactly—she'd been my best friend, until puberty—but I'd spent the last three years at Bartley doing everything humanly possible to separate my home life from my school life, and a thing I remembered very clearly about Holiday was that back when we were kids, she'd been the kind of person you could always rely on to say the quiet part out loud. I could just imagine it now: *Hi, I'm*

Holiday Proctor! Michael's mom washes my unmentionables for a living. I'd worked too hard to fit in with these people. I'd worked too hard, period, to risk her messing it up.

"Well, it was cool to run into you." I reached out to touch her arm in a friendly way, only I kind of accidentally punched her instead, like we were on the same high school football team in 1950. Fuck, I needed to get out of this conversation. "I guess I'll see you around," I said at the same time that Holiday said, "We should get coffee and catch up for real."

"Oh!" I froze. "Um, yeah, totally."

"I mean, only if you want to," she said, looking at me a little strangely. "No pressure, et cetera."

"No, no, that sounds great," I lied. In fact, it did not sound great—it sounded awkward and boring and like a waste of an hour I could otherwise be spending at the beach or in the pool or taking a particularly luxurious bathroom break—but then I thought about what my mom would say if she found out I'd blown Holiday off after all this time, and found myself nodding like a dashboard bobblehead doll on a particularly bumpy stretch of road. "Day after tomorrow, maybe?" I hoped the whole thing might slip her mind by then, though it seemed unlikely. Holiday had always been like an elephant that way: she never forgot.

"Sure thing." She smiled, toothy and sincere. "Let's do it."

"Who was that?" Jasper asked when I rejoined the group. They were sprawled in various states of repose on the blanket, passing around a flask that Wells had pulled out of his hoodie pocket.

I shook my head. "Just somebody I know from home."

"Long-lost love?" He waggled his eyebrows.

"Fuck you," I replied. I wasn't sure which one of us he was making fun of, Holiday or me, or if he wasn't making fun of either one of us and I was just being touchy. I glanced uneasily over my shoulder, but Holiday had rejoined her friends down at the far end of the beach. She was probably just as glad to be rid of me as I was of her, I reassured myself: after all, nobody in their right mind wanted the son of the household help crashing their tony beach vacation. And granted, Holiday had never once treated me that way in all the time we'd spent together, but what did I know? I hadn't talked to Holiday in years. "Our moms know each other."

Jasper nodded distractedly. I was worried he'd press me, but he didn't seem to care, handing me the flask and taking a hit from the joint that Wells was holding out. "Sit down," he instructed. "We're playing Lies."

"Okay," I said with a laugh, the liquor burning in my throat and chest. "What are the rules, just lie your fucking face off?"

"Exactly," Eliza confirmed. "We used to do Two Truths to go along with it, but that got boring, so we trimmed the fat."

"Very market-focused of you," I said.

Eliza smiled. "Thank you."

"The trick is to make them believable," Jasper explained, a halo of smoke around his face. "So, for instance, if I were to say, *I saw Wells jerking off to a picture of a prominent Republican senator in women's underwear,* you would say, *Yeah, that seems legit,* and—"

"Fuck you," Wells said, but he was laughing. "I'll have you know he was wearing a suit, like a gentleman."

"Best lie wins," Jasper said cheerfully. "Doc, you start."

Doc nodded. "Let's see," he said, leaning back on his palms

and crossing his ankles, his canny gaze flicking around the circle before finally lighting on me. "When he's not getting his ass fully trounced at lacrosse, Linden lives a double life back in Boston as a part-time hot dog vendor at Fenway and an extra in Masshole movies directed by Ben Affleck."

I burst out laughing along with the rest of the group, trying to ignore the embarrassment and annoyance flaming in my face. Doc was kidding around, obviously—that was how the game worked—but hadn't Jasper just said the whole point was to make your lies believable? Also, fuck that guy! He'd beaten me at lacrosse *one time*. Still, "I actually work the drive-through at a Dunkin' Donuts in Dorchester," I corrected as good-naturedly as I could manage, reaching for the flask and wondering for the hundred thousandth time if that was how I seemed to these people, like some sweatsuit-wearing stereotype. If it was how I seemed to Eliza. "Have some respect." I turned to Jasper. "So what, it's my turn now?"

We played a few rounds, Eliza accusing Jasper of sending dick pics to the perpetually sweat-stained woman who airbrushed souvenir T-shirts at a kiosk in town and Wells suggesting Doc sat down to pee. When it was Jasper's turn, though, he didn't hesitate. "Meredith," he said grandly, turning to where she was perched on a hollowed-out log, scrolling her phone industriously; I wasn't sure if I was imagining that something in his voice suggested he'd been waiting for this opportunity, had perhaps even orchestrated the entire game with it in mind. "*Meredith* spends her days desperately trying to avoid getting chlamydia from her cocksmack boyfriend because, apparently, she's too stupid to cop onto what everybody else with two brain cells already knows, which is that the only person he's ever given a steaming shit about is himself." He paused, then frowned theatrically. "Whoops," he said, "sorry. For a second I forgot that was supposed to be a lie."

Meredith didn't laugh. Neither, to our small credit, did anyone else, all of us staring slack-jawed across the circle at the way the air had suddenly changed; I had never, in all the time I'd known him, heard Jasper say anything like that to anyone. "Fuck you, Jasper," Meredith said, her green eyes flashing; she got to her feet, jamming her phone into her shorts pocket and stalking off across the sand.

"Fuck *you*, Meredith," Jasper called after her. "You have a good night, now!"

Eliza scrambled upright. "Why do you have to be like this?" she asked Jasper, her whole body coiled with temper. "For fuck's sake, she's not even the one who *did* anything."

"She fucks around with that guy, and then she comes back to our house—to *Dad's* house—and eats our cereal," Jasper shot back immediately. "Personally, that's enough for me."

Eliza shook her head. "You're an asshole," she announced, then turned and headed off across the beach after Meredith, kicking up sand as she went.

Once she was gone, I looked around the circle for an explanation, but none seemed to be forthcoming. Jasper was reaching for the flask, looking a little bit sheepish; Wells was whistling the chorus to "We Are Family" under his breath. "Okay," I muttered to Doc finally, "what the fuck just happened?"

"Dude," he said quietly, "you don't want to know."

The shine kind of came off the game after that, but we stayed where we were anyway—getting progressively drunker, talking cheerful trash. I figured Eliza had followed Meredith back up to the house, but at some point I glanced down the beach and spotted her a few hundred yards away, sitting in the dunes, looking out at the dark, endless water. I got up and headed over; she'd sifted through the sand until she found a flat, round seashell, was turning it over and over her knuckles like she was practicing a coin trick. "What happened to your friend?" I asked as I approached.

Eliza shrugged. "She left."

"To . . . go see the cocksmack?" I asked.

That made her smile, but only faintly. "We used to all be so close," she told me softly, pushing her sea-swept hair out of her face. "Us, and Meredith's family, and the Hollimans—Greg Holliman, that's the cocksmack in question. Our parents grew up together, you know? We used to spend all day together every single summer and then go sleep at each other's houses at night. And I thought it would always be like that—like eventually we'd all grow up and bring our own kids out here and they'd all grow up and marry each other and bring *their* kids, just like our parents had." She shook her head, like she couldn't believe her own stupidity. "So incestuous, right?"

It was, but it wasn't unusual. A thing I'd learned at Bartley was that the same complicated, sprawling rich-person ecosystems that got undeserving people into the Ivy League and elected to the presidency also operated in a thousand smaller, more pedantic ways. Even the ones who didn't know each other from decades of idyllic summers on the Vineyard might as well have: They docked their boats at the same marinas and boarded their horses at the same stables, played tennis and golf at the same exclusive country clubs. They spoke the same dialect. I spoke it too now, sort of, though I was still working to train the accent—*Fuck Tom Brady,* I thought with a grimace—out of my voice. "Maybe a little incestuous," I agreed.

"Incestuous and delusional, it turns out." She glanced at me sidelong. "Greg's dad is the one who flipped, in case that wasn't abundantly clear."

I hesitated, not wanting to let on that I wasn't totally sure what she was talking about.

"In the . . . court case?" I finally guessed.

Eliza nodded. "He and my dad had the same financial advisor," she explained. "Greg's dad was the one who hooked our dad up with him in the first place. And then when everything happened, Greg's dad made a deal with the DA. He got probation and community service, on the condition that he testified." She shoved the shell back down into the sand, like the blade of a knife. "Our dad got ten months in jail."

Holy shit. I did everything I could to keep my face neutral just then, but my brain was ricocheting wildly around inside my head. Suddenly a million tiny, seemingly insignificant moments fell neatly into place: Mr. Kendrick's conspicuous absence from family weekend last semester. The way Mrs. Kendrick had thanked me earlier tonight. The random, midweek trip home Jasper had taken right around the time of my accident, even though it was only a couple of weeks until reading period.

Eliza was still looking at me, expectant: "Yeah," I said finally, not wanting to let on that I hadn't known. "That's . . . fucked up." Right away I wondered what else I didn't know about the

Kendricks, what else Jasper had kept to himself in the three years we'd been roommates. It made me feel a little shitty that he hadn't trusted me enough to tell me what was going on.

On the other hand: I guess there were a lot of things I hadn't trusted him with either.

"Yeah," Eliza said now, sinking back onto her elbows and tilting her chin up, gazing at the dark, velvety sky. "It wasn't great. I mean, it would have been one thing if Greg had just been like, *Hey, sorry my dad's a giant weeping dick who ruined your lives,* but instead he just decided to like, lean into every single one of his worst impulses? Which meant, of course, that my brothers did too."

"Woof," I said, glancing back in Jasper's direction. "And Meredith stayed with Greg anyway?"

"I mean, they've been together forever," Eliza pointed out, "and it's not like *her* dad went to federal prison. Also, apparently, he's amazing at oral sex, although that has always seemed like an *incredibly* dubious claim to me." She grinned, presumably at the blush that was making its way up the back of my neck and migrating around to my face. "It would have been nice to have a little bit more loyalty on her part, but what was I going to do, tell her she couldn't stay here? She's spent basically just as much time at this house as I have." She trailed her hand through the sand for a moment, sifting it through her fingers. "I don't know. I guess there was a part of me that thought maybe this summer would be a way for us all to find our way back to each other, but instead it's just been, like, an eight-week emotional horror show the likes of which all of us will probably be working out in therapy for the rest of our adult lives." She cleared her throat then, a little bit sheepish. *"Anyway,"* she said, "sorry to word vomit all over you. You came out here for a vacation, not to listen to some random girl tell you all her champagne problems."

I don't know why I didn't contradict her. To this day, I wonder what would have happened if I had—if I'd looked at her that first night in the moonlight and said, *I want to know everything you want to tell me; I want to hear everything you have to say.* If maybe it would have changed everything that went down afterward. If maybe it would have saved us both.

Instead I waited a beat too long and the moment slipped by as silent as a submarine, the two of us staring out at the water. I tipped my head back and breathed in the smell of salt water and woodsmoke, catching sight of August House glowing warmly on top of the bluff like a beacon for passing ships. It didn't *look* like the kind of place where anyone's dad got jammed up by the law, that was for sure. I wanted to think I was immune to that kind of stuff—the romance of it, or whatever—but after what had happened with Greer, I knew I wasn't. It worked on me sometimes, like a witch doing a glamour spell. It made it so I couldn't see what was happening right in front of my face.

All at once Eliza stood up, brushing the sand off the seat of her shorts and pulling her tank top up over her head. "I'm going in," she announced. Her features were just visible in the gleam of the bonfire as she took off in the direction of the water, her body half in shadow, half in light. Right at the line of the surf she looked behind her, holding her hand out. "You coming or what?" she hollered.

I laughed. "I'm coming," I told her, reaching back and yanking off my T-shirt. I chased after her into the dark, chilly waves.

We all stumbled up from the beach sometime around two-thirty, Eliza catching my hand as we tumbled through the back door of August House. Her fingers were chilly against mine as she peeled me away from the rest of the group and pulled me up the back stairs from the kitchen, then down the hall and around a corner before pausing at the doorway of her bedroom, her narrow back flattened against the jamb.

"Hi," she said.

I smiled, leaning against the wall partly to look cool and casual and partly to keep myself upright. "Hi." Over her shoulder I could see a full bed with a fluffy white duvet cover, a canvas-covered reading chair big enough for two people at least. The air smelled like sunscreen and like girl. I could hear everyone else trying to be stealthy as they settled down—the floorboards groaning in protest, someone tripping on the stairs.

"Shh!" I heard Jasper hiss, but when I looked back at Eliza, she wasn't laughing.

"You should try to kiss me goodnight," she advised.

The floor pitched a little, the beer and the anticipation. I hadn't kissed anyone since Greer. "I should, huh?"

Eliza nodded, taking a step closer so our chests were almost touching. I reached out and curled one hand around her waist. She tipped her face up to mine, lowered her eyelashes—and feinted at the very last second, turning her head so I caught her cheek instead.

"I said you should *try,*" she reminded me with a smile, then reached down and yanked my belt loop before stepping back inside her bedroom and shutting the door behind her.

I stood there for a moment, my forehead against the doorjamb, the hallway starting to spin all around me, before shuffling up to the third floor alone. I steadied myself on the bedpost in the turret room—ugh, I was really drunk—then crossed the creaking floorboards and opened the window to the cool, salty air. I could see a sliver of beach from up here, could hear the waves slamming themselves against the rocks as the tide came in. I breathed for a minute, then blinked, my heart doing a startled, squirrelly thing inside my chest: there was somebody standing on the sand down there, face tipped up to gaze at August House.

I swallowed hard, not totally trusting what I was seeing. My brain was sloggy and forgetful sometimes since the concussion, but I'd never just fully *hallucinated,* and sure enough, the figure was still there a moment later, solid and corporeal. I squinted, trying to figure out if it was anyone I recognized. It was a guy, I thought, though I wouldn't have sworn to it, a bulky hooded sweatshirt making it impossible to tell. I glanced down at the clock on my phone: it was almost three o'clock in the morning. When I looked up again, whoever had been there was gone.

4

I WOKE UP BEFORE DAWN WITH A SAVAGE HANGOVER
pulsing at the backs of my eyeballs, my mouth cottony and gym-sock rank. I shuffled dizzily into the bathroom and drank some water out of my cupped hands, then turned the faucet on full blast and stuck my whole head underneath it for good measure. I straightened up, blinking in the blue predawn light trickling in through the window before turning toward the door and sklonking the shin of my busted leg on a decorative step stool. I swore under my breath—at least, I meant to swear under my breath, but it must have been louder than I thought because a moment later I heard a door creak open down on the second floor, the investigative click of Whimsy's nails on the hardwood followed by a set of human footsteps. Mr. Kendrick peered up at me from the landing.

"Uh-oh," he said with a laugh. He was already wearing his bathing suit, plus a light pink polo shirt and a Black Dog baseball cap. He looked like the slightly manic string-bean character in a children's cartoon about a gang of mischievous vegetables. I tried to picture him in jail—even minimum-security, country club-esque, Martha-Stewart-knitting-a-poncho kind of jail—and emphatically could not. "You kids overdo it a little bit last night?"

"Oh no," I said quickly. The last thing I wanted was to get busted for being obliterated my very first night in his house. "We weren't—I mean, we didn't—"

"Relax, Linden." Mr. Kendrick cut me off. "I was young once. And I always say to my guys, we'd rather you do it here." He smiled. "A quick jump in the ocean will sort you right out."

"Uh." I shook my head. "Thanks, but I think I'm just going to head back to bed."

"Bullshit," he said cheerfully. "Go grab your suit; I'll wait."

Which was how I wound up bobbing neck-deep in the freezing-cold Atlantic before the sun was even all the way up, my balls trying to retreat all the way into my body and my headache significantly worse than it had been when I woke up.

"Better, right?" Mr. Kendrick asked once we'd finally waded in toward shore, a spring in his step as he crossed the wet, chilly sand. I trudged along behind him, trying not to shiver. "There's nothing like it."

Birdie was already in the kitchen when we got back up to the house, coffee gurgling away in the fancy machine on the counter. "How about a couple of egg white omelets, Birdie?" Mr. Kendrick asked. "And a Bloody Mary for my friend here."

"Oh, that's okay," I said immediately, "I'm good." I'd met Birdie and her husband, Dean, the day before; they were the housekeepers and caretakers at August House, and lived on the island year-round in a cottage that had been converted from a barn down the road. Birdie was probably about my mom's age, a little older than the

Kendricks, and having her around doing stuff for me—picking up my empty water glass, setting out little enamelware bowls of chips on the patio—made me feel hugely uncomfortable.

Also, it was seven o'clock in the morning, and Bloody Marys are gross.

But Mr. Kendrick was undeterred. "Don't be ridiculous," he said in the same jocular voice he'd used to cajole me down to the beach. "Hair of the dog, et cetera." He smiled, but I couldn't tell if I was imagining something steely underneath it. All at once I remembered a phrase we'd read in history that year: *an iron fist inside a velvet glove.* Which was ridiculous, right? Even if he *had* been in prison, it wasn't like Jasper's skinny, slightly nerdy dad was about to force me to chug a vodka cocktail against my will first thing in the morning.

But: I drank the Bloody Mary.

"There you go." Mr. Kendrick nodded as Birdie slid a perfectly cooked omelet onto my plate, complete with a little tuft of parsley from the garden as a garnish. "Like I always tell the kids," he said, "better to do it in the house."

After breakfast I limped back upstairs and passed out for another hour, the kind of sweaty, restless sleep that doesn't actually make you any less tired. I probably would have kept my head stuffed underneath the pillow until noon, but Jasper banged on my door before letting himself into the bedroom and kicking lightly at the four-poster bed.

"Come on," he said, "I want to go into town and get chips and stuff for later. And the girl who works at the coffee place on Friday mornings is extremely fucking hot."

That was . . . enough to lure me out of bed, honestly. "Get more avocados," Eliza instructed as we passed through the living room. She was lying on the sofa in running shorts and a tank top, her tan feet slung over one side. "And take the big car."

Jasper pulled a face. The Kendricks had three cars that stayed on the island full-time and referred to them all by size, like the Three Bears; the big car was a Land Rover that looked like something Prince William would take on safari, but none of them liked to drive it because it handled like shit. "Why?" he asked.

"Because," Eliza replied. She wasn't looking at me; she hadn't looked at me since we'd come into the room, and I wasn't sure if it was because I'd tried to kiss her last night outside her bedroom, or because I hadn't managed to get the job done. "Meredith and I are going to yoga."

"Oh, well, in that case," Jasper said, "far be it from me to inconvenience you and *Meredith*." He said her name the same way he had yesterday, like it had spoiled in the fridge and he hadn't realized until he'd swallowed a huge mouthful. I remembered the way his easygoing features had twisted last night when we were playing Lies around the bonfire. I remembered what Eliza had told me about how everything had gone to shit.

The girl behind the counter at the coffee place was, in fact, extremely hot—though, I suspected, out of both my league and Jasper's, with dark hair braided into a rope so thick you could have used it to hoist sails, and sleeves of colorful tattoos snaking up both arms. We got bagels for second breakfast and ate them at a table outside, watching the late-morning crowds stroll by. The whole island looked like the set of a TV show about precocious teenagers trying to lose their virginity while up-tempo pop songs played in the background: the tiny bookstore, the homemade ice-cream stand, the souvenir shop with its racks of pastel sweatshirts and locally drawn postcards out front. The sidewalks were all lined with cobblestones. Brightly colored flowers spilled from terra-cotta pots.

"So," I ventured finally, swallowing the last of my bagel. All morning I'd been trying, and failing, to figure out how to bring this up casually. My hangover was mostly gone, but my head felt dull and slow from the nap; there was an anxious feeling gnawing away at my synapses, the sneaking suspicion that I had forgotten something important. "Last night at the bonfire."

Jasper raised his eyebrows behind his Wayfarers. "What about it?" he asked.

"No, nothing." I hesitated, trying to figure out a diplomatic way to say this, or if I really wanted to say it at all. "I don't know. When we were playing Lies, you just kind of seemed—"

"Like a total fucking dick?"

That made me laugh. "I mean, yeah," I agreed, relieved that he'd been the one to put it out there. "Maybe a little."

"Yeah," he admitted, leaning back in his patio chair and not sounding particularly sorry, "you're probably right."

"Eliza said—"

"Eliza said what?" Jasper's mouth thinned.

"No, no, nothing," I said quickly. "Just that you guys all used to be really good friends? You and Meredith and Greg and everybody?"

Jasper seemed to consider that for a moment. "That would be a fair assessment," he conceded, "yes."

"And now?"

I was trying to give him an opening to tell me himself what had happened with his dad—I had a million questions, starting with *What other shit are you keeping to yourself, exactly?*—but Jas just shrugged.

"Now?" he said, crumpling up his waxed-paper wrapper and boosting himself to his feet. "Now we are not."

When Jas said *get chips and stuff for later,* I was picturing an actual supermarket, but instead we pulled into the jam-packed parking lot of a tiny specialty-food store, the kind of place with old-fashioned schoolhouse lights hung above the sandwich counter and plastic tubs of lobster salad that cost forty-five dollars a pound. "I want Pirate's Booty," Jasper announced as we edged our way down the narrow aisles, past wicker baskets of freshly made baguettes and displays of expensive Brie that smelled like the locker room at Bartley. The local public radio station piped in over the speakers, James Taylor strumming blissfully away. "Don't you love Pirate's Booty? It's like eating cheesy Styrofoam."

"I mean, sure," I said dubiously. "I wouldn't say that's what I personally look for in a snack food, but you do you."

"Oh, come on, how it squeaks on your teeth? How do you not like that?" Jasper grinned. The weird, tense energy that had been radiating off him ever since I'd mentioned what had happened at the bonfire had fizzled away, and just like that, he was himself again, good-natured. "Pirate's Booty," he said again, "and Bagel Bites."

"And avocados," I reminded him.

Jasper's eyes narrowed in a way that made me wonder if possibly he was onto me insofar as his sister was concerned. "And avocados," he allowed.

He peeled off to go get limes, which Wells had requested to make caipirinhas. "The guy spends one week going to clubs in Brazil," Jasper muttered, "and all of a sudden he's an international mixologist." I turned down the chips aisle and almost crashed straight into the waitress from Red's.

"Oh!" I said, raising a hand in greeting. She was wearing cut-offs and a V-neck T-shirt with the sleeves pushed up onto her shoulders, a bag of kettle corn tucked under her arm. "Hey."

She looked over at me blankly. ". . . Hi."

"Last night," I reminded her. "At the restaurant."

The girl raised her eyebrows. "Oh, don't worry," she said, "I remember."

I cringed. I wanted to apologize, but what would I have said? If I was going to object to how Meredith had acted, I should have done it last night at the table. But I hadn't, because I hadn't wanted to draw attention to myself. *Michael,* I could hear my mom saying, *that is small behavior.*

"Right. Um." I nodded at the kettle corn. "Good choice, anyway."

Jasper came around the corner just then. "Linden!" he yelled. "Get Doritos." Then he saw the waitress. "Hey!" he greeted her, like they were old friends. "It's you. Listen, sorry Meredith was raised in a fucking barn and doesn't know how to eat in a restaurant without embarrassing herself and everyone around her. You want to come to a party tonight?"

That made her smile, the same way girls always smiled at Jasper, like in spite of themselves, they were won over by his earnestness and his energy and his always-messy hair. "Maybe," she said, slipping one foot out of her flip-flop and using it to scratch the back of her opposite calf. "Now you want to talk to me, huh?"

"I always want to talk to you," Jasper said, smiling like he was asking for her vote in this fall's congressional election. He looked like he was about to say something else when he suddenly remembered I was standing beside him, jerking his head in my direction. "This is my buddy Linden. He'll be at the party too, but as you can see, he's not as good-looking or charming as me. Linden, this is Aidy. I once saw her open a beer bottle with her teeth."

Aidy laughed, warm and maybe a little embarrassed. "I'm sorry, *that's* my defining quality in your mind?"

"Nope," Jasper said immediately, and winked. "August House, nine o'clock."

Once she was gone, I turned to look at him, shaking my head. "I *knew* you were checking that girl out last night," I said with a laugh. "I didn't realize you knew her, though. Like, from before she was our waitress?"

Jasper busied himself looking at all the different shapes and flavors of Wheat Thins. "I might have had a little thing for her at the beginning of the summer," he admitted, "at which point Holliman realized I was interested and like, gave her the full-court press for the explicit purpose of fucking with me, because he's a good buddy like that."

I blinked, though it wasn't like anything anyone had told me about Greg so far suggested he was a particularly steadfast monogamist. *Incestuous,* Eliza had said. "Does Meredith know?"

Jasper shrugged. "I mean, you saw her at Red's last night," he said, tossing a jar of salsa into the basket. "If you had a gun to my head, I'd say yeah, I think she probably copped the fuck on at some point."

"So I'm sure she's going to love that you just invited Aidy to the party, then."

"Dude, it's my fucking house," he said cheerfully. "Besides, anything I can do to ruin that girl's night is more than worth it, as far as I'm concerned."

We finished our shopping, Jasper putting the groceries—all 314 dollars' worth of them—on his parents' account like it was 1942. "Hey," he said as we loaded the bags into the trunk of the Land Rover, "you want to invite your friend tonight?"

"Huh?" I blinked. "Who?"

Jas looked at me a little bit oddly. "Your friend from the beach," he said. "The one who was dressed like Ms. Singh."

"Oh." I shook my head, feeling the back of my neck get a

little warm. "Nah, that's cool. I don't really think she's the partying type." That wasn't actually fair: In fact, I had the vague impression that Holiday was pretty popular at Greenleaf, her arty Cambridge day school where they were always putting on all-female productions of Shakespearean tragedies and nobody shaved their armpits. But somehow I couldn't picture her drinking caipirinhas with Eliza and Meredith, or even Aidy the waitress from Red's. Holiday was, and always had been, in a category all by herself.

Jasper shrugged again. "Whatever you want, man. The more the merrier, is all."

"In bed," I replied reflexively. Then, the word sending some synapse firing off deep inside my brain, the memory sparked: "Hey. You didn't go back down to the beach after we all came upstairs last night, did you?"

"Are you kidding?" Jasper snorted. "I was so messed up it was a miracle I found my bed the first time." He glanced at me curiously as he slammed the trunk. "Why?"

"No reason," I lied, pushing whatever drunken, still-concussed head trip I might or might not have had to the back of my mind and climbing into the passenger seat of the Land Rover. "I was too."

The fog and the clouds burned off by the time we got back to August House, and suddenly it was another perfect beach day: the sun round and bright and yellow, the rays almost visible like a little kid would draw. Birdie made BLTs and potato salad for lunch. Mr.

and Mrs. Kendrick left for the ferry once we were finished, the two of them headed for a black-tie wedding in Truro.

"Be good," Mrs. Kendrick said, taking a lap around the patio table and dropping kisses on everyone's foreheads, including Meredith's and mine.

Jasper smiled. "We always are."

Once they were gone, Meredith biked over to Greg's house and the rest of us drifted out to the pool, Eliza reading a Joan Didion novel on one of the lounge chairs and Jasper scrolling his phone. Wells lay faceup on the hot concrete beside the pool, eyes hidden behind a pair of mirrored sunglasses. He was a tricky guy, Wells: I hadn't spent that much time with him back when he was at Bartley, but I remembered him being a pretty mellow dude. I didn't know if it was everything that had happened with his dad or just being around all the blowhards at Harvard, but there was something about him that seemed suddenly brittle to me, just this side of mean. He'd been the drunkest of all of us when we gamboled up to the house last night, and it seemed like he was probably headed in that direction again now, a can of hard seltzer sweating on the patio beside him. "Mom's going to be pissed if you drink all her special juice," Jasper had warned the last time he disappeared into the pool house for another, to which Wells had lifted one middle finger in reply.

"Yo, Linden," he called now, still lying supine on the pool deck. "You ever play Orange?"

Eliza sighed loudly. "Wells," she said, marking her place in her book with her index finger, "come on."

"Don't start with that shit," Jasper put in.

"Why?" I asked, sitting up on my own lounge chair. I'd purposely left an empty seat between Eliza and me, not wanting to look like I cared one way or the other about . . . anything. "What's Orange?"

"It's a stupid game," Eliza informed me, "for stupid people."

"Aw, sis," Wells told her, "you say the sweetest things." He lifted his chin, half peering back at me. "Come on, Linden. You in, or what?"

"I—yeah, okay," I said slowly, swinging my feet over the side of the lounge chair and standing up. I was curious now, if a little bit nervous. "Sure."

Wells smiled. He got up from the patio in one smooth movement, padding barefoot into the house before returning a minute later holding an orange the size of a softball—there was a bowl of them sitting on the kitchen island, along with fuzzy local peaches and bananas that never seemed to brown. He held it out to me and I took it like an instinct, feeling the weight of it in my hand as he walked around to the other side of the pool.

"Okay," he announced, turning around so that his back was facing me. I could see the sharp ridges of his spine through his skin. "Now hit me with it."

I laughed out loud, then realized he wasn't kidding. "Wait," I said. "Seriously? Dude, what the fuck."

"That's the whole game," Eliza informed me, peering at us over the tops of her sunglasses. "And then you're going to turn around and he's going to hit *you* as hard as *he* can, and you're going to go back and forth like that until one of you cries uncle or the orange explodes, whichever comes first." She gazed balefully at her brother. "Am I forgetting anything?"

Wells smirked. "Nope," he admitted. "That about covers it." He looked at me over his shoulder. "What do you say, Linden? Still want to play?" His tone was friendly, but after three years at Bartley I knew exactly what kind of bargain was on offer here: Wells wasn't going to give me a hard time if I told him I wasn't interested. But he wasn't going to forget about it either.

So. I said okay.

I turned the orange in my hand for a moment, rubbing my thumb over the bumpy skin, then wound up and tossed it—hard enough so it cleared the width of the pool, but not hard enough to do any real damage. It connected with a dull thud against Wells's back before dropping to the patio and rolling for a second, coming to rest a few feet away. Wells, for his part, barely winced.

"He's going easy on you," Jasper informed his brother. "He knows you're delicate."

Wells didn't like that. "Were you?" he asked me, bending to retrieve the orange. "Don't."

I shrugged, turning around and facing the garden. Already I was regretting this, some kind of weird *Fight Club* pissing contest. I should have just told him to go screw. "Just warming up, I guess."

"Okay," he said, then lobbed the orange back across the pool, hitting me in the back hard enough that I flinched. "Better hurry up and get warm."

I felt anger flare in my chest, a muscle in my jaw twitching.

The next time, I threw it as hard as I could. It left a mark right away, a bright red splotch just to the right of Wells's backbone.

"That's more like it," Wells said, sounding satisfied. Eliza sighed again and went back to her book.

"This is fucking dumb," Jasper announced, unfolding himself from his lounge chair. "I'm gonna go eat a string cheese and jerk off."

He disappeared into the house, but Wells and I kept at it, going back and forth half a dozen more times. Red marks bloomed on his lower back and underneath his shoulder blades. He hit me so hard that I coughed. I was just about to bail out—fuck this, it was asinine and I was asinine for agreeing to it, I was every embarrassing stereotype about dudes who went to private school—but thankfully, the orange gave out just then, smashing to a wet, pulpy mess on the patio.

"Shit." Wells grinned, turning back around to face me. "Guess this round is a draw."

"Whatever you say, man." My back was burning; I felt idiotic and disproportionately rattled, like I'd accidentally done something a lot worse than just play a boneheaded game with my buddy's dipshit brother. Out of nowhere I thought of Greer and the accident, ambulance lights flashing on the winding road that led to Bartley. Pushed it all out of my mind.

"Are you going to clean that up, at least?" Eliza asked as Wells strolled back across the patio toward the house; she'd been ignoring us pointedly for the last several minutes, lying on her stomach with her head bent over her book.

"I'll tell Birdie," Wells promised easily, sliding the kitchen door shut behind him.

I did it myself in the end, scooping it up off the concrete and immediately wishing I hadn't. It felt like picking up roadkill bare-handed, heavy and slippery and somehow deeply wrong. I brought it inside as fast as I could without looking like I was running and tossed it into the kitchen garbage, then came back with a can of grapefruit LaCroix for Eliza.

"Is this so I won't tell you what a moron you are?" she asked, taking it from my hand with a smile.

"Nah," I said, sitting down on the chair beside her and crossing my ankles. "I figured you were going to tell me that whether or not I brought you a drink."

"That fancy private-school education is paying off." She was still lying on her stomach, propping herself up on one elbow to look at me. "How's your back?"

"Fine," I lied. In fact, I felt . . . well, like I'd been pelted with an orange over and over. Even with Wells gone, I was still a little uneasy, my bones jangling around inside my body like I was one of those full-size plastic skeletons from the Halloween store. "I'm really manly, so. Barely felt it."

Eliza's lips twisted. "You realize you're going to have to explain those bruises over and over every time you get in the pool all week long," she pointed out. "Citrus injury, et cetera."

"Probably." I grimaced at the thought of it. "Maybe I'll start swimming in a full wetsuit, avoid that problem altogether."

"Now, *that* would be a waste." Eliza grinned. "Wells is an asshole," she continued, moving on to the second thing before

I could process the first one. "He took it the hardest, you know? Everything that happened with my dad. Which makes zero sense, because it's not even like he was living at home for any of it. Neither of them were, him or Jasper. I'm the one who had to go into my mom's bathroom at night and count her Xanax."

She said it so casually I wasn't sure if she was kidding or not, crossing her arms in front of her and dropping her head down. Mostly I was just relieved she didn't seem to be mad at me anymore. "That sucks," I said finally, sounding like a dumbass even to my own ears.

Eliza shrugged, reaching behind her to unhook the back clasp of her bathing suit. "Don't peek," she instructed me firmly.

I cleared my throat, glancing back at the house. "Wouldn't dream of it."

"I mean," she said, turning her face to look at me, "you can *dream* of it, if you want." She rubbed her nose against the crease of her elbow. "So what's your story, Michael Linden?"

I shook my head like an instinct. "You know," I told her, "there's not much to tell."

Eliza hummed, skeptical. "Somehow I don't think that's true."

We stayed like that for a while, quiet, the sun making patterns across the water in the pool. I waited for my back to stop throbbing. Eliza turned the pages of her book. At last she got up in one smooth motion and—not bothering to put her top back on, the fabric dangling between two elegant fingers—she got up and headed across the patio. I watched the long line of her backbone as she disappeared into the house.

I sat in the lounge chair for a long time once she was gone, trying dazedly to figure out if she'd been issuing me some kind of silent invitation, and telling myself I was being ridiculous for feeling too edgy and rattled to go find the hell out. I was still gathering my courage when all at once I noticed something moving on the patio. I got up to investigate, then stopped short with a shudder halfway to the back door: There was a giant clump of ants crawling all over the wet, juicy stain the orange had left on the flagstone, hundreds of them scuttling in tandem around what was left of the pulpy mess. I watched them for a long, gross moment, weirdly hypnotized, until Jasper's voice startled me alert.

"Yo!" he yelled from one of the upstairs windows. "You want to go take the boat out?"

"Uh," I called back, still watching the ant colony, "sure thing."

"Cool," Jasper said. "Be right down."

I stared at the swarming ants for another minute—transfixed by the sheer number of them, how from a distance they looked like one dark, vibrating mass. Then I left them to their business and went inside.

5

PEOPLE STARTED SHOWING UP AT AUGUST HOUSE around nine that night, wandering over in twos and threes; by ten-thirty the yard was full to bursting, the overflow trickling down the wooden staircase and onto the beach. Jasper was known around Bartley for throwing a pretty good party—Drinkin' for Lincoln in February, Last Gasp every spring—and clearly his reputation had followed him to the Vineyard. "Do we need to be worried about your neighbors?" I asked, watching with some interest as he pulled two giant handles of vodka out of the Sub-Zero.

Jasper blinked. "Worried about my neighbors doing what?" he asked.

I thought of Mrs. Le back in Eastie banging on the ceiling if I played video games too loud. "Nothing," I said. "I'm gonna get a beer."

I dug one out of the cooler on the patio and looked out at the crowded yard. Eliza was sitting in the hammock with Doc, I noted grimly, the two of them talking with their heads bent close together. Aidy the waitress had shown up after all—she'd brought a couple of friends with her, all of them tequila-drunk and laughing in the deep end. Jasper had made a beeline in their direction, hopping into the water and slinging a slightly-more-than-friendly arm around Aidy's neck. A pretty girl in a bright red bikini looked like she was trying to keep Wells's attention over on the patio, but he didn't seem particularly interested; at one point I caught him sneaking a glance at the clock on his phone, like possibly he was waiting for her to finish talking so he could go watch the newest episode of his favorite nighttime soap in real time.

The night blurred by, the smell of weed and chlorine, the bass from the outdoor speakers reverberating down my spine. Around eleven-thirty I went inside to pee and passed Eliza lying on the couch in the library with her ankles crossed, almost at the end of her Joan Didion book. "What are you doing in here?" I asked from the doorway.

Eliza shrugged into the throw pillows. She was wearing a white eyelet sundress that skimmed her smooth, tan knees, her hair loose and wavy to her shoulders. "Hiding," she said.

"Fair enough." I nodded at her book. "Should I leave you to it?"

"Nah," she said, sitting up and tucking her feet underneath her. "You're acceptable." She made a face. "Jasper's been throwing these tasteful little gatherings all summer like he thinks it's the last days of Rome or something. And I kind of hate parties to begin with, honestly."

"Really?" I asked. "I wouldn't have guessed that."

Eliza smiled. "I'm a very good actress."

I remembered what she'd said last night, about the toll this summer had taken on all of them; still, I didn't press her, taking a sip of my beer and leaning back against the bookshelves. The library seemed like the kind of place Teddy Roosevelt might smoke a cigar after dinner, with a deep leather sofa and two green velvet chairs. There was a piano in one corner, a baby grand with a stack of old music books on the bench. "Can you play?" I asked.

"Of course I can play," she said. "What am I, a hobo?" She shook her head. "I'm kidding. But yeah, we all took lessons. My mom is old-fashioned about that kind of thing. She had to do it, so I have to do it, et cetera."

Mrs. Kendrick hadn't struck me as old-fashioned, but I could see what Eliza meant as I looked around the library: the classics and prizewinners on the bookshelves, the abstract art on the walls. A thing about August House was how weirdly timeless it felt, like you might at any moment look up and realize you'd accidentally traveled back to the thirties or the sixties or the eighties. I kept glancing down at my phone, half expecting not to have a cell signal.

Eliza nodded at my beer then, holding one manicured hand out; I passed it over obediently, sitting down on the sofa beside her. "When do you leave for France?" I asked. She was going to Paris for her fall semester, she'd told me last night, to live with a host family in the 12th arrondissement.

She took a sip of the beer, the muscles in her throat moving as she swallowed. "Not until the third week of September," she said.

"And you'll just hang out here until then?"

"I might," she allowed, her fingers brushing mine as she passed the bottle back. "Unless a better offer comes along."

"What's the thing you're looking forward to most?"

"What, about being abroad?" I was expecting her to say the food or the culture, maybe make some joke about a French affair, but instead Eliza seemed to consider it for a moment. "The thing I'm looking forward to most, Linden," she said finally, her pink lips twisting, "is being someone entirely new." Then, before I could answer: "We should get in the hot tub," she announced, setting her book aside and standing up on the thickly piled rug. "Do you want to get in the hot tub?"

I blinked at the conversational whiplash of it, then nodded. "I would . . . love to get in the hot tub," I told her, and she laughed.

The hot tub was set into the far end of the swimming pool, steam rising off the surface of the water and curling up into the air. "Out," Eliza said to the couple that was currently using it as their own personal Playboy grotto; she smiled, satisfied, as they hauled themselves up and out of the water, then pulled off her sundress to reveal a pale pink swimsuit and hopped in herself.

"Can I ask you something?" I asked once we'd gotten ourselves settled. I leaned back against one of the jets, trying to act like I casually sat in hot tubs with pretty girls all the time and not like I was concentrating extremely hard on not getting a boner, which I was. I liked her, Eliza, but even as her feet brushed mine under the water, there was a part of me that knew I also liked her life: She spoke three languages. She smelled preternaturally fresh. She gave off the subtle but unmistakable impression of ease, like as long as you were around her, you'd never need to rush for a train and there would always be a pile of fresh towels still warm from the dryer waiting for you when you got out of the shower. "You and Doc."

Eliza gazed at me across the hot tub, something that wasn't quite a smile playing at the very corners of her mouth. "That's not really a question, Linden," she pointed out wryly. "Are you jealous?"

"I—yeah," I admitted after a moment, ducking my head and laughing. "A little bit."

Eliza smiled for real this time, sliding one foot up my shin under the water. "Well," she said, "don't be. We messed around a couple of times last summer, but we're just friends now." Her foot crept up a little bit higher. "Besides, I might have just met somebody I like."

I smiled back—and yeah, now I definitely did have a boner. "Okay."

I was about to slide closer and kiss her when all at once Eliza straightened up, her attention snagging on something over my shoulder: "Oh, dirt," she said, hoisting herself elegantly up out of the hot tub in one smooth movement. "What the fuck is he doing here?"

"Wait," I said, momentarily disoriented, "what?" I took a second to admire the view of her from behind—and, okay, to readjust my sails—before scrambling out after her. I trailed her through the crowd over to the patio just in time to see Jasper push past Meredith and step between Wells and some kid I didn't recognize.

"Holliman, dude," Jasper was saying as we approached, lopsided smile belied by the broken-glass edge in his voice, "is there any particular reason you can't stay on your own beach? I mean, I know ours is nicer, but fuck."

Holliman, I realized belatedly—as in Meredith's boyfriend, Greg. I startled in spite of myself. Seeing him in the flesh felt

strangely like catching a glimpse of a celebrity, someone whose reputation preceded him: he was tall and broad and gym-rat muscley
in a green-and-white striped rugby shirt, wavy brown hair tucked
underneath a backward Sox cap. He shrugged, looking completely
and admirably unbothered by all three Kendricks staring poison in
his direction, by the fact that he was clearly unwanted in this place.
"Just wanderlust, I guess."

"In that case," Wells said, shoving past his brother and getting
right up into Greg's face, "why don't you *wander* yourself on back
where you came from?"

"Wells," Jasper said quietly. "Easy."

He said it like he was calling off a dog, and to my surprise,
it actually seemed to work—Wells's posture relaxed a little, his
shoulders coming down from around his ears. "Get the fuck out
of here, Holliman," he said.

Greg smirked. "You keep him on a pretty short leash, huh?"
he asked Jas.

That was a mistake: Right away Wells was ready to go again—
his chest getting bigger, hands balling into fists at his sides. He was
more than a little bit drunk. "You know what, man? Why don't
you and I finally just—"

"*Wells,*" Jasper said again, more sharply this time. "Let it go."
His gaze flicked to Greg. "He's leaving."

But Wells wasn't buying. "Let it *go*?" he demanded, rounding
on his brother. In the second before he schooled his expression
into anger, I thought he looked legitimately hurt. "Is that what
you think I should do? Or forget me, even: Is that what you think
Dad should do?"

Jasper flinched. "Dude," he started, "I'm just saying there's no point in letting him ruin the whole—"

"He's just saying, don't be such a little bitch all the time, Wellsy," Greg interrupted helpfully. "Girls don't like it."

"Can you shut the fuck up?" Jasper demanded, whirling on him. A crowd had started to gather by now, Doc and me both inching closer to offer backup. Meredith looked utterly miserable, her sharp gaze flicking nervously back and forth between Greg and the Kendricks as she twisted her hands together. I didn't envy her, caught between both sides. "For fuck's sake, man. Did you come here specifically to get the shit beat out of you, or what?"

"What, by you guys?" Greg laughed at that, looking almost fond of them. "I mean, you can try." As much as I hated to admit it, he had a point. Not only did he look like he could take Wells and Jasper in a fight, but he kind of looked like he could bench-press them both and maybe me for good measure without even breaking a sweat. It was funny, though: Most of the dudes I knew at Bartley played a couple of sports, but they weren't meatheads, and rather than being threatening, the whole aesthetic kind of had the opposite effect. It gave Greg the look of somebody who was trying hard to be intimidating. And if there was one thing I knew about these people, it was never to let any of them see you try.

Still, I couldn't help but feel a little bit uneasy. I knew plenty of guys like Greg at school, the kind who'd spent their whole lives walking around protected by a hard shell of privilege. Jasper was that way too, sort of, though with him it was more like the candy coating of an M&M: apply a little heat, it would melt away and he'd become a regular person. This guy, clearly, was all jawbreaker.

"Look," Jasper said now, his voice reasonable. He hated Greg, maybe, but he liked a party more, and he wasn't about to let anyone, not even his sworn enemy, ruin this one. "Can we just—"

"Can we just *what*, exactly?" Wells asked, his face twisting into an ugly snarl. "What the fuck is your problem, Jasper? Can you pick a fucking side, for once in your life? Are you part of this family or not?"

For a moment Jasper just reeled, his reaction as physical as if his brother had decked him. "Fuck you, Wells," he said, and his voice was so quiet.

Greg liked that: "Yeah, Wells," he said cheerfully. "Fuck you."

That was when Wells hit him.

It was a sloppy fight, both of them drunk and neither one of them a particularly experienced fighter, shoving each other roughly and landing the occasional messy punch. Jasper tried to pull them apart, catching an elbow to the throat for his trouble; he stumbled, letting go of his brother with a sharp, surprised cough. I jumped in to help him, pushing Wells up against the exterior of August House as gently as I could. "Dude," I tried, "just—"

"Get your hands off me, Linden." Wells shrugged me off, then went after Greg one more time. His fist connected with the side of Greg's face with a nauseating crack, but Greg only reeled for what felt like a second before hitting him back.

It took all three of us—Doc, Jasper, and me—a long time to pull them apart, Meredith and Eliza screaming at them to cut it out while the rest of the party catcalled gamely; by the time they were finished, Greg's nose was bleeding and Wells had a nasty-looking gash below one eye, his navy-blue polo ripped at the collar as he stormed off across the yard. "Oh my god," Meredith said, reaching her hand out in Greg's direction, "are you okay?" He batted her away.

Jasper turned to Greg then, looking more exhausted than I'd ever seen him, even during finals or after a particularly brutal crew practice. "Dude," he said. "Just go, okay?"

Greg blinked at that, dazed or drunk or both, then nodded. "Yeah," he agreed, "seems like it's about that time." He was smiling that same smug, self-satisfied smile that seemed to be his trademark, but I thought there was something hollow in his voice, like possibly the fun had gone out of it for him. He nodded at Meredith, clearly expecting her to take off along with him; when she hesitated, her gaze cutting guiltily to Eliza, he muttered something I didn't catch and stalked off alone across the yard.

Once he was gone, Eliza clapped her hands together, sunny as a camp counselor on the first day of summer. "Well!" she said brightly. "I think it's probably time for everybody to get the fuck out of our house, don't you all agree?"

That broke it up, all right, people heading home or down to the beach or off to another party somebody knew about closer to town. Doc and I helped Jasper gather up the trash strewn around the deck, tossing it all into the bins hidden discreetly at the back of the pool house. "What happened to your brother?" I asked, glancing around for Wells, but Jasper only snorted.

"Oh, come on," he said, a lightness in his voice I was almost sure he was faking. "Does he really strike you as the kind of person who helps clean up after a party?"

It was a little after one by the time we were finished; I went upstairs to the turret and stared at the poisonous plants while I changed into a pair of basketball shorts and a T-shirt. I dicked around on my phone for a while. Finally I got out of bed. "Dude," I muttered to myself, then went into the bathroom and swallowed a giant gulp of mouthwash. "Nut up already."

I glanced at myself once more in the mirror above the sink, then made my way as quietly as I could down the creaking steps to the door of Eliza's bedroom. I took a deep breath, and I knocked.

6

I WOKE UP TO THE SOUND OF SOMEONE SCREAMING.

I scrambled out of bed so fast I got tangled in the covers, my heart a bloody fist slamming away at the back of my throat. For a second I had no idea where I was. I thought it was my mom, that there was someone in our house I needed to protect her from. I thought it was Greer, and the car was starting to skid.

Then I realized it was Eliza.

I grabbed for my glasses—I was basically blind without them, though I usually put my contacts in first thing—shoving them onto my face and stumbling down the stairs in the muddy-gray dark. My busted ankle gave as I turned the corner into the kitchen, and I landed face-first on the floor.

"Shit," I hissed. Eliza was still screaming, one high, panicked shriek after another. I boosted myself upright, wincing at the icy-hot pain careening up and down my leg. I burst through the open door and out onto the patio, where I found her standing illuminated by the warm, tasteful glow of the backyard lights, hands clenched into fists at her sides.

Crumpled on the pool steps, slumped like a shipwreck just above the waterline, was a body.

"Oh, fuck." Wells was right behind me—pushing past his sister and running across the patio, crouching down by the edge of the pool. "Linden!" he barked. "Help me."

I startled. I'd been standing there staring; for a moment the whole scene seemed enormously, ostentatiously fake to me, like something that was happening on TV or in a movie. Like something I had no realistic frame of reference for at all.

"*Linden!*" Wells said again, and this time I moved. Together he and I wrestled the body out of the water, my hands sliding slickly over its damp arms and shoulders. Its skin was cold and clammy under my palms. I thought of the orange from the previous afternoon, the overwhelming feeling that I was touching something I shouldn't be. I thought of the phrase *dead weight*.

"It's Greg," Wells said as we turned him faceup on the concrete. "*Fuck*, what the fuck is Greg doing here?"

"Is he breathing?" Eliza demanded shrilly.

"I have no idea," Wells said. "Call 911."

She shook her head back and forth about a dozen times. "I don't have my phone."

"Well, go get it!" he roared. "Shit!"

"What the fuck is going on?" That was Jasper running through the sliding door out onto the patio, Aidy—*Aidy?*—at his heels and Meredith close behind them. They stopped short when they saw Greg lying motionless on the ground, his arms and legs sprawled in all different directions like a little kid's action figure left on the playground. Right away, Meredith started screaming too.

"He was in the pool," Wells explained, sounding completely baffled. "I don't—why was he in the pool?"

"Is he dead?" That was Meredith, down on her knees at Greg's side.

"No," I said, finding my voice for the first time since I'd come out onto the patio. Greg was breathing, but barely, the rise and fall of his chest just visible in the dim predawn light. There was a gash in his head, I saw now, like he'd hit it on something. When I looked down, there was blood on my hands. "He's alive."

"They're on their way," Eliza reported shakily, coming back out through the kitchen with the phone pressed to her ear. "Yes, I'm still here."

"Buddy," Meredith was saying softly, touching Greg's face and chest and shoulders as tears and snot ran down her face. "Hey, buddy, please wake up."

Things seemed to happen in flashes after that: the paramedics tromping in through the garden, carrying a bright orange backboard between them. Aidy clutching Jasper's hand while the dawn came up red and sudden and overripe. Meredith pulling a borrowed fleece over her head and climbing into the back of the ambulance beside Greg, her bangs sticking up at a funny angle; the burst of static from a walkie-talkie as—oh Jesus—two cops from the Edgartown Police Department turned the corner into the yard.

Their names were Reyes and O'Neal, a man and a woman; O'Neal did most of the talking, taking notes in a little book not much bigger than a credit card. "All right," she said once we'd all introduced ourselves. Birdie had arrived just as the ambulance was leaving, was pressing hot cups of coffee into everyone's hands. "Can you all tell us what happened here this morning?"

Wells spoke first. "Greg is a friend of ours," he began, his voice surprisingly steady. "He came over last night to hang out by the pool, but he went home a little after midnight. I don't . . ." His gaze flicked to the rest of us, then back at the police officers. "I don't think any of us have any idea what he did after that."

O'Neal nodded. "Was there anyone else at the house we should know about?"

"No," Eliza said immediately, and I felt myself startle. There'd been at least two dozen people in the pool alone. I didn't want to get hauled off to jail either, obviously, but still I was surprised by how easily the lie seemed to roll off her tongue. "Just us—and my friend Meredith, Greg's girlfriend. She's at the hospital with him now."

"You all were having a bit of fun, I'm assuming?" That was Reyes, both hands in his pockets as he looked around at the quiet, neatly manicured backyard. We'd done a final sweep for abandoned beer bottles before we went to bed, thank god, though from my vantage point by the patio table I could see the glint of one lonely can hiding under Mrs. Kendrick's rosebushes.

"You mean, like, drinking?" Eliza asked, her eyes wide and innocent. "No, not at all."

"I mean, I guess we don't know what Greg did after he left here," Wells pointed out. "But none of us are legal yet, so."

Reyes nodded faintly, his face impassive. I glanced from Eliza to Jasper to Aidy, waiting—and waiting some more—for someone to mention the fight, or the fact that Greg hadn't so much *come* over to hang out as *shown up drunk and uninvited*. And sure, I could have mentioned it myself; I knew that even as I was standing there on the patio like a tree stump. But I couldn't get my mouth to make the words.

"We'll need to talk to your parents, obviously," O'Neal said finally. "You said they're on their way back?"

Wells nodded. "I called them," he said. "They're getting on the first ferry out."

"Have them give us a call when they get in," Reyes said, handing Wells his card as O'Neal tucked her notebook back into her pocket. "In the meantime, you kids take care of yourselves, will you? You must have had quite a scare."

Take care *of yourselves?* I blinked. I'd been bracing myself for a full interrogation, something out of the *Law & Order* reruns my mom liked to watch while she folded laundry, but before I knew what was happening, Reyes and O'Neal were saying their goodbyes and pulling out of the driveway of August House, the police car disappearing down the road like maybe it had never been there at all. I thought of the cops at my middle school back in Eastie, resource officers who stood like sentries in the hallways, tasers and batons tucked neatly into holsters on their hips. Twice I'd seen them pick kids up and haul them out of class kicking and screaming. Once I'd seen them wrestle a girl down onto the linoleum floor. I wasn't stupid enough to think everyone had an equal shot when it came to law enforcement. But *take care of yourselves* was . . . something else.

After they were gone, Jasper whirled to look at his sister, his hair and his expression both wild. "Eliza," he said, "what the *fuck*?"

"What?" Eliza's eyes widened. She was still in her pajamas, a matching set printed with little off-white stars. "Don't look at me like that."

"I mean, you just fully lied to the cops, so I think if I'm looking at you a little funny—"

Right away, Eliza held a hand up. "First of all," she interrupted, eyes cutting to Aidy, "I didn't lie. They asked if there was anyone else here that they needed to know about, which there wasn't."

"And the part about how none of us were drinking?"

She made a face. "Oh, I'm sorry," she said, "do *you* want Mom and Dad to know we threw a gigantic fucking party while they were gone?"

"Since when do Mom and Dad give a shit about that kind of thing?" Wells asked.

"Since Greg fucking Holliman wandered drunk into our pool, and his trash parents are going to rain even more shit down on this family than they already have!" Eliza exploded. "Also, 'Greg is a friend of ours'?" She rolled her eyes. "I'm sorry, *which* one of us was lying, exactly?" She sank down into a patio chair, scraping her hands through her sleep-messy hair. "Look," she said, "obviously this is fucking horrible. Like, I don't even know how to begin to—" She broke off. "But it was his own fault. And I'm not about to let any more of them drag any more of *us* down with them."

None of us said anything for a moment. I could hear the seagulls cawing down on the beach. Birdie slid the door halfway open, a blast of cold air from the AC whooshing out into the muggy morning. "Breakfast is ready," she reported, her voice perfectly even. "You all should come have something to eat."

The four of us shuffled inside obediently, taking our seats around the island. I was expecting Birdie to follow, but instead she slipped past us out into the yard, her strawberry-blond hair catching the sunlight. I watched through the window as she made her way across the patio, discreetly pulling the beer can from beneath the branches of the rosebush and dropping it into the recycling bin before coming back into the kitchen.

"Syrup's on the counter" was all she said.

7

BY NOON, LIFE AT AUGUST HOUSE HAD RETURNED AL-most to normal. Mr. and Mrs. Kendrick got home as we were finishing Birdie's pancakes; Mr. Kendrick shut himself in the office basically as soon as they walked in the door, his voice muffled as he talked on the phone—to his lawyer, I assumed, trying to gauge the family's legal exposure. "None of you gave that kid anything to drink, did you?" he asked when he emerged. Greg was in a coma, Meredith had reported from the hospital; the doctors thought he'd probably tripped, drunk or high or some combination of both, and hit his head on the edge of the pool before tumbling over. "You're sure?"

The Kendrick siblings looked at each other, just for a second. This time it was Jasper who spoke. "No, Dad," he said. "Come on, you know how that kid is. You think we're inviting him over and offering him the good Scotch?"

That made Mr. Kendrick smile, just faintly. "You shouldn't joke," he said, though his lips were still quirked. "It's a tragedy. Obviously, he's a troubled guy."

"How could he not be, coming from a family like that?" Mrs. Kendrick shook her head. She looked daisy-fresh for a person who'd been awoken before dawn to the news of a comatose teenager floating in her swimming pool, her golden-blond bob pulled into a springy ponytail and her white button-down shirt tucked into a pair of red khaki shorts. Already she'd called the market that Jas and I had been to yesterday and had a tray of sandwiches sent over to the hospital. "Not that it makes this any less awful."

Now she and Mr. Kendrick were gone again, taking Whimsy for a long walk along the water. Birdie was baking a blueberry crumble to go with dinner, humming along to Blossom Dearie on the stereo. A company had arrived to clean the pool.

I found Jasper sprawled in the yard with his earbuds in, one flip-flop dangling from his toes over the side of the hammock. "Dude," I said quietly, "should I go home?" My nerves felt brittle and rattly, a bad-seafood kind of queasiness in my stomach. Every time I blinked, I saw Greg slumped like a deflated inner tube on the steps of the pool.

"What?" Jasper pulled out one earbud. "Dude, no. Why? You just got here."

"No, I know, but—" I broke off. I didn't know what to say, exactly: *Pulling your unconscious neighbor out of the water first thing in the morning kind of takes the fun out of paddling around in the deep end? The casual relationship you and your family suddenly seem to have with the truth makes me a teeny bit uncomfortable? I'm desperate to leave this idyllic seaside playground and spend the last dregs of the summer bagging groceries in the sweltering city heat?*

"Greg's going to be fine," Jasper promised, all confidence. "And if he's not . . . not to be a dick or anything, but it's kind of his own fault for getting fucking obliterated and creeping around our yard in the middle of the night like some kind of giant psycho."

"Yeah," I agreed, though there was a part of me that couldn't get over the notion that it wasn't quite that simple. "No, totally." All at once I didn't want to talk about it anymore. "So," I said instead, raising my eyebrows in his direction, "you and Aidy, huh?"

Jasper grinned. "Me and Aidy, huh." She'd taken off before his parents got home, though not before the rest of us caught an eyeful of them saying a decidedly prolonged goodbye on the side porch. "Get a room!" Eliza had yelled, banging on the window as she passed by.

"Yo!" That was Wells coming through the back door in his swim trunks, blue-and-white striped towel slung over one tan shoulder. "You ready?" he called across the yard.

"One sec," Jasper called back. "I'll meet you down there."

"Hold up," I said, even as Wells headed through the gate and down the steps that led to the sand. "You guys are going to the beach?"

I didn't mean to sound like such a little bitch about it, but I must have, because Jasper looked sheepish. "I mean." He ruffled his hair with his hand. "I don't know if we'll *swim* or anything."

I laughed at that, but only to avoid some other, more awkward reaction. I didn't know why the idea seemed so profoundly appalling to me, or what exactly I thought they should be doing instead. After all, what *was* the socially appropriate itinerary for the day after your sworn enemy almost drowned in your pool? Still, I couldn't get over the seasick feeling that the rules were somehow different for the Kendricks, and for people like them, than they were for everyone else. I kept thinking of the way the cops had acted this morning, the *all in this together, sorry we even have to ask you this* quality of their questions. It was as if Jasper and his family were untouchable, like they had some kind of invisible missile shield of power and privilege around them that nothing—not even something like this—could penetrate.

"Look," Jas said, boosting himself upright with the practiced ease of a person who'd clearly spent a lot of time getting into and out of hammocks, "I get it. I don't want you to think that, like, shit like this happens all the time around here and we're a bunch of sociopaths who are immune to it or something. The whole thing is super fucked up."

I breathed a sigh of relief at that, hearing him say it out loud. "It is, right?"

"Of course it is!" Jasper laughed a little. "It's creepy as shit! But also, like . . . sitting around feeling bad about it all day isn't going to change anything. And you going back to Boston definitely isn't." He shrugged. "Obviously I'm not going to say anything fucking corny like *Greg would want us to go on with our lives* or whatever. But if the situation was reversed, and I was the one in the hospital right now? You can bet your ass that kid would be out here drinking a frosty watermelon margarita and working on his tan."

I had to admit, Jas had a point. I didn't know Greg at all, but it wasn't like I needed to scrutinize the results of his Myers-Briggs personality test to figure out that the guy was a total douchebag. And he *had* kind of brought the whole thing on himself.

Hadn't he?

"Go get your suit and meet us down there," Jas advised now, tucking his earbuds back into their charging pod and slipping them into the pocket of his shorts. "Seriously, bro. What else are you gonna do all day, lie in bed with a finger in your belly button, contemplating the cruel randomness of the universe?"

"Of course not, asshole," I replied immediately. "You know I only do that on my birthday."

I could hear Jasper laughing all the way down to the beach.

I was headed back across the patio toward the house—maybe I'd get my suit after all, I thought, and stop being such a delicate flower about the whole thing—when someone called out behind me. I turned and saw it was one of the pool guys, his polo shirt stitched with a logo of three little waves. "This belong to you?" he asked. He was holding something I couldn't make out in the glare of the midday sunlight. "It was stuck in the filter."

I held my hand out like an instinct, flinching a little as he dropped it into my palm: a necklace, a rose-gold chain strung with a delicate charm in the shape of a tiny anchor.

I felt my heart do a weird, stuttering thing inside my chest. It didn't mean anything, I reminded myself immediately: after all, there'd been a million people in the pool last night, and it could easily have fallen off any one of them. But the clasp was broken, the metal bent at a weird, violent angle.

Almost like it had been yanked off someone's neck.

"I'll ask around," I said, tucking the necklace into my pocket. I wondered if anyone had told the pool guys why the Kendricks had called them out here on such short notice. "Thanks."

Inside the house was cool and quiet, save for the modest hum of the dishwasher. Birdie's crumble sat cooling on a rack beside the stove. Eliza was perched at the kitchen island, eating leftover blueberries and scrolling her phone. "Did the boys leave for the beach without me?" she asked, peering past me out the sliding door into the yard. "Those two fuckers." She paused with her fingers in the ceramic dish, then frowned. "Wait," she said, "are you not going?"

"No, I will," I assured her. I curled my hand around the necklace inside my pocket, rubbing my thumb over the charm. *Any idea who this belongs to?* I thought of asking her. Then I thought again. "I just—you know."

Eliza tilted her head to the side. "You should come," she said, pulling one elegant foot up onto the barstool and resting her chin on her knee. She was wearing a pair of white shorts and her bathing suit top, two white triangles connected by a length of nautical rope. "I mean, let's be real, it's not like Greg would be sitting vigil if it was one of us who wound up in the pool."

"That . . . is pretty much exactly what your brother said." I smiled, though suddenly there was a tiny part of me that wondered if they'd come up with that line together. "I'll catch up with you guys, I promise. I think I'm just gonna lie down for a little bit first. I didn't sleep that much."

"No kidding." Eliza smirked at that, her green eyes sparking hot. "Want company?" she asked. Then, before I could answer: "Birdie likes to snuggle."

I nodded wryly, waiting for the familiar thrill of the tease to hit me. Instead I just felt kind of ill. "Good to know." I headed for the doorway, then stopped short just before I got to the dining room. "Hey," I said, turning to face her again. "Can I ask you something? What were you doing outside so early this morning?"

Eliza looked surprised for a second, then shrugged. "Whimsy had to pee," she said, popping a blueberry into her mouth. Her tone was totally unbothered, but I thought I saw a flicker of something—annoyance? Suspicion?—cross her sharp, canny face. "Why?"

I shook my head. "No, no reason." I didn't actually remember seeing Whimsy in the yard that morning, but that didn't necessarily mean anything. After all, it wasn't like I'd been paying a ton of attention. I was letting my own uneasiness get the better of me, that was all. "Was just lucky. For Greg, I mean."

Eliza unfolded herself like a cat and slid off the barstool, padding barefoot across the hardwood floor. "He can thank me when he wakes up," she said lightly, then slipped out the door onto the patio.

I stood in the doorway for a moment, watching her go. There was a part of me that wanted to follow—to toss her over my shoulder and run us both into the ocean, to bury my feet in the warm sand and let the sun bake this weird, briny guilt right out of me. What was I even feeling guilty about? It wasn't like I was the one who'd pushed Greg into the pool.

The more I thought about it, though, the more I was starting to wonder if maybe somebody else might have.

I went upstairs to the third floor and lay down on the four-poster bed, the antique frame creaking a bit under my weight. I looked at the ceiling for a while. I stared at the poison plants on the wall. I kind of wanted my mom, in all honesty, but I knew if she got even the faintest whiff of any of this, she'd have an existential crisis about the kind of murderous Republican element she was exposing me to by sending me to Bartley in the first place. She'd probably drive down the Cape, get on the next ferry out of Woods Hole, and drag me back home herself. Forget bagging groceries; I'd be spending the rest of the summer listening to socialist protest anthems and running errands for the neighborhood mutual aid group.

I was still flat on my back, trying not to feel like the tasteful shiplap walls of August House were creeping ever-so-infinitesimally closer, when my phone buzzed on the nightstand. *Hey!* Holiday had texted. *Still up for coffee today?*

"Oh, fuck me," I muttered. I'd completely forgotten, and honestly, the whole thing sounded even less appealing now than it had two nights earlier. Not only was it basically guaranteed to be excruciatingly awkward, but there was also no way I could make an hour's worth of inane small talk without Holiday figuring out that something was going on. I knew her—and, more to the point, *she* knew *me*. She'd sniff me out in ten seconds flat.

I stared at the screen for a moment, trying to figure out the best way to bail. The last time I'd messaged her was two full years ago, when she'd texted to ask if I remembered the day we'd found a lost puppy in her backyard in Cambridge. We'd fitted it with a leash and collar and made signs to put up all over the neighborhood before my mom caught us and whisked us both to the pediatrician to get checked for rabies exposure, as our puppy was in fact a surprisingly good-natured baby possum.

Haha, I'd replied two days later.

So, fine, I thought now, cringing a little: It was probably mostly my fault that our friendship hadn't exactly held steadfast through the ages. On top of which, the more I thought about it, the more I felt like a piece of shit about how I'd basically blown her off at the beach the other night. Still, all at once it occurred to me that maybe she wouldn't be the worst person in the world to talk to about what had happened at the Kendricks' this morning.

And as soon as I had *that* thought, I realized there wasn't actually anyone else I could imagine talking to about it at all.

Coffee sounds great, I typed, then tapped the button to send before I could convince myself not to. *Where should I meet you?*

"Holy shit," Holiday said an hour later, her gray eyes wide behind her enormous round glasses. She'd suggested a coffee shop near her parents' house, a brand-new-but-made-to-look-old-fashioned kind of place with a wide variety of non-dairy milk alternatives and fourteen-dollar avocado toast sprinkled with a million different kinds of seeds. "You think somebody tried to kill him?"

"What? No!" I looked around, afraid somebody would overhear her. The walls were white and bare in here, the ceilings tall and echoey. It seemed like even a whisper would carry clear to the counter, though nobody actually seemed to be paying us any mind: Two women in tennis dresses sipped iced tea and pored over wallpaper swatches. A young couple looked on adoringly as their toddler ate a yogurt parfait with his hands. The same local radio station as yesterday piped in over the speakers: Bonnie Raitt this time, "Something to Talk About." I looked back at her. "That's not what I'm saying at all. When did I say anything like that?"

"I mean, how is that not the logical conclusion to draw here?" Holiday frowned, her thick eyebrows knitting. "A guy that everyone hates winds up unconscious in the pool at the house of his former-best-friends-turned-worst-enemies?" She looked almost insulted. "If you're not saying that somebody pushed him, what *are* you saying?"

"I'm not saying anything! I just—" I broke off. When I'd told her about Greg, I think there was a part of me that that been hoping she'd tell me I was being dramatic—that it was a tragedy but that tragedies happen, that secretly I didn't trust rich people and it was showing. But I'd forgotten that Holiday loved a mystery like nobody else I'd ever met. If there wasn't one to solve, she would invent it: a weird neighbor who turned out to be a perfectly harmless actuarial assistant; common city vermin as beloved missing pet. In middle school she'd become absolutely convinced that two members of her favorite boy band were secretly dating each other and set out to prove it in a series of escalating gambits that culminated with her talking her way onto their floor at the Mandarin Oriental in Boston by convincing the hotel concierge she was the youngest granddaughter of the Commonwealth's most prominent political family. She wouldn't tell anyone what she'd seen there—"It was messed up of me to use my considerable powers of investigation to snoop on people's private lives like that, and I shouldn't have done it" was all she'd say—but six months later, they came out as a couple.

Still—Holiday's *considerable powers of investigation* aside—no way was I about to start accusing my friends of having anything to do with what had happened. That was ridiculous. That was insane. That was—

—the same thing you've been secretly wondering all morning, asshole.

"I don't know what I'm saying," I hedged finally, scrubbing a hand over my face.

Holiday nodded, stretching her long legs out underneath the table so her ankle bumped, not particularly gently, against mine. A thing I had noticed about her, both the other night and today, was that she didn't seem to care how much space she took up. It wasn't just her physical body, although that was definitely part of it—she was almost taller than me, with broad shoulders and wide hips, her stomach soft and round under the boxy short-sleeved dress she was wearing—but it was the way she carried herself. Her overstuffed tote bag. The way she'd asked the barista a thousand questions before she ordered. How tightly she'd hugged me when she saw me on the beach. Sometimes it seemed like the girls at Bartley were all in some kind of silent contest for who could be the most sleek and smooth and optimized, like they'd all been engineered at the Apple headquarters in Cupertino. Holiday was . . . analog.

"Well, I'm glad you texted, anyway," she said now, taking a sip from her heavy ceramic mug—after much deliberation she'd ordered a London Fog, a latte made with Earl Grey tea. It smelled like libraries and cloudy days and, actually, kind of like Holiday herself. "Because it kind of seemed like maybe you weren't that glad to see me at the beach the other night."

Right away I felt about two inches tall. I should have known there was no way she was going to act like she hadn't noticed. "No no no," I said quickly. "It wasn't that. It's just . . . complicated, that's all."

Holiday nodded, her full lips quirking. "Sure," she said, sitting back in her chair.

"I'm serious," I insisted. "I know all these people from school, you know? And none of them know, like . . ." I trailed off.

Holiday ducked her head, low and conspiratorial. "That you're Superman?" she whispered across the table.

I rolled my eyes. "That I'm broke."

"Okay." Holiday straightened up. She didn't look convinced—in fact, she looked like maybe she thought I was being a dick to her on purpose even more than I had been the other night.

"What," I said, "you don't believe me?"

"No, I one hundred percent believe you," she countered with a shrug. "It's just that you say it like you expected me to stroll up to this random group of total strangers and immediately lead with the fact that you're not, like, the heir to a private prison fortune. It's—what does your mom always call it? *Small behavior.*"

"Okay, can we not bring my *mom* into this, please?" I pushed my iced coffee away, feeling my temper flare. "I don't think it automatically makes me a piece of shit to want to be careful about keeping private things private. Do you have any idea what it's like to show up to a place like Bartley—or a place like this island, even—knowing you don't actually fit in?"

Holiday fixed me with a deeply unimpressed look across the table. "No," she deadpanned. "Please, tell me more about it."

"I—okay," I said, feeling myself blush. She was right. Things were fine for her now, maybe, but I remembered plenty of bullshit from back when we were kids—a birthday party nobody had come to, my mom mentioning some crap with some girls at her school. Once I stopped to think about it for even half a second, it was obvious she wouldn't have ratted me out to Jasper or Eliza or anyone. She was way more loyal than that. "You're right. I'm sorry."

"I'm teasing you, Michael." Holiday smiled. She had a nice smile, wide and unselfconscious, her teeth white and rich-girl straight. "I can tease you a little, can't I? I think we've known each other long enough for that."

"Yeah." I exhaled, rubbing at the back of my neck. Holiday had stayed over at our house a couple of times when we were really young, when her parents—both of them professors at Harvard, her dad in criminology and her mom in Shakespearean lit—were out of town at seminars or conferences. For a second I remembered the two of us running naked through the sprinkler in my small, scrubby backyard, then felt my face get even warmer and abruptly stopped remembering it. "I guess we have."

"My mom told me about your ankle," she said, wrapping her hands around her mug. Her nail polish was a deep red, and chipped. "That sucks."

That surprised me, the baldness of it. "It sucks," I agreed with a laugh. It was a relief to say it and not have to worry about her reaction.

"Does it hurt?"

I opened my mouth to tell her it was fine, or that it would be, some variation on what I'd been telling everybody since it happened. That I was in better shape now than I'd been before the accident. That I'd be back on the field in a few weeks.

"Yeah," I admitted quietly. "It hurts a lot."

Holiday looked at me for a long minute, her expression inscrutable for the first time since she'd sat down at the table. Then she nodded.

"So," she said, reaching back and scooping her hair into a curly knot on top of her head, securing it without the benefit of an elastic. "Just, like, hypothetically speaking. If what happened to this Greg guy wasn't a drunk accident. If somebody *had* wanted to hurt him. Do you have any idea who?"

"No," I said immediately.

Holiday snorted, flopping back in her chair. "Liar."

I huffed a breath. "These are my friends, Holiday! Not to mention the fact that they're the people that I'm *staying* with. I'm not just going to start running my mouth accusing them of who the fu—"

"I'm not asking you to accuse anyone of anything!" Holiday interrupted. "I'm just curious, that's all. From what you've said, Greg wasn't exactly anyone's best buddy. I'm just wondering if there's anyone in particular who might have—again, *hypothetically*—been looking for payback."

I thought of Eliza lying to the cops about who'd been at the Kendricks'. I thought of Wells's fist connecting with Greg's jaw. I thought of how cagey Jasper had been when I brought up Greg outside the bagel place, and I let out a quiet, involuntary groan.

"That's the thing," I confessed finally. "I think it might be, like . . . kind of a long list."

Holiday nodded again, focused as a clockmaker, her gray eyes shades of brown and green and blue. She reached down into her overflowing bag and pulled out a notebook with *Holiday Proctor* embossed in gold on the cover and the same kind of purple ballpoint pen she'd been writing with since second grade.

"Well then," she said brightly, opening to a fresh sheet of paper, "I guess we better get started."

We sat across from each other at the coffee shop for the better part of the afternoon, wandering back up to the counter first for refills of our drinks, then for turkey-and-cheddar sandwiches to soak up some of the caffeine, then for a couple of moon-size oatmeal chocolate-chip cookies because Holiday said she couldn't possibly be expected to reason deductively without a sugar hit. She made me tell her the story of last night over and over while she scribbled furiously in her notebook: peppering me with questions about Greg and the Kendricks and the police who'd showed up at August House, about what exactly I'd seen when I'd stumbled sleepily out onto the patio that morning. The more I heard myself talk, the more ridiculous and far-fetched the whole thing started to sound—and the sillier I started to feel for dragging Holiday all the way out here to listen to me spout some bonkers conspiracy theory when we'd barely talked at all since the onset of puberty.

What happened to Greg had been an accident, obviously. People got drunk and hurt themselves all the time.

"I don't know," I said at last, rattling the ice in my compostable coffee cup. It felt like my whole body was full of bees. "I'm probably making too big a deal about this. I mean, the police didn't seem to think it was suspicious, and they'd be able to recognize a potential crime scene a whole lot better than I would."

"Probably," Holiday agreed absently. "Though if I had to guess, the Kendricks are also the kind of people who send fruit baskets lined with cash down to the station on every major holiday to prepare for this exact eventuality. Nobody's going to want to bad-cop them." She tugged speculatively at one dark curl, then let it go so it bounced back like a cartoon spring, a habit of hers that I suddenly remembered from when we were kids. "Tell me again how he looked when you got out there?" Then, as if perhaps I'd encountered more than one injured, unconscious bro this fine morning: "Greg, I mean."

I shook my head. "Holiday, maybe—"

"Michael." Her gaze was steady. "Just humor me."

I took a deep breath, then described it one more time as best I could—Greg's head just barely above the waterline, his broad body slouched like a punctured raft on the steps—but Holiday still didn't look satisfied. She squinted at me for a moment, then slid her notebook across the table, thrusting her purple pen at me. "Draw me a diagram."

I sat back without entirely meaning to, like she was handing off a poisonous snake. "Seriously?" I laughed.

But Holiday nodded. "I want to be sure I'm picturing it right," she said, waggling the pen in my direction. "Besides, you're a good artist."

I made a face. "I'm sorry, you're basing that on *what*, exactly? All those drawings of Pikachu I used to do when we were seven?"

"They were very realistic renderings," Holiday said primly. "Also, don't be fake-modest—it's not cute. Didn't you win like a hundred art contests back in middle school?"

I shrugged, oddly embarrassed that she'd remembered. I never drew anymore, not really. It was a hobby I'd left behind when I went to Bartley, along with taking out huge stacks of manga from the East Boston branch of the BPL every week and stealing shopping carts from the Market Basket parking lot. Kid stuff.

Still, a thing I had forgotten about Holiday was how hard it could be to say no to her, and after a moment I found myself taking the pen from her outstretched hand and putting it obediently to paper. My grip felt awkward under her watchful eye, like when you sign your name too many times in a row and the letters stop meaning anything, but finally I pushed the notebook back across the table. It was all there: the carefully landscaped yard with the lights strung up in the trees, the bean-shaped outline of the pool. I'd done quick sketches of me and all three Kendrick siblings, drawn little arrows to indicate where everyone had come from. A stick-figure Greg sprawled on the steps.

Holiday's fingertips brushed mine as she picked up the notebook and looked at it closely. "Very sophisticated," she commented. "I especially like the little *x*'s over his eyes."

"You know what, screw you," I said with a laugh. "You're the one who wanted me to do this."

"I did," Holiday agreed. She was smiling as she said it, but her expression got serious as she studied the drawing for another moment, chewing speculatively on her bottom lip. "This is exactly how he was lying?" she asked. "You're sure?"

I thought back, suddenly skeptical of my own recall. My memory wasn't always the most reliable since the accident, and already I could feel the previous night going fuzzy in my brain, smearing like wet ink on glossy paper. Still, when I closed my eyes, I was pretty sure I could picture Greg exactly: the sag of his shoulders, the slump of his spine. "Yeah," I said. "I'm sure."

"Then somebody must have moved him."

My eyes popped open again. "Wait," I said, sitting up so straight my knees bumped the tiny table; our empty dishes rattled loudly, and I felt myself blush. "What?"

"Think about it," Holiday urged, pushing the notebook back in my direction and tapping my little illustration with one fingernail. "Imagine you're Greg, right? You're drunk, maybe stoned, you come back to the Kendricks' yard either through the side gate here or up the stairs on the beach side. You're looking for Meredith, or to find Wells and yell *And another thing!* or whatever. You're messed up enough to trip and take a header into the pool." She walked her fingers along the narrow lines of the paper. "There's no way you just casually land on the steps in a way that miraculously keeps you from drowning."

"Well, no, of course not," I said, a little defensive. "But he could have conceivably fallen in, hit his head, dragged himself over there, and *then* lost consciousness."

"I mean, I guess." Holiday looked unconvinced. She plucked

a fancy kettle-cooked chip from the bag on the table between us, crunching thoughtfully. "Logically, he would have fallen forward, though, if he was alone. So then how did he wind up with the blood on the back of his head?"

"I have no idea!" I exploded, the words way louder than I meant for them to be. I sat back in my chair, scrubbing a hand over my face as Holiday regarded me across the table. I felt edgy and tense, overwhelmed by the sharp and uncomfortable notion that by bringing her into this, I might have inadvertently set something in motion that I wouldn't be able to stop later on. Another thing I'd forgotten about Holiday: she wasn't the quitting type.

"Sorry," I mumbled finally. "I'm being a dick. Maybe I got it wrong, I don't know. It was hard to tell where the blood was coming from, exactly. I didn't really stop to check."

Holiday seemed to sense that I was about two seconds from pulling the plug on this whole endeavor. "Okay," she said, holding her hands up. "Fair. We'll put a pin in that for now." She stretched her arms up over her head and shook her wrists out, then flipped to a fresh page in her notebook. "Let's talk about suspects instead." Then, anticipating my protest: "*Hypothetically*, I mean."

I hesitated. "I mean, Wells," I said finally. "He and Greg literally beat the shit out of each other right before this happened. And he hates Greg's guts because of what happened between their dads."

Holiday nodded, writing carefully in her notebook. "The other two would have motive too, then," she pointed out. "Jasper and Eliza."

But I shook my head. "I know Jasper," I said. "And before you tell me I'm full of shit, yeah, I hear how that sounds. But I've been listening to that kid fart in his sleep every night since we were freshmen. He didn't do anything." Even as I was saying the words, I couldn't help but remember that, apparently, he'd spent the better part of the last year lying to my face about what was going on with his family, but still. Jasper's preferred method of conflict resolution was, and always had been, avoiding it altogether. I couldn't imagine him getting into a physical fight in the first place, let alone shoving somebody as big as Greg hard enough that he ended up in the pool with a serious head wound. "He doesn't have it in him."

"I mean, I would argue that everybody has it in them, if you push them hard enough."

I laughed at the true-crime gravity in her voice. "That's dark, Proctor."

"What?" Holiday blushed—just faintly, the tips of her ears and nose getting pink. "You don't agree?"

"It's not that I don't *agree,* exactly." After all, if there was one thing I'd learned for sure while I was with Greer, it was that all of us, myself included, were capable of way more than we liked to think. "I'm just surprised by your grim view of humanity, that's all. And I think Jasper should be pretty far down your list."

Holiday shrugged. "Okay," she said, turning back to her notebook, "probably not Jasper, then. And Eliza?"

"Not Eliza either." Prickly heat crept up the back of my neck. "She's . . . got an alibi."

"Does she now?" Holiday's full mouth twitched. "I'm sorry, and who might that be?"

I made a face across the table. Eliza had taken her time answering my knock the night before, leaving me standing outside her door like a dumbass for long enough that I thought it was possible she'd fallen asleep and I'd missed my chance entirely. I should have known she was just making me wait.

"I was wondering when you were finally going to get your act together," she said when the knob finally turned, her eyebrows and mouth just barely quirking. She'd changed into her pajamas, a crisp cotton set with white piping along the cuffs and collar. Her lips were slicked with something that just missed being shiny.

"I'm slow," I admitted with a grin.

"Evidently," Eliza agreed, then popped up onto her tiptoes and pressed her mouth against mine. She yanked me into her room, shutting the door behind us with a tidy click and walking me backward toward her mattress. Her sheets were clean and starchy and smelled like her—sand and summer, perfume and possibility.

We kissed for a long time, both of us shifting around infinitesimally until I was lying fully on top of her, her body warm and soft under mine. She rubbed the sole of her foot against my calf. I was sliding one careful hand up underneath her pajama top, my fingertips just grazing the smooth skin of her rib cage, when someone knocked on the door.

I sprang back so fast I almost fell off the bed, my reflexes conditioned by years of house parents at Bartley popping their heads into our rooms to make sure everyone had at least one foot on the floor at all times. "Um, yup?" Eliza called, clearing her throat and adjusting her pajama shirt. The palm of my hand felt like it was on fire. "Come on in!"

The door opened and Meredith poked her gingery head in. "Hey," she said, then "Oh," her eyes widening when she saw me. She was still in the outfit she'd been wearing at the party, high-waisted shorts and a bathing suit top printed with tiny pineapples. "Sorry. I didn't realize you were—" She nodded at me. "Otherwise engaged."

"You're totally fine," Eliza said, her tone so convincing I wasn't sure if I should be offended or not. "We were just talking. What's up?"

But Meredith shook her head. "Just dumb shit," she said with a rueful roll of her eyes. "I'll catch up with you in the morning."

For a moment I thought Eliza was going to argue, that I was going to wind up sandwiched between them on the bed while they gossiped about Aidy's ugly outfit or the patriarchy or whatever girls liked to talk about late at night, but instead she just nodded. "Okay," she said, blowing Meredith a kiss across the fluffy white carpet. "Sleep tight."

Once Meredith was gone, Eliza turned back to me, quirking one perfect eyebrow. "Boner killer?" she asked with a smile.

In fact, as far as I was concerned, the answer to that question was emphatically no, but Eliza seemed to have decided the mood was ruined, because she tucked her long legs underneath her and reached for her phone, fiddling with it for a moment until some quiet, plinky music started piping from the speakers on the bookshelf. "So," she said, curling up like a delicate bird in the giant nest of pillows at the head of the bed. The pillow budget alone at

August House must have been more than what my mom paid for rent on our entire apartment in a year. "Linden. Did you have fun tonight?"

"I mean, yeah," I said, leaning back beside her and wondering in spite of myself how to steer this conversation back around to a hookup-adjacent place. "Parts of it were fun. You?"

Something about the look on Eliza's face suggested the distinct possibility she was humoring me. "Parts of it were fun," she agreed, not bothering to hide her smile.

"Why don't you like parties?" I asked, reaching out and running one finger over the soft crease at the inside of her elbow. I could see the veins there, the blood blue and faint through her skin.

Eliza shrugged into the pillows. "I just get tired," she said quietly. "Of having to be a certain way."

"What way is that?"

She seemed to consider that for a moment, her features gone sharp and canny in the warm glow of the bedside lamp. "Civilized," she finally said.

Something about her answer startled me, like strolling into calm, placid-looking water and suddenly realizing the undertow was a lot stronger than you'd thought, and I let out a reflexive laugh. "Me too," I joked. "Everyone at Bartley is so fucking squeamish. You can't even eat a human heart in the dining hall anymore without getting cancelled."

Eliza smirked at that, though I couldn't tell if I was imagining she looked just the tiniest bit disappointed in my answer. "What a bunch of prudes," she agreed.

I didn't remember falling asleep in her bed, but I must have, because the next thing I knew, I was blinking awake again—Eliza breathing softly beside me, her warm body curled against my side. When I dug my phone out of my pocket, the clock on the screen read 3:42. I got up to pee, then stood in the hallway debating for a long minute before finally heading back up the stairs to my own room. Even if Eliza was pissed at me for sneaking out, I reasoned, it was better than one of her brothers catching me walk-of-shaming it out of her room in the morning. Up on the third floor I collapsed face-first onto the creaky mattress, which is where I stayed until I heard the screaming a little bit before five.

"It doesn't matter," I told Holiday now—shaking off the memory, reaching for the last of the cookie and shoving it into my mouth for the sake of having something to do. The truth was I felt enormously awkward just *thinking* about Eliza in front of Holiday, let alone trying to explain whatever was happening between us. The last time Holiday and I had had anything approaching a real conversation, we'd been kids. I didn't know how to talk to her about girls, or if girls were the kind of thing we *could* talk about, even. It felt like talking to my sister, if I'd had a sister, only it also really did not feel like that at all. "Let's just say it's pretty airtight."

"For the whole night?"

"For all the parts that matter."

Holiday's expression was utterly inscrutable, but she didn't press me. "Okay," she decided finally. "It's your rodeo." I thought she'd ask me for other suspects, but instead she turned the page of her notebook—a little more violently than strictly necessary, I thought, but possibly I was projecting. "You said something about a necklace?"

I shifted around in my seat and pulled the tiny rose-gold anchor out of my pocket, both of us staring at it for a moment as it swung gently from my fingers like a hypnotist's watch. "Well, it's a Georgette McKeown," Holiday said at last, reaching out and plucking it from my grip to examine more closely, turning it over in the palm of her hand. "So that's one place to start."

I blinked. "I'm sorry, a who now?"

"She's a famous Vineyard designer," Holiday explained patiently. "She makes this really intricate, really expensive jewelry with like, New England themes. It's a status symbol if you are, perhaps, a certain kind of girl."

I had a feeling I knew exactly what kind of girl she was talking about, but I also knew better than to take the bait. "New England themes?" I echoed instead. "So what, like, Pilgrim hats? Iced-coffee cups?"

"Small but intricate busts of David Ortiz," Holiday fired back, then smiled. "No, like, leaves and shells and stuff, I don't know. Nautical shit. They're all one of a kind, supposedly, but I feel like I've seen this one before." I could almost see her mind working as she peered at it, weights dropping and levers being pulled. "Can I ask you something?" she said suddenly. "The other night at the bonfire—" She broke off.

"What?" I prodded, but Holiday shook her head.

"Nothing," she amended. "Just thinking, that's all." She tucked the necklace—excuse me, the *Georgette McKeown*—into the inside pocket of her tote bag for safekeeping. "So, next steps. I think the logical thing to do is talk to some of these guys, right? See if they let anything slip about last night that they haven't already mentioned?"

"Wait wait wait." I held my hands up, startled. When I'd sent Holiday that text this morning, I hadn't for a second actually imagined us going around doing interviews like a couple of crack private detectives from a film noir on the classic movie channel. It felt like a ridiculous, farcical endeavor, like we needed trench coats and magnifying glasses and theme music, and also for someone to tell us to grow the fuck up. "I mean—no. These are my *friends*, Holiday. I can't just stroll back into their house and start asking all kinds of weird, nosy questions."

"I'm not suggesting interrogation lights and zip ties, Michael," Holiday said reasonably. "Ninety percent of good detective work is shutting up and letting people say what they want to say anyway. I just want to hear what that might be."

"Holiday—"

"Michael." She fixed me with a look across the table; just for a second I remembered what it was like to be the focus of all her attention, to feel like there was nothing about me she hadn't already figured out. "Look," she said. "Clearly, we haven't really hung out in a while. And if I had to guess, you probably thought long and hard about bailing on coffee today. But I still know you well enough to know that you wouldn't have told me about any of this to begin with if you didn't think there was at least an outside possibility something weird was going on." She shrugged. "Also, it'll be fun. I'll bring chips."

I hesitated. On the one hand, she wasn't *wrong*, exactly. On the other, in addition to the absurdity of this particular enterprise, there was still some part of me that felt strange bringing her around the Kendricks in the first place, and it must have shown on my face because Holiday rolled her eyes. "Okay," she said, reaching for her notebook. "Well, it was good to see you. You can tell your mom you did your due diligence, or whatever—"

"No," I said immediately, my voice cracking a bit. "You're right." As soon as the words came out of my mouth, I realized they were true—I *had* come to her looking for help, even if I didn't want to admit it. "You're right."

Holiday gazed at me for a long moment, looking faintly but unmistakably amused. "I mean," she reminded me, "I usually am."

Neither one of us said anything then, a weird, awkward gulf opening up between us. Holiday cleared her throat. When I glanced at my phone, I realized that we'd been sitting here for hours, the time evaporating while we talked and argued and theorized. There were empty plates and glasses scattered all around us; the other tables were mostly empty, and the sun had taken on that late-afternoon toastiness through the wide glass windows at the front of the shop. Jasper had texted forty minutes earlier: *Dude,* he'd said, *what happened to you?*

"Okay," I said, swallowing down a feeling that I'd gotten caught doing something embarrassing. I could remember plenty of afternoons like this from when we were kids, Holiday and I losing whole days in elaborate adventures of our own making. But we weren't little kids anymore. We were way too old to be playing pretend. "I should probably get back."

"Me too," Holiday said, gathering up her supplies and tucking them back into her overstuffed tote bag as I bused our plates and cups to the counter. "You need a ride?"

I shook my head. "I'm good," I said, holding the door open for her. The sun may have been waning, but the heat hit surprisingly hard after sitting in the AC for so long, the air thick and humid and salty. "I'll text you about whatever's going on tonight."

Holiday nodded quickly. "Okay," she said, though I could tell there was a part of her that didn't entirely believe me. I guess I couldn't blame her—in that moment, I wasn't even sure if I entirely believed myself. "See you, Linden."

She waved, then hitched up her bag on her shoulder and headed across the parking lot. She was almost to her car when I yelled her name.

Holiday turned and looked at me. With her big hair and lipstick she looked like some kind of old-fashioned movie star, on the Vineyard for a quick rendezvous with a Kennedy before heading out west to film her next major motion picture. Holiday Proctor, I thought, live in technicolor. "What's up?" she called. "You remember something else?"

"No, it's not that." I shook my head again. "I guess I just wanted to say thanks? I don't know if it showed, but I was like, pretty rattled this morning."

"Oh, it definitely showed," she admitted, her smile bright and almost mischievous. "But you don't have to thank me. We're friends, right?"

"I—yeah," I said, realizing that it was still true even as it made me feel a little built guilty to hear her say it out loud. If I was being honest with myself, I wasn't sure if I'd have shown up for Holiday if the situation had been reversed. Probably not, actually. But—even after all this time—somehow I wasn't surprised that she'd shown up for me. As I waved goodbye and headed for the bike rack in brilliant afternoon sunshine, I promised myself I wouldn't take that for granted again. "We're friends."

8

"WHAT HAPPENED TO YOU?" JASPER ASKED WHEN I got back to August House twenty minutes later. He was lying on the couch in the den in a still-wet pair of swim trunks, balancing a bowl of cereal on his stomach while he looked at his phone. "I thought you died." Then, both of us grimacing at his choice of words: "Uh. Just . . . kidding?"

"Sorry," I said, blinking in the mausoleum dimness. "I should have texted. Just got some food with a friend."

"Ms. Singh?" Jasper asked with a grin.

"Ms. Singh," I agreed, though I felt a little bad about calling her that now that we'd spent some time together. "I actually told her to come by and hang out later tonight, if that's cool?"

"Yeah, dude," Jasper said distractedly, shrugging into the throw pillows. "Whatever."

"What's going on here?" I asked, sinking down into an over-stuffed lounge chair.

"Not much," he reported. "Meredith's at the hospital still. Eliza's outside reading Proust or whatever the fuck. And I don't know where Wells is." He lifted his cereal bowl. "Really the most important news of the day is that Birdie bought Cookie Crisp."

I felt myself brighten. "Fuck yeah she did!" I exclaimed, then frowned as I was immediately hit with that same uncomfortable, slightly sick sensation from this morning—the grim suspicion that it was somehow fundamentally wrong to be doing something as mundane as eating junk cereal after everything that had happened here the night before.

On the other hand: I was starving. The sandwiches at the coffee shop had been expensive but tiny, their filling more microgreens than anything else. Not to mention the fact that Cookie Crisp is fucking delicious, so I went to the kitchen and poured myself a giant bowl, and Jasper and I spent the next hour in comfortable silence watching shows we'd both already seen, just like we'd spent any number of lazy afternoons back in the dorms at Bartley.

We were just starting a new episode of *The Simpsons* when Eliza came in from the yard in denim shorts and a breezy white button-down, her hair tied back in a brightly colored scarf. "Gentlemen," she said with a nod. She was looking at me in the same cool, canny way she had this morning, all held tongue and sharp cheekbones. I wondered if she was mad at me for sneaking out of her room last night. I wondered if there was a tiny part of her that suspected me of something too. She turned to Jasper. "Mom wants you to get your shit off the kitchen counter so Birdie can make dinner."

Jasper made no move to get up. "Are you sure?" he asked. "Because I think it sounds like Mom wants *you* to get *your* shit off the kitchen counter so Birdie can make dinner."

Eliza opened her mouth to answer just as the front door opened and Meredith walked in. She looked pale and drawn, the color leached from her cheeks and hair and eyebrows; even her clothes, the same pajama pants and borrowed hoodie she'd been wearing at five this morning, somehow looked threadbare and washed out. "Hey!" Eliza said, scurrying across the room and wrapping her in a tight, fierce hug. "What's the latest?"

Jasper heaved himself off the couch as they disappeared up the stairs, the creaky treads shrieking. "Not to be a total douche," he muttered as he shuffled off in the direction of the kitchen, "but I'm *pretty* sure we pay Birdie a salary to do literally this exact thing herself." He was gone before I could figure out how to reply.

I stayed where I was in the den for a moment, listening with some interest to the muffled hum of voices coming from the second floor, then the sound of a door shutting and the shower turning on. Eliza reappeared in the den a few minutes later, sinking down on the sofa beside me with a quiet exhale. "How's she doing?" I asked, nodding in the direction of the stairs.

Eliza shook her head. "Not great," she reported, reaching back and pulling the scarf out of her ponytail, raking her hands through her hair. "He's in a coma. And it sounds like his brain function is . . ." She made a face.

I winced. When I'd been trading pet theories with Holiday this afternoon, it had been easy to think of this entire situation as almost theoretical, like back when she and I were ten and spent every Saturday night in her living room eating Bugles and playing Clue. I'd imagined making my various accusations with a theatrical flourish: *Wells, in the backyard, with the swimming pool.* But Greg—obnoxious or not—was a flesh-and-blood person. And none of this was actually a game.

"Did they say anything else about what they thought happened?" I couldn't resist asking. "The police or the doctors, I mean?"

Eliza looked at me a little strangely. "Besides what we already know?" she asked, tucking her long, smooth legs up underneath her on the sofa. "Not really. Meredith said he probably wasn't in the water more than an hour or so, which was good because otherwise he could have gotten hypothermia."

"I thought the pool was heated," I said, and Eliza nodded.

"It is, but it's on a timer, so the temperature drops at night." She smiled wryly. "I think you'll find we're very serious about the environment here at August House."

I grinned. Holiday would like that, I knew; it gave us a neat, compact timeline to work with. It also, of course, meant Eliza's supposedly airtight alibi didn't quite track—after all, I hadn't actually been with her in the hours just before dawn—but I pushed that thought out of my mind. There were plenty of people with way more motive to hurt Greg than Eliza had, I reminded myself. There was no reason to think . . . anything.

I took a deep breath. "Listen," I said—moving a little bit closer, taking a little bit of a chance. "About last night."

Eliza tipped her head to the side, pale eyebrows barely arcing. "I'm sorry," she said, "what about it, exactly?"

"I just wanted to say that I had fun," I told her. "You know, like . . . before the terrible part."

"Oh, Linden, don't be so hard on yourself," Eliza said cheerfully. "Your kissing isn't *that* bad."

That made me smile. "Oh, you think you're very cute."

"I do, thank you."

"What are you two whispering about?" Mrs. Kendrick asked, coming into the den in a tailored dress and cardigan, her blond hair clipped back with a tortoiseshell barrette.

"Linden was just asking what I thought he should get you as a hostess gift," Eliza replied without missing a stitch. "Don't worry, I told him how much you like gerbera daisies. The brighter the better, I said."

Mrs. Kendrick made a face. "Dear god, don't even joke." She braced one hand on the bookcase, reaching down and adjusting the strap on her shiny metallic sandal with the other. "Listen, Daddy and I are going to go meet the Grahams in town for something to eat. We weren't sure we'd be back in time when they invited us, but since we're here . . ." She trailed off, frowning. "Unless you want us to stay in?"

Eliza shook her head. "We'll be fine," she promised lightly, and I couldn't tell if she was faking it or not. "We always are."

Jasper's parents were in good spirits as they headed out to dinner in Vineyard Haven, seemingly placated by whatever conversations they'd had with their lawyers that day: "The gate on the pool is up to code, and the kid was trespassing," I heard his dad saying to his mom as they headed out the door. "It's a horrible thing, but according to Barnes, in terms of liability, our asses are covered." Birdie grilled chicken for the rest of us, slathering it with dill-and-yogurt sauce and putting together a brightly colored salad with fat slices of tomato and peach. We ate outside around the patio table under the party lights once she and Dean were gone for the day, none of us commenting on the fact that what probably looked from the outside like a perfectly curated Instagram post had been full of police officers and paramedics not twelve hours before.

Then again, maybe I was the only one even thinking about it.

"So," Wells said finally, sitting back in his chair and lifting his chin in an impression of his father that was almost uncanny. He'd reappeared just before dinner, though nobody seemed to know where he'd been. "How was everyone's day?"

Eliza rolled her eyes, then cut a glance at Meredith, who was picking silently at her dinner. "Don't be a dick, Wells."

"Hey now," Wells chided mildly. I thought he'd seemed more worried than anyone about getting in trouble with Reyes and O'Neal this morning, but he seemed almost jovial now. Though, I realized, catching sight of the ice cubes in his tall, frosty glass, it was possible that actually he was just drunk. "I'm only trying to make conversation with you kids. Highs and lows of the day? Anyone?" Then, when no one answered: "Nobody?" he asked. "Okay then, I'll start. My high is the truly delectable local feta in this salad right now. And my *low*—"

Meredith shoved her chair back and bolted from the table. Eliza shot her brother a look that could have taken the paint right off the little car. "Dammit, Wells!"

Wells sat back in his chair. "What'd I say?"

"Dude," Jasper said, "you're an asshole." Still, I couldn't help but notice that he was smirking too. Any leftover tension between them from last night seemed to have seeped away. Not for the first time, I wondered if that was just how it worked when you had siblings—fights that burned out as quickly as they started, a blood bond that was stronger and more important than anything else.

I'd texted Holiday before we sat down to eat, and she came through the gate at the side of the yard just as we were bringing our plates inside. "Hey," she called, her dark gaze flicking around the group of us on the patio, and I thought I saw a moment of uncertainty cross her expression before she smiled. She'd changed her clothes since this afternoon, was wearing cropped jeans and a boxy T-shirt. Her hair was long and wild down her back. She looked . . . *pretty*, and by the way Wells was eyeing her, I could tell he thought so too.

"Guys, this is Holiday," I announced, swallowing down a weird flash of protectiveness and lifting a hand in greeting. "We've known each other since we were zygotes."

"Hey there," Wells said, suddenly friendly in a way that immediately raised my hackles even though I knew that was ridiculous. "Pull up a raft."

No matter what I'd told Holiday about wanting her to come over, I was fully expecting this whole endeavor to be excruciatingly, cringingly awkward, but in fact, I was surprised by how easily she seemed to fit in with the Kendricks: chatting gamely with Jasper, flirting idly with Wells. Eliza had coaxed Meredith back outside at some point, and the two of them and Holiday knew a couple of girls in common—the New England Rich Kid Network strikes again, I thought with a smirk. I tried not to eavesdrop too closely as they talked, but all at once I heard the pitch of Eliza's voice rise in excitement. "Hold on a second," she said, gazing at Holiday with open admiration. "*You're* the girl from the Mandarin Oriental?"

Holiday ducked her face, bashful. "It would be unladylike of me to confirm or deny," she said with a grin.

"Linden," Eliza announced, looking utterly delighted, "your friend here is an absolute fucking After Hours fandom legend."

"Wait a minute," I said, shaking my head in realization and disbelief. After Hours was the cheesy boy band that Holiday had been so obsessed with when we were younger, the one whose two most eligible members were now raising a blind, three-legged rescue dog in cohabitational bliss. "You're an After Hours fan?"

Eliza shrugged primly. "I contain multitudes," she informed me. I snorted. "Clearly."

"Don't be misogynist," she fired back, hopping up in one smooth motion and crossing the patio in my direction. "First of all, I'll have you know the Beatles were a boy band."

"After Hours are hardly the Beatles."

"Spoken like someone who's not terribly familiar with either," Holiday put in, and Eliza grinned.

"My dad got us backstage passes to the Past Midnight tour when I was in sixth grade," she recalled, settling back in a lounge chair and crossing her delicate ankles. "I wrote *I love James* all over myself with Sharpie and then it wouldn't come off, so I had to go to school like that until it faded."

"Rubbing alcohol," Holiday said absently. "Takes it right off."

"Oh, *now* you tell me." Eliza grinned. "Where were you when I was playing dodgeball with two full DIY *Future Mrs. James Harper* sleeves?"

"Seriously?" I laughed, trying to picture Eliza as an awkward preteen superfan and not quite getting there. She seemed like the kind of person who'd come out of the womb perfectly assured, who'd never had a bad hair day or a breakout or an unfortunate favorite outfit. And sure, of course there was a part of me that knew even then that it wasn't true, that I was projecting my own hot-girl fantasy onto her, but looking across the patio at her luminous skin and sharp cheekbones—and, okay, the pale shadow of cleavage at the neckline of her shirt—it was hard to make myself stop.

"So you know Linden from when he was a little kid?" Wells asked Holiday now, beer bottle dangling from his fingers as he settled himself at the edge of the deep end of the pool. "Tell us something really fucking embarrassing about him."

I cringed. There were plenty of stories for her to choose from, if she was inclined to take me down a peg or two—the time I'd peed my pants in the Government Center T station on the way to the circus, the six months I'd spent carrying a Captain America shield to school every day—but Holiday just laughed. "I think he's unembarrassable," she said, which was deeply untrue and both of us knew it. "He's too cool."

"Holiday's being very generous to me right now," I said, shooting her a grateful look across the patio. "What she's not telling you is that I talk a pretty big game for a guy who lovingly kisses his After Hours poster every night before bed."

That got a laugh and also redirected the conversation, just like I'd been pretty sure it was going to; never mind that it wasn't anything real. "I knew it," Jasper joked, cueing up the band's latest album on his phone.

I felt myself relax after that, listening to the conversations wandering all around me and the faint crash of the waves down at the beach. Eliza taught Holiday to play the Minister's Cat, the two of them side by side on the lounge chairs; Jasper turned idle somersaults in the pool. And yeah, I wasn't exactly sure how any of this was going to help us figure out what had happened to Greg, but as I took the joint that Wells handed over, it occurred to me that maybe that didn't matter. Maybe there really was nothing to figure out in the first place.

I was thinking about getting into the pool—after all, I consoled myself, it *had* just been cleaned—when I heard the sound of the sliding glass door to the house whooshing open. Up until now Meredith had been sitting mostly silent at the patio table, looking at her phone, but I turned just in time to spot a glimpse of her gingery red hair as she disappeared into the kitchen.

Holiday noticed too—and, to my surprise, she got unobtrusively to her feet a moment later. "Bathroom?" I heard her ask Eliza, who directed her to the powder room off the kitchen. Holiday caught my eye as she went, shooting me a pointed look that definitely meant either *Follow me ASAP* or *Stay exactly where you are and don't mess this up for us,* though unfortunately I had no idea which.

In the end my curiosity got the better of me, though, and I heaved myself up off the pool deck and handed the joint back to

Wells in what I hoped was an extremely casual and unsuspicious manner. "Who needs a beer?" I asked, brushing my palms off on the back of my shorts.

"I do!" Jasper called cheerfully; Eliza's hand went up across the patio, and Wells called out detailed instructions for how to make a vodka tonic just the way he liked it as I padded into the cool, quiet house.

I stepped into the kitchen just in time to see Holiday holding the necklace out in Meredith's direction, the charm swinging gently as it dangled from her hand. "This isn't yours, is it?" she was asking, her round face open and guileless. "I just saw it floating in the pool, and I thought I remembered seeing you wearing it at the beach the other night." She grinned. "I *love* Georgette McKeown."

Meredith's eyes widened in surprise. "Oh jeez, yeah, it is. Thank you." She glanced at me over Holiday's shoulder. "Aidy the trash bag pulled it right off my neck."

"*Jasper's* Aidy?" I blurted before I could stop myself. Holiday whirled around, and I realized too late that she'd probably intended for me to stay outside after all. "Really?"

Meredith laughed at that, a short mean cackle. "First of all, that girl has hooked up with basically every trust fund on this island, so if I were you, I'd take a breath before I called her *Jasper's* anything." She plucked the necklace from Holiday's outstretched hand, frowning darkly at the broken clasp before tucking it into her pocket. "Second of all, you saw her at that party last night. She was totally shit-faced. I know you guys all love to eat up that little Cinderella act she puts on, but get a couple of drinks into her and believe me, her townie starts to show." She reached up and scooped her hair off her shoulders: sure enough, there was a trio of livid red scratches on the side of her neck.

"Oh my *gosh*," Holiday said, and I suspected her alarm was probably real. "What were you guys fighting about?" Then, affecting a slightly dorky sheepishness: "Sorry. It's fully none of my business."

Meredith shrugged. "Whatever," she said, jerking her chin in the direction of the patio, "it's not like it isn't everyone's favorite thing to talk about out there. I'm sure you'd hear about it eventually. Greg—my boyfriend, the guy who got hurt—had like, a moment of insanity with that girl at the beginning of the summer, which he admitted to and apologized for and which, not for nothing, has never mattered less to me than it does in this moment when he is actively fighting for his freaking *life,* but Aidy like, can't let it go." She huffed a breath. "She thinks he's the one that got away, or some other Taylor Swift sad-sackery. Never mind the fact that he's told her to get lost like a thousand times."

I blinked, the contents of my brain reshuffling like a deck of cards in the hands of a boardwalk huckster; beside me, Holiday had gotten very still. I'd hardly given Aidy a second thought since the party—she'd barely even come up when Holiday and I were talking this afternoon—but all at once, I couldn't believe our mistake. After all, it made perfect sense: At some point late last night, she and Greg must have argued about him going back to Meredith. Tempers flared, the situation escalated, and Greg wound up in the pool. "You don't think—" I blurted before

I could stop myself, then clamped my jaws abruptly shut: the last thing I wanted was for Meredith to get suspicious, or to tell Eliza I'd been pestering her with a million weird questions about Greg.

But Meredith just looked at me blankly. "I don't think what?" she asked. Then the penny seemed to drop. "Wait, like do I think she pushed him into the *pool*?" She laughed again then—louder now, the sound of it faintly hysterical; just for a second, I was afraid it was going to turn into a sob. "Oh my god," she said— almost to herself, it seemed like, pushing the heels of her hands into her eye sockets. "Oh my *god*, how is this my life right now?"

I opened my mouth to backpedal, to tell her she definitely didn't need to talk about it, but this time the look that Holiday shot me was clear: *Don't say another word.* Sure enough, a moment later Meredith pulled herself together, taking a deep breath and shaking her head. "Look," she said finally, "I'd be the first person to tell you if I thought Aidy had anything to do with what happened to Greg last night. That girl is fully garbage, and I hate her fucking guts, and honestly, the only thing that keeps me from smacking her across her smug face most of the time is the knowledge that she's going to be stuck on this tourist-trap island forever, slinging fish sticks to support her six children who all have different fathers."

Holiday's eyes widened. "That is . . . evocative," she said.

"Thank you," Meredith said, though I was pretty sure Holiday hadn't exactly meant it as a compliment. "In any case, she and Jasper were going at it like they were auditioning for a low-budget porno all night long. I don't know if she was hoping it would get back to Greg and he'd be jealous, or what, but I don't think they came up for air long enough for her to have done anything like that." She was quiet for a moment, scrubbing her hands roughly over her face. "I feel like roadkill," she announced when she looked up again, and I noticed for the first time how exhausted she was—bluish hollows blooming under her eyes, her eyelashes pale and mascaraless. A generous spray of freckles stood out across her nose and cheeks. "Thanks for bringing me the necklace," she told Holiday, then turned to me. "Will you tell Eliza I went to bed?"

I nodded so hard and fast it was a miracle my head didn't pop off and go rolling into the pantry. "Of course," I promised, feeling both oddly guilty for prying into her personal life and deeply exhilarated that it had worked. The second she disappeared down the hall, I whipped around in Holiday's direction. *"Dude,"* I started, but she held up a fierce hand to stop me, then put her finger to her lips and motioned for me to follow.

"Right." I trailed her out onto the wide wraparound porch of August House, the two of us plunking ourselves down on the front steps to debrief in the pale glow of the porch light. "Sorry about that," I said, "and also about barging into the kitchen back there. I didn't mean to like, salt your investigative game."

Holiday waved me off. "No, no," she said, "it's fine. We're better as a team anyway. I definitely wouldn't have been able to get all that out of her on my own."

"How the heck did you notice Meredith wearing that necklace

at the beach the other night?" I asked. "You only saw her for like five seconds."

Holiday shrugged. "I notice everything," she reminded me, looking out at the fireflies flickering lazily near the tree line. "I can't help it." From the tone in her voice it didn't necessarily sound like a quality she liked in herself.

"So you knew it was hers when I showed it to you this afternoon?"

"I had a hunch," she admitted.

I wasn't sure whether to be impressed or annoyed that she hadn't told me, though I guessed I wasn't actually surprised. Holiday had been one step ahead of me more or less our entire friendship; she'd been the one to tell me the truth about Santa Claus and the Tooth Fairy, not to mention where babies came from. I might still have believed in the stork if it wasn't for her.

"So, okay," I said quietly, glancing over my shoulder to make sure nobody could hear us. The crickets were noisy up in the trees, the moon round and white and full through the dense, leafy branches. "Not Meredith or Aidy, then?"

"Not *Aidy*," she corrected. "Clearly, Meredith isn't what you'd call her biggest fan, so it's probably safe to assume that we can trust her if she says Aidy couldn't have had anything to do with it. But we don't know for sure that she's telling the truth about the necklace." She tugged on a strand of dark hair, twisting it around one finger. "I also kind of don't understand why a girl like her was with Greg to begin with," she mused. "Or like, why she took him back after he cheated."

"He's great at oral," I reported before I could stop myself. Then, feeling the heat creep up my neck: "I mean, so I've heard."

"I will . . . be sure to put that in his personnel file," Holiday said with a smirk. "But somehow I don't think it's *quite* enough."

I shrugged. The ins and outs of Greg and Meredith's relationship weren't particularly interesting to me, probably because I'd seen so many variations of it play out at Bartley over the last three years. "Girls like douchebags," I reminded her. "Sometimes that's just how it goes."

"Do you think that's true?" Holiday asked pointedly. "Or do you think it's just a thing guys tell themselves when they feel entitled to a date but can't get one?"

The screen door squealed open behind us before I could reply. "Fuck you guys," Jasper said, crossing the creaking porch holding a fresh bag of Pirate's Booty. "Nobody told me the party moved out here." He sat down on the step above us, holding the cheese snacks out like an offering.

"Yes, please." Holiday helped herself to a handful. "I love this stuff," she said once she'd swallowed. "It's so good. The way it kind of squeaks against your teeth?"

Jasper's mouth dropped open. "Do you want to get married?" he asked, visibly delighted.

"I don't think you could handle me," Holiday fired back with a grin. She stood up then, brushing her fingers off on the back of her jeans. "I should go," she said, gesturing at her car in the driveway, then looked back at me. "Lunch tomorrow?"

I hesitated, my gaze cutting to Jasper and then to Holiday again; she was working out a plan, obviously, though I had no idea what it might be, and it wasn't like I could ask now. "Tomorrow," I agreed, and she nodded her approval before waving goodbye and taking off.

Once she was gone, Jasper turned to me, eyebrows waggling suggestively. "What's up, Ms. Singh?" he crooned, licking his lips like a pervert. I rolled my eyes and flipped him the middle finger, then followed him back up the stairs and into the house.

9

HOLIDAY TEXTED ME TO MEET HER AT RED'S THE FOL-
lowing afternoon. When I pulled up on my borrowed bike, she
was waiting for me at the host stand, looking particularly art
teacher–esque in a long black dress and lace-up sandals. "I already
scoped out Aidy's section," she announced, then turned to the
hostess before I could answer and pointed to a shady corner of the
patio. "Sorry," she said with an apologetic smile, "would you mind
if we sat over there?" She rolled her eyes in an exaggerated way,
jerking her head in my direction. "My friend here is very sensitive
to the sun."

Aidy appeared in her Red's uniform a few moments after we sat
down at the rickety plastic patio table, lifting her chin in recogni-
tion. "Oh!" she said. "Hey, Linden." Her golden hair was up in a
tall, messy bun today, giving her the look of an aerobics instruc-
tor or an Instagram influencer who specialized in wellness prod-
ucts. The polish on her short, bitten-down nails was a bright neon
white. "How's it going?"

"It's going," I said, then gestured across the table. "This is my friend Holiday. We were wondering if maybe we could ask you—"

Holiday kicked me so hard and so precisely in my busted ankle that I almost yelped out loud. "—for a couple of Cokes," she finished for me, smiling her most innocuous smile. "I think we need another couple of minutes with the menu."

"Sure thing," Aidy said with a nod. She had that same look on her face as she'd had the other day at the market in town, like possibly there was something about me she found slightly ridiculous. "I'll be right back."

Once she was gone, Holiday turned to look at me, her gray eyes wide. "What the fuck are you doing?" she hissed.

"Wait," I said, "what?" All at once it occurred to me that maybe I'd misunderstood the purpose of this entire outing—that Holiday didn't have a plan at all, that she'd only brought me to Red's in the first place because she really liked fried calamari. "I thought the whole reason we came here was to cross-check Meredith's story."

"I mean, yeah," she agreed, "but we can't just barrel right into it like a couple of amateurs. You said yourself that these people are your friends, right? We should be using that if we can—for a lot of reasons, but mostly because it's the only leg up we've got. If it gets back to everyone else that you're sniffing around trying to figure out what really happened the other night . . ." She trailed off.

"Oh," I said, feeling my face get hot in spite of the leafy green canopy shielding us from the midday sunshine. Holiday was right, obviously; I'd just gotten excited, like a dog peeing on the rug. "Yeah, totally."

"Just slow-play it a little bit, that's all," she continued. "Let her come to you."

That made me smile. "Like I always do with the ladies, you mean."

"Oh, brother." Holiday rolled her eyes. "Just don't make it weird, okay?"

"No, no," I promised, "I'll be totally cool. Put on a little smooth jazz music, ask a couple of casual murder questions . . ."

"Gee," Holiday said, looking pointedly at her menu even as she tried and mostly failed to stifle a laugh, "maybe I'll get the scallops!"

Aidy dropped off the drinks a minute later, plucking a pen from behind her ear. "So hey," I said once we'd ordered. "How crazy was all that shit at August House the other night?"

Her gaze flicked back and forth between Holiday and me, cautious. "I mean, *crazy* is one word for it," she agreed. "I heard Greg's pretty fucked up."

"Sounds that way." I nodded. "Meredith mentioned you guys used to . . ."

Aidy's eyes narrowed. "Oh, did Meredith mention that?" she fired back, her voice all salt and sarcasm. "I'm sure that's not all she mentioned."

"I mean, no," I admitted, and I didn't have to feign my own embarrassment. "She might have also mentioned something about a necklace."

Aidy made a face. "I'm so sick of that girl, you know that?" she said, then turned to Holiday as if for validation. "She doesn't even *live* here, and she's spent the entire summer going all up and down the island telling everyone what a skank I am and how I chased after her boyfriend and blah blah blah. First of all, I didn't even know Greg had a girlfriend when we started hanging out. And second of all, nobody forced her to take him back after things ended between us. She's the one who can't let it go." She clicked her pen once before tucking it neatly back behind her ear. "Besides, I did her a favor. Georgette McKeown is basic as hell."

Holiday laughed at that, loud and genuine. "I mean, fair enough," she said with a grin—allying herself with Aidy, I realized, the same way she'd done with Meredith last night. "Kind of fits her whole aesthetic, though."

"That girl suuuuucks," Aidy singsonged, clearly enjoying the pleasure of a captive audience. "And she's *mean*! Honestly, I wouldn't be surprised if she was the one who pushed Greg into the pool."

I almost choked on my soda. "Wait, seriously?" I blurted. I thought of what Holiday had said back at the coffee shop, about how most detective work was just letting people say what they wanted to say anyway; still, I'd never expected Aidy to just come right out with a bald-faced accusation.

"I mean, no, not seriously." Aidy laughed too, and then— presumably off my overeager, slightly sweaty expression—looked at me a little strangely. "Like, yes, she's the kind of person who steals dalmatian puppies from loving homes to make into fur coats. But she's not a stone-cold killer. Besides, I actually saw her passed out on my way to the bathroom at like four a.m.—snoring like a fucking trucker, I might add. So much for being a lady." She held up her notepad then, waggling it a little. "Anyway," she said, "I'll put your order in."

Once we were alone again, Holiday knocked her plastic cup gently against mine, smiling. "I must admit," she said grudgingly, "that was nicely done."

"Just like I always do with the ladies," I reminded her. "So do you think she's telling the truth?"

Holiday shrugged. "I mean, obviously those two hate each other," she said thoughtfully, "so yes, probably. You said Eliza told you that Greg went into the water sometime in the hour before dawn, right? So the timeline clears her."

"Yeah." I was surprised by the sharpness of my own disappointment just then: That necklace had been our only concrete piece of evidence, and it turned out it was just an accessory in a fight over a guy who, by all accounts, was a total boner. On top of which, I wasn't entirely sure when I'd gotten invested enough to be bummed out in the first place: After all, didn't I *want* there to be nothing to find here? Didn't I want this whole thing to have been an accident, to go back to my own vacation guilt-free?

Holiday turned to watch as Aidy dropped the check at a nearby table. "Her and Jasper, huh?" she asked thoughtfully, twisting her straw paper between two fingers. "That's why she stayed over at the house the other night?"

"Apparently, he liked her way before anything happened between her and Greg," I explained. "Which, not for nothing, but how fucked up is that? I mean, one summer the guy is your best friend for life, and by the next his dad put your dad in jail and he's hooking up with your crush just to mess with you?"

Holiday shrugged, not quite looking at me. "I mean," she said quietly, "friendships change."

I winced at that—I couldn't help it. "Yeah," I admitted, knowing all at once that we weren't talking about Jasper and Greg anymore. "I guess you're right." The more I'd thought about it the past few days, the shittier I'd felt about how things had gone between Holiday and me way back when: It wasn't like I'd ever consciously decided to ditch her, though looking back, I was pretty sure that was how it had seemed from the outside. Even back in middle school, I knew in theory that Holiday's commitment to being exactly who she was, no matter the context—her habit of singing show tunes on the Red Line, or the time she spent my entire twelfth birthday party speaking in a nonspecific Balkan accent and convincing half the kids in my class she was an exchange student from Montenegro—was admirable, but it was also . . . a lot. I wasn't exactly sure when I'd started to notice, or when it had become a thing that bothered me, but either way, by the time we turned thirteen, I'd stopped bringing her around my friends from school.

The last time we really hung out was the summer after eighth grade; my mom had dropped me off in Cambridge to meet Holiday for lunch, one of the first times our parents had agreed to turn us loose in the city without them. I'd been hoping for burgers, but instead we'd gone to a sushi place that Holiday liked, where she'd greeted the waitress in confident Japanese and ordered for the both of us without asking. It wasn't until the food came out that I realized there were no forks or knives on the table.

I only hesitated for a second, but Holiday was onto me right away. "Do you not know how to use chopsticks?" she asked, pulling her set from their red paper sleeve and breaking them apart. She was wearing a dress that was printed with bright yellow moons and stars and looked like she'd dug it out of Ms. Frizzle's closet. Something about it had annoyed me the second I saw her waiting outside the restaurant, though I couldn't explain exactly what— the nerve of it, maybe, her confidence that either she wasn't going to get made fun of or that it would be fine if she did.

"No, I do," I lied. "I'm just like, slow at it."

Holiday wasn't buying. "I can show you," she offered gently. "It's really not that hard."

"It's fine," I said, yanking the chopsticks apart like a wishbone at Thanksgiving with enough force that they snapped unevenly, one of them significantly longer than the other. "I got it."

"Michael—"

"*What?*" I sat back in the booth and dropped them on the table, my whole body suddenly itchy and hot. "I'm not even that hungry."

"Don't be ridiculous," she said reasonably. "I'm paying, anyway. My mom gave me her credit card to take you out."

And that—that did it. All at once I was sliding out of the booth and stalking out of the restaurant, pretending I couldn't hear Holiday calling my name. I'd gotten myself a burger and fries at a place around the corner—I could pay for my own lunch, thanks—and eaten them on a bench inside the Harvard Square T stop while a drunk guy yelled obscenities across the platform. Then I got on the train and went home, where my mom, who'd been planning to pick me up at Holiday's house at five o'clock, looked at me with great suspicion. "Everything okay?" she asked with a frown.

"Yep," I'd reported shortly, then went into my room and played *Minecraft* for the rest of the afternoon.

Holiday and I patched things up, ostensibly, and we'd seen each other a couple of times before I left for my first year at Bartley in September; still, things were never quite the same between us after that. It was like we'd outgrown each other, or something. It was like everything that had always been different about us was suddenly too big to ignore.

At least, that was what I'd told myself. If there was anything I'd learned in the years since Holiday and I had been inseparable, it was that there were a lot of different versions of the truth.

Now I looked at her across the wobbly fish-shack table, pulling my mind—and hers, I hoped—back to the present. "So if it wasn't Meredith," I said, "and it wasn't Aidy—who, then? We're back to square one?"

Holiday seemed to consider that for a moment. "Not necessarily," she countered.

I raised my eyebrows, immediately recognizing her expression as the one she got when there was something on her mind she wasn't telling me. "Meaning what, exactly?"

She shrugged. "Meaning I'm hungry" was all she said, smiling as Aidy dropped a basket of popcorn shrimp on the table between us. "Let's eat lunch."

I got up before dawn the next morning, lacing up my sneakers and taking off down the winding, tree-lined road that snaked away from August House. The birds called out their wary-sounding warnings in the branches high above my head. Last spring before the accident, I'd been doing seven miles every morning with no problem, all the way into town and back before breakfast and my first class of the day. Now, though, I barely made it a mile before I had to quit, the pain shrieking up my ankle with enough heat to power the entire Massachusetts Steamship Authority. I swore under my breath, useless rage at my own body coursing through me as I looked around frantically for a non-awkward place to sit down before finally giving up and plopping myself at the shoulder like a smashed-up slab of roadkill. I was drenched in sweat, my heart thumping with exertion; my ankle was swollen and squealing and hot. "Fuck," I muttered, something that felt hideously, dangerously, like tears rising at the back of my throat and sinuses. *"Fuck."*

I don't know how long I'd been sitting there, trying to figure out if I could even make it back to August House at a hobble or if I was going to have to endure the mortifying ordeal of calling Jasper to come get me, when I heard quick footsteps echoing closer down the pavement, the fleet, familiar sound of rubber meeting road. I lifted my head just as Doc slowed to a stop a few feet away.

"Hey, Linden," he said cautiously, pulling out an earbud. He was wearing running shorts and sunglasses, a hat from Yale Med School turned backward on his head. "You okay?"

I nodded maniacally, jumping to my feet so fast and enthusiastically it was a miracle I didn't take out my other ankle in the process. "Oh yeah," I assured him, "I'm totally fine." The last thing I wanted was for Doc of all people to be catching me like this, weak and pathetic and out of ideas. It was . . . fucking emasculating, to be honest, though already I could see Holiday rolling her eyes at the thought. "You can go."

"Nah, it's fine. I was about to cool down anyway," Doc said, pulling out the other earbud and dropping the pair of them into the pocket of his shorts. "I'll walk back with you."

Well, shit. What the fuck was I going to do? If I'd had my way, I would have stayed on the side of the road for the rest of the day, waiting for some native Vineyard wildlife to come along and make me into their dinner, but I wasn't about to let Doc see me being a weenie for a second longer than absolutely necessary. I brushed my palms off on the back of my shorts, ignoring the cacophony of pain singing its way up my shin and hoping I was projecting a robust picture of health and hardiness. "Cool," I said loudly. "Let's go."

At first neither one of us said much: it was taking the better part of my concentration just to stay upright without groaning, and Doc seemed happy enough to listen to the birds and the far-off crash of the ocean as we walked. Just as August House came into view in the distance, though, the morning sun rising above the roofline, he looked at me sidelong. "So," he said, "you and Eliza seem to be pretty chill."

Right away I felt my hackles go up. "I guess," I said, more roughly than I meant to. "Is that a problem?"

Doc shook his head, laughing a little. "Not at all," he said easily, holding his hands up. "She's a friend of mine, that's all. I like to look out for her."

I nodded slowly—remembering the shame of slinking off the field once Doc's team had finished with us in the championships last fall, wincing at the hot surge of pain in my ankle every time I gave it any weight. "I don't know, man," I said, knowing full well I was being an asshole and not entirely able to help it. "She seems like the kind of girl who can look out for herself."

"Yup," Doc agreed. "I'm sure she does."

I didn't know what that meant, but I didn't like the way he said it—like he had access to inside information, like he knew her so much better than I ever could. And all of that was probably true, I reminded myself: After all, Doc belonged here, had grown up spending summers on this jagged shoreline same as the rest of them. I could only ever hope to be a guest.

"Whatever you say, man," I told him finally, hobbling up the front steps of August House with as much dignity as I could muster. "I'll see you around."

"Yeah, Linden," Doc said. "You will."

Back inside the house, I limped into the empty kitchen, digging a bag of peas out of the freezer and slapping them onto my ankle. I was still staring sulkily out the window twenty minutes later when Birdie let herself in through the sliding door, a couple of canvas grocery totes slung over her sturdy shoulders.

"Good lord, Linden," she said, eyes wide across the kitchen island, "you scared me." Then, before I could apologize, she motioned to my leg. "War wound?" she asked.

I sighed, easing the peas off my red, chilly ankle. "Something like that."

Birdie nodded, setting the bags down on the marble countertop and heading toward the coffeemaker—then looking back at me, eyebrows lifted, when she realized I'd already made a pot.

"I helped myself," I admitted, raising my mug in her direction. The coffee cups at August House were the wide, brightly colored enamel kind, all of them monogrammed with a blocky uppercase *K* and a little bespoke doodle of the house itself. "I hope that's okay."

Something approaching a smile crossed Birdie's no-nonsense face. "I like self-sufficiency in a young person," she said. "Or an old person, for that matter."

"That's what my mom always says," I told her before I could think better of it, easing myself up off the stool and staggering across the kitchen to help her unload the groceries. "She's the housekeeper for a family back in Cambridge."

I watched the surprise flicker over Birdie's face in the moment before she turned to set a jug of organic milk in the fridge. "Is that so?"

"Uh." I cleared my throat, immediately filled with deep and scalding regret at my own disclosure and wishing for the millionth time that I knew how to quiet the constant low-grade hum of shame around who I was and where I came from. "Yup." I thought of my mom, who'd spent the last seventeen years cobbling together an income so I could pay for shit like cleats and uniforms and whose own life would have had a significantly different trajectory had I not come along in the first place: *Small behavior*, I reminded myself grimly, and plunked a bunch of bananas into a giant bowl on the counter.

Thankfully, Birdie didn't seem to have any interest in unpacking my various childhood neuroses. "So, Linden," she said, setting a wide cast-iron skillet on the stove and reaching for an onion; I watched as she chopped it and a red bell pepper into tiny, uniform pieces, her movements practiced and precise. "Is this your first time on the Vineyard?"

"Pretty much," I said, deciding to spare her the story of my mom's doomed ex-boyfriend. I pulled the last few groceries from the bags, then hung the empties on the hook in the pantry.

"Are you liking it so far?"

"I am." I sat back down at the island. "I mean, I guess it's been a little intense—with everything that happened the other night, you know?"

Birdie tossed the vegetables into the pan with some butter. "I do know." She added a generous amount of salt and pepper, then plucked a bowl from the cupboard and opened a carton of giant brown eggs. "It's a terrible thing," she allowed.

I hadn't actually been fishing for intel—*Well, why the heck not?* I could hear Holiday ask—but something about the tone of Birdie's voice caught my attention. All at once I remembered something my mom had told me once, about nobody knowing a family's secrets quite like their housekeeper. "The night of the party," I began, trying to sound as offhanded as humanly possible. "I mean, I'm assuming you know we had a party."

Birdie finished whisking the eggs and poured them into the skillet with a noisy sizzle, then turned to look at me with a gimlet eye. "I might have guessed at something like that, yes."

"Might have guessed something like what?" asked a deep voice behind me. I whirled around, heart pounding, as Wells shuffled sleepily into the kitchen.

So much for trying to get the inside scoop in secret. "That I was the one who finished all the Cookie Crisp," I replied quickly. "I was just apologizing to Birdie for eating all your food."

"Yeah, you're a fuckin' freeloader," Wells agreed, reaching up and scratching one bare, tan shoulder. I couldn't tell if he was kidding or not, but his words stung. It was something I was perpetually conscious of back at school: the casual way Jasper threw down a credit card for the entire table whenever we went to dinner off-campus, and how I could never quite afford to do the same.

I didn't answer, watching as Wells opened the fridge and poured himself a glass of orange juice. He drank the whole thing in one long gulp, the muscles in his throat moving in a way that reminded me of a snake eating a field mouse. He set the glass down on the counter, then strolled out of the kitchen in the direction of the patio. "Birdie," he called over his shoulder, "make some bacon too, will you?" He winked at her, obnoxious. "And can you do it the way I like it this time?"

I was quiet for a moment once he was gone, watching as Birdie slid the frittata into the oven and set a timer. Then I got up and put my mug in the dishwasher, doubling back at the last second and sticking Wells's glass in there too.

Birdie caught me doing it, nodding at the gesture. "Thank you," she said softly.

"No problem," I told her, then: "How *does* he like his bacon, exactly?" I couldn't help but ask. "Like, with fourteen-karat gold dust sprinkled on it, or . . . ?"

Birdie pressed her lips together, but it didn't quite tamp down her smile. "This might be hard to believe," she told me conspiratorially, "but he's not even the worst one."

I grinned back at her, torn between vague queasiness at the fact that I had used a combination of my mom's job and basic manners to nation-build with the Kendricks' housekeeper and satisfaction that, apparently, it had worked. "Who's the worst one?" I asked, wanting to know and not wanting to in equal amounts.

"Now, *that* I'll never tell." Birdie opened the refrigerator and pulled out a package of bacon, plucked a pair of scissors from a drawer. "One thing I will say for Wells," she continued, arranging the strips in neat rows on a couple of sheet pans, "is that he's been coming and going so much this summer I've barely seen him. I don't know what that boy is doing sneaking out at all hours, but I certainly don't mind one less bed to make in the morning."

I whirled around to stare at her so fast I whacked my ankle on the corner of the island. "Um, what about the other night?" I asked, too busy trying not to swear at the fresh pain squealing up my shin to be particularly casual about the question. "The night of the party, I mean. Did you wind up making his bed the morning after that?"

Birdie looked at me a little oddly, but in the end she just shook her head. "No," she said slowly, "I guess I didn't." Her eyes narrowed then, like possibly I wasn't the only one who suddenly regretted their own candor in this conversation. "Why do you ask?"

Eliza's footsteps echoed down the stairs before I could come up with an answer; pretty soon the rest of the Kendricks had trickled in behind her, the kitchen filling with the clinking of coffee cups and the clang of Keb' Mo' on the Sonos. I joked around with Jasper and smiled at Eliza over a bowl of freshly sliced fruit, but all the while my mind was reeling: if Birdie was telling the truth—

and there was no reason to think she wasn't—Wells hadn't slept in his bed the night of Greg's accident.

Which, of course, begged the obvious question: Where the fuck had he been?

The timer went off on the oven a few minutes later, and I was following the Kendricks out onto the patio to eat when Birdie laid one firm hand on my arm. "Linden," she said quietly, tugging me backward and away from the others. "Before you go."

My breath caught. For a moment I was sure she was about to tell me something else about Wells, or backpedal entirely and say she'd made a mistake, or warn me to be careful, but instead she just turned back to the freezer and dug out a bright blue ice pack.

"Next time," she said, handing it over before plucking the bag of now-melted veg off the counter and tossing it back into the drawer, "don't use my peas."

10

"I THINK WE SHOULD LOOK AT WELLS," HOLIDAY AN-
nounced grandly.

I frowned. "Wait," I said, momentarily taken aback. It was
later that afternoon; we were sitting on the patio at an ice cream
shop she liked in Edgartown, the kind of place where even just one
scoop in a cup cost eleven dollars and they only had weird flavors
like green tea and everything bagel. "You have?" I'd been looking
forward to seeing the surprise on her face when I told her what I'd
learned from Birdie that morning; in fact, I'd spent the whole ride
over here practicing my delivery. It was a tiny bit disappointing,
if not a giant shock, to find out I was still a step behind. "Why?"

Holiday shrugged. "I mean, all the reasons you mentioned the
other day, to begin with," she said reasonably, licking the back of
her spoon. She'd gotten a scoop of lavender, which she insisted was
delicious, though when I'd tried it myself, it tasted like a dusty bar
of soap or the kind of candle they'd burn for ambience in a night-
gown shop for old ladies. "Plus I stalked him a little bit on my

phone, and let's be real, if anybody at August House gives off the faint whiff of expensive shampoo and violent sociopathy, it's him."

I glanced down at my pretzel cone, which held two unpleasantly spicy scoops of something purporting to be chipotle–chocolate chip, and remembered the sting of the orange against the naked skin of my back. "I mean, you're not wrong."

"The problem is we have zero proof." Holiday sat back in her chair, her broad shoulders pink and freckled in the afternoon sunlight. "Like, yes, it definitely seems like he's capable of hurting someone, but for all we know, his deepest, darkest secret is an extensive collection of vintage Hello Kitty memorabilia. We can't just stroll into the police department like *Don't worry, professional law enforcement officials, here we are with our big weird hunches!* We have to have actual, incontrovertible evidence."

I felt myself startle at that. I guess I hadn't really thought about what might be waiting at the end of this particular trail of bread crumbs; that day on the patio, the idea of turning Wells—or anyone else—over to the police still felt vaguely ridiculous and far-fetched. As far as I knew, nobody at August House had heard anything from Reyes or O'Neal since the morning after the party, which I could only suppose meant they were satisfied that whatever had happened to Greg had been an accident. Whatever proof we brought them—assuming we could find any—would need to be pretty convincing.

Still: "I might have a place for us to start, actually," I told Holiday, then filled her in on what Birdie had said in the kitchen that morning.

By the time I was finished, Holiday's dark eyes were shining. "I knew you had it in you," she told me, her smile wide and white and dazzling across the table.

"And what's that, exactly?" I raised my eyebrows.

Holiday lifted her cup, tapping it gently against the remains of my cone in a dorky little toast. "Truly brilliant detective work," she said.

I made a face, but the truth is I was weirdly flattered. It had given me an unexpected rush, what Birdie had told me this morning; more than that, it was a thrill to have something of value to bring to Holiday, even if it did make me feel a tiny bit like a dog dropping a dead squirrel onto its master's doorstep. This whole time I'd been telling myself this was Holiday's circus—that I wasn't even convinced an actual crime had been committed, that I could walk away whenever I chose. But it turned out that I was invested now too.

We tossed our trash and headed down the tourist-clogged street, which was lined with tiny jewel-box shops that sold organic soaps and ethically made Montessori toys and a six-hundred-dollar designer raincoat that Holiday pulled me inside the store to properly admire. "Oh, that's cute," she said, reaching out to gently touch one rubbery sleeve.

"I mean, sure," I said, "if you want to spend half a month's rent to look like the Gorton's Fisherman."

"It's an Oak and Thunder," the salesgirl informed us, footsteps echoing on the wide wooden planks of the floor as she hurried over. "Isn't it fantastic?"

"I love it," Holiday said—or something like that, anyway. I had already drifted boredly across the shop. I remembered this from when we used to hang out all the time: the occasional stark reminder that, as unaffected as Holiday acted by her parents' wealth, at the end of the day she had a hell of a lot more in common with the Kendricks than she ever had with me. Sure, her mom and dad went to fundraisers for Democratic candidates and plunked a Black Lives Matter sign on the lawn of their three-million-dollar house in Cambridge, but how different was she from any other rich girl on this island, really? Privilege was privilege. Wealth was wealth. And being comfortable in a store where even the simplest leather key ring cost more than I'd made in a week all summer long was something I couldn't quite imagine, no matter who I was trying to become.

"You ready?" I asked, my voice sounding loud and rough in the genteel quiet of the shop. Holiday raised her eyebrows, didn't reply.

At last we headed back out onto the crowded sidewalk, Holiday grabbing my arm and yanking me out of the way as I almost got mowed down by a little kid on a scooter. My ankle gave briefly underneath me and I stumbled into her side, swearing under my breath. "Shit, Michael," she said as she steadied me, "are you okay?"

I nodded even as my eyes watered. "Yup," I promised, waiting to get my breath back. "I'm good."

"Are you sure?"

"I said I'm fine, Holiday."

Holiday let out a low whistle that might as well have been a whole entire song about toxic masculinity, and we both knew it; still, she didn't press me, and in return I tried to swallow down my suddenly sour mood. "Okay," she said instead, "back to the night of the party. Walk me through it one more time, will you?"

"Which part?"

"I mean, all of it," she said, "but let's start with what Greg looked like when you found him in the pool. What was he wearing?"

I thought about it for a moment. "Red shorts?" I guessed. "And boat shoes, obviously."

"Obligatory. Any shirt?"

"No, actually." I'd been able to see the pleats of his backbone through his skin, I remembered suddenly, the ridges of them weirdly vulnerable-looking even on such a beefy person. I thought again of Greer and the night of the accident, the terrifying fragility of a human body. "No shirt."

"But he'd been wearing one at the party?"

I hesitated. ". . . Yes?"

"Are you asking me or telling me?"

"Telling you," I said, though in truth I wasn't totally sure. The more I went over that night in my head, the less clear it felt to me, like a letter that's been handled so much that the writing has started to blur and smudge and soften. "He wasn't swimming."

"And he's not just one of those guys who takes his shirt off randomly?" Holiday asked. "He seems like he might be the type."

"He does," I agreed with a smirk, "but he was dressed at the party."

"In what?"

"That I don't remember." I shook my head at her barrage of

questions; just for a moment, it felt a little like she was interrogating *me*. "Why does this matter again?"

Holiday blew out a breath. "Everything matters, Michael," she said in a voice like that should have been obvious. I remembered this about her, how she could be a little bit of a know-it-all when she felt like other people weren't keeping up. My ankle ached; the shine of Birdie's revelation had worn off by now, and I found myself wondering what fun shit Jasper and Eliza were up to that I was currently missing out on.

"Okay," Holiday announced suddenly, digging her car keys out of her back pocket and holding them aloft. "Time for a field trip, then."

I blinked. "To where?"

"Wells's room," she said pleasantly. "Lead the way."

I stared at her. "Are you fucking kidding me right now?"

"I never kid," she informed me. "Come on, Michael. No risk, no reward. Let's go."

Which is how we wound up back at August House, making our way as quietly as possible through the cool, empty corridors. Birdie was baking a berry pavlova in the kitchen. Mrs. Kendrick was reading a magazine by the pool. Mr. Kendrick was in his office, I was pretty sure, judging from the closed door and the low murmur of conversation on the other side of it. And everybody else was down at the beach—at least, that's where Jasper had said they were headed as I'd limped out to meet Holiday earlier this afternoon.

Wells's room was down at the end of the hall on the second

floor, past Jasper's and Eliza's and around the corner from his parents' suite and the guest room where Meredith was staying. I put my hand on the knob, then hesitated. Crossing the threshold into Wells's room meant violating an actual, physical line of demarcation; once we went inside in search of concrete evidence, there was no way to excuse away whatever we were doing as *just messing around.*

"I feel like it's going to be booby-trapped," I said, and Holiday laughed.

"With like, one of those networks of lasers that we have to do ballet moves to get between?" she asked. "In that case, my friend, you will be on your own. If he has an invisible hair taped over his diary, on the other hand, I feel confident in my ability to dismantle it undetected."

"Fair enough." I twisted the knob, eased the door open. I hadn't had any reason to visit Wells's room since I'd been staying at August House, but it had the same familiar, slightly funky smell I recognized from my friends' rooms—and, let's be real, mine too—back at Bartley. It was decently neat, which I knew now was Birdie's doing; the bed was made with the same striped sheets from the guest room upstairs, a hairbrush and a stick of deodorant lined up neatly on the dresser.

Holiday stood at the center of the tasteful, neutral area rug, turning a slow circle like she was committing her surroundings to memory. "What are we looking for, exactly?" I asked.

She shrugged. "What's that saying about porn?" she shot back. "You can't describe it, but you know it when you see it?"

"I'm pretty sure I could describe what porn is," I replied absently, then immediately felt myself blush.

"I'm sure you could," Holiday said with a smirk. "And judging by that little Kleenex-and-lotion situation on the nightstand over there, so could Wells."

"Oh, *gross.*"

"Shh," she said mildly, squaring her shoulders and getting to work. I watched as she moved purposefully around the room with the quick precision of a master surgeon, taking careful inventory of its contents: rifling efficiently through the closets, getting down on her hands and knees to peer under the bed. I didn't trust myself to be quite so meticulous, so I kept watch in the doorway, head tipped for the sound of anyone coming; Holiday was squinting through the blinds to see which parts of the property were visible from the window when I heard someone's footsteps on the stairs.

"Shit," I hissed, even as Holiday whirled around, panic written all over her face. Without thinking, I grabbed her arm and yanked her into Wells's closet—the two of us staring at each other wide-eyed, holding our breath in the inky dark. I imagined I could hear her heart beating. I thought I could feel it right through our clothes. We listened, Holiday's nails digging into the thin skin on the underside of my arm as whoever it was—Mr. Kendrick, I thought, based on the solid but slightly springy tread—headed down the hallway in the opposite direction, opening another door and moving around noisily for a moment before finally retreating back downstairs.

"Holy crap," Holiday breathed once we'd eased the closet door back open, blinking like baby ducks in the sudden light. "That was—"

"Yeah." I felt light-headed with leftover adrenaline, dizzy with relief. "It was."

"Did you even have a plan?" she asked, laughing a little bit giddily. "Like, how were you going to explain it if Wells opened the closet door looking for his sneakers?"

"That—" I broke off abruptly. *We were making out and couldn't wait until we got upstairs,* I almost said, but something about that felt deeply unwise. "I had no plan," I amended, scrubbing a hand through my hair. I was sweaty, even though the temperature at August House was always kept at seventy-two degrees exactly; my ankle felt like it was on fire. "You ready to get out of here?"

Holiday nodded. "In a second," she said calmly. Then, with no more urgency than she had displayed before we were almost interrupted, she continued her search. I stared at her in disbelief as she headed for the dresser, peeking inside a smooth wooden accessory box sitting on top before turning her attention to the furniture itself.

"Holiday," I warned, glancing nervously over my shoulder, "come on."

"I'll be quick," she promised, poking through Wells's T-shirts and bathing suits. "But who knows when we're going to get this chance again?"

"That's what I'm saying," I whispered urgently. "We were lucky once. Not to mention the fact that I don't really think we're going to find a smoking gun in the back of Wells's—"

"Underwear drawer?" Holiday asked, pulling something out of the dresser with a showy, theatrical flourish.

I gaped at her, my eyes flicking wildly back and forth between her delighted face and the prize she was holding aloft like a kid who'd caught a giant fish their first time casting into the water. It was a rumpled, threadbare rugby sweatshirt, monogrammed on the pocket with the initials *GTH*.

And there was a streak of blood on the collar.

"How the fuck did you just do that?" I asked, my heart slamming away in wonder inside my chest.

"I'm magic," Holiday deadpanned, and for a moment I 100 percent believed her. If she had pulled a snow-white rabbit out of the dresser along with the sweatshirt, then sawed it in half and promptly put it back together again, I would not have been more impressed. "Is this what Greg was wearing at the party?"

I tried to think, but try as I might, I couldn't pull up a clear picture of him in my mind. "It could have been?" I asked, cringing at my own shitty memory. I wanted to be as impressive as she was, to wow her the same way she wowed me, but my fuzzy brain wouldn't cooperate. "It had to be, right? Wells must have hidden it after he pushed Greg into the pool."

"And what, like, wrestled it off his wet, comatose body?" Holiday frowned. "Why go through the trouble? Like, obviously the blood *came* from someplace. Whoever found Greg was going to know that he had hit his head somehow, whether they saw blood on the shirt or not."

"Maybe it's not Greg's blood, then?" I guessed. "It could be

Wells's, right? From the fight? And he didn't want there to be any evidence."

"But why keep the sweatshirt in the first place, then?" Holiday persisted. "And in his room, of all places? Why not just toss it, or burn it, or literally anything else?"

"I don't know," I admitted, irritated at her for taking the wind out of our collective sails so quickly. Shouldn't we have been celebrating right now? "Because he's a big dumb weirdo, conceivably. But it doesn't matter why. The fact of the matter is he's got Greg's bloody sweatshirt hidden in his bedroom. And we need to get the fuck out of here."

Holiday nodded. She took a few photos of the sweatshirt on her phone before placing it carefully back where she'd found it and shutting the drawer. "So what do we do?" she asked as we headed back down the stairs. "Do we bring the sweatshirt to the police? I'm pretty sure there's going to be a chain-of-custody issue or something, but I have to Google to be sure."

"Google to be sure about what?" Jasper asked, padding into the hallway from the direction of the kitchen.

"Whether Michael's haircut makes him look like Macklemore," Holiday said immediately.

"A little bit it does," Jasper said, looking at me speculatively. "Not as handsome, though." He turned to Holiday. "Are you coming to the thing tonight?"

"What thing?" she and I asked in unison.

Jasper grinned a curly grin. "Aw, you guys are cute." Then, looking at me: "Illumination Night, remember?"

I did suddenly—he'd mentioned it this morning, a Vineyard tradition where a cluster of tiny Victorian cottages near the water in Oak Bluffs were decorated with thousands of Japanese lanterns—but I'd completely forgotten about it until right now. Before I could respond, Holiday answered, "I am!"

I walked her out to her car not long after that. "Hope it's okay that I'm coming tonight," she said quietly. "It's just probably a good chance to get our eyes on Wells, is all."

"No, totally," I agreed. "I'll see you there."

Jasper was waiting in the kitchen when I got back inside, eating a plum. "I didn't know you guys were here," he commented. "What were you doing hiding upstairs?" It was pretty clear from his tone that he'd drawn his own conclusions, and that they definitely weren't *snooping through my brother's room looking for evidence.* I felt myself blush.

"Nothing," I said, bumping his shoulder with mine as I headed for the refrigerator; all that detecting had left me starving. "It's not like that."

"Oh no?" he asked, a knowing smirk on his face. "What's it like?"

I opened my mouth, shut it again. "She's like my sister," I said finally, because I knew Jasper would understand that, though in truth it didn't feel like Holiday was my sister at all. But it wasn't anything like it was with Eliza either, the way all my nerve endings perked up whenever she was in the house. With Holiday it was just . . . whatever it was.

"Sure thing, dude," Jasper said. He finished the plum and tossed the pit into the garbage, wiping his hands on his shorts. "Whatever you say."

11

"YOU'RE GOING TO LOVE ILLUMINATION NIGHT, LIN-den," Mr. Kendrick promised on the drive into Oak Bluffs later that evening. The sun was just setting out the window of the big car, the late-summer breeze cool on the back of my neck. "It's a Vineyard tradition that goes all the way back to just after the Civil War."

"And by the end of the night," Jasper chimed in from the front seat, "you too will feel like you've been experiencing it for one hundred and sixty years."

"My son is something of a naysayer," Mr. Kendrick said cheerfully. He'd swapped out his swim trunks and ball cap for khaki shorts and driving moccasins, the thinning patch of hair at the back of his head the only visual clue that he was Jasper's dad and not his older brother. A sleek silver Breitling winked from his wrist. "And I get it, you know? He's a teenager; he's gotta give his old man a hard time. But between you and me, I think he'll be singing a different tune when he remembers how much he loves the dulcet musical stylings of the Vineyard Haven Band."

"I mean, that's true," Jasper admitted with a snort. "I do own all their records."

I laughed distractedly, glancing over my shoulder out the back window. We'd split up into two cars, so Mrs. Kendrick was following in the Volvo along with Eliza, Meredith, and Wells. I couldn't stop thinking about the sweatshirt, turning it over and over in my mind like a Rubik's Cube with no solution. On the crime shows my mom liked, this would be the point where the grizzled detective would send the sweatshirt off to the lab for analysis, the source of the bloodstain neatly resolved during commercials for cat food and Viagra. But this was real life, and after the adrenaline rush of our supposedly game-changing discovery, it was still just Holiday and me, bumbling around like a couple of amateurs.

We'd wanted actual evidence, and now we had it. But I had no idea what to do next.

"Linden?" Mr. Kendrick said, and I snapped to attention, suddenly aware from the tone of his voice that this probably wasn't the first time he'd said my name.

"Sorry," I said, smiling my most affable, dopey-pal smile. "Daydreaming."

"About Ms. Singh?" Jasper asked quietly. I kneed the back of his seat.

"I was just pestering you some more about the lax season," Mr. Kendrick continued. "Whose asses are you most excited to kick this year?"

We spent the rest of the ride in lacrosse land, Mr. Kendrick asking about my coaches and talking smack about other boarding schools. He'd played himself back when he was at Bartley in the late '80s, and I tried to answer his questions as gamely as I could, but I could feel my blood pressure rising the longer the conversation went on. *I don't know if I'm going to be able to play ever again,* I wanted to tell him. And *I don't even know where I'm going to go to school if I can't.*

Also, not to make it awkward or anything, but I think your son might have tried to murder someone.

"Should be a great season," I said instead. "I'm really psyched to get back on the field."

The campground in Oak Bluffs was already mobbed by the time we showed up—tourists mixing with locals, everyone milling around on the springy green grass as they marveled at the elaborately decorated gingerbread cottages. The western sky was streaked with pinks and oranges and purples, and the smell of expensive perfume mixed with freshly cut grass hung heavy in the air.

We met up with the others near the bandstand, the group of us picking our way through a maze of blankets and lawn chairs as we looked for a place to settle down. Clearly, this thing was a way bigger deal than I had realized: people had laid out elaborate picnics on pop-up camping tables, complete with linens, candles, and bottles of wine chilling in tasteful-looking coolers. Birdie had sent us with dinner too: cold fried chicken and a zingy slaw made with purple cabbage; potato salad flecked with green onion and what I thought might have been dill.

Jasper wolfed his food with impressive gusto, then peeled off to go meet up with Aidy, who was hanging out with some friends across the campground: "Don't wait up," he said cheerfully, tossing a wave over one shoulder as he trotted away through the dense, moneyed crowd. Meredith rolled her eyes as she watched him go, then turned back to her phone. She'd been spending most of her days at the hospital, where Greg was still unconscious in the ICU; she'd been headed back over there tonight as we were leaving, but Mrs. Kendrick had convinced her to come with us instead. "You're not helping anyone by running yourself ragged," she'd pointed out as we'd gotten settled on the blanket, discreetly pressing a plastic cup of sparkling wine into Meredith's hand.

Now I glanced around for Holiday—she wasn't, typically, difficult to spot—but in the end she didn't seem to have shown up after all. I thought about texting her to find out for sure, but there was another, bigger part of me that couldn't help but feel relieved at the chance to take the night off from our little investigation—not to mention the opportunity to spend some time with Eliza.

She was leaning back on her palms with her ankles crossed, her face half in shadow and half aglow in the warm light of the hanging lanterns. She was wearing a short, patterned dress that seemed to float ethereally around her, her shoulders bare in a way that made me want to put my mouth on her skin. "So, here's a question," I began, leaning over and murmuring in her ear as inconspicuously as I could manage. "As much as I appreciate the considerable talents of the Vineyard Haven Band—and believe me, I sincerely do—you want to get out of here and go for a walk with me?"

Eliza's face broke open into a grin. "Oh god," she said immediately, holding her hand out so I could pull her to her feet, "yes please."

We made our excuses to her parents, then headed across the grass, the back of Eliza's hand brushing against mine as we went. "Not a huge fan of Illumination Night?" I asked.

Eliza shrugged. "I mean, it was fun the first dozen times," she said. "The last five, not as much." She glanced at me out of the corner of her eye. "It makes my parents happy, though. Especially my dad. And I've sort of been trying to do more of that kind of stuff lately—make it up to them, or whatever—since . . ." She trailed off.

"Right." I wasn't entirely sure if she meant because her dad had been away or because she was leaving for Paris in a few weeks or something altogether different. It seemed safer not to ask—at least, it did in the moment. Much later, it would occur to me to wonder which one of us I thought I was trying to protect.

"Anyway." Eliza seemed to sense my hesitation; she smiled a goofy, reassuring smile, reaching down and taking my hand for real. "The company's not so bad this year, I guess. With the obvious exception of my brother's boring friend who's visiting."

"Ugh, that guy sucks." I grinned, tugging her over to an empty bench at the very end of the campground. "I can't stand him."

"Yeah," Eliza agreed, settling close enough so that our arms were touching, "he's the worst."

We sat there for a long time, the hum of the crowd and the murmur of the music drifting languidly through the deep blue evening; from this distance, the cottages were a warm, glowing blur. Eliza was a good storyteller, unexpectedly funny as she told me about the summers she'd spent with her family at August House: the pranks she and her brothers used to play on Dean and

Birdie; the time Jasper hadn't gotten off the ferry with the rest of them and nobody had realized until he was halfway back to Woods Hole. For the first time since I'd run dazedly out onto the patio the other morning, I wasn't thinking about Greg at all.

"So how come Jas is at Bartley and you're back at home?" I asked finally, stretching my legs lazily out in front of me. "Not into the whole boarding-school thing?"

Eliza's eyes widened. "Oh *god*, no," she said, waving a hand in front of her face like the idea was a visible cloud of stink she could bat away. "I mean, I did it for a little while—some frilly fucking place in Connecticut where my mom supposedly made, like, 'the greatest friends of her whole life!' But five hundred girls in plaid all getting their periods at the exact same time? It was . . . not for me." She shuddered. "I mean, the plumbing situation alone was like something out of a horror movie."

"I . . . would imagine," I said with a grin. "So what *is* for you, then?"

I just meant it as a throwaway question, flirtatious, but to my surprise, Eliza seemed to stop and consider it. "Bookstores," she said, ticking a list off on her fingers. "Train travel. The way Birdie's garden smells at the very end of the summer. Old dogs. Staying at hotels for long enough that the concierge gets to know who you are. Chronic insomnia, regrettably. Museums right before closing time. Being the kind of person other people want to tell secrets to." She leaned into me for real then, just for a moment. "And, you know. Occasional troublemaking."

When she was done, I just gazed at her for a moment, ensorcelled. "That's . . . a good list," I finally said.

"Thank you," Eliza said primly. "What about you?"

I thought about it for a beat, wanting to paint a picture that was at least half as beguiling as the one she'd made for me. I should have been able to do it no problem—after all, I'd spent the last three years inventing a brand-new version of myself mostly from scratch—but it was strange to be called upon to deliver an oral report on the person I'd created. I wanted to repeat everything she said, to live the kind of magical, romantic life she'd laid out so cleanly. "I don't know, exactly," I admitted, frustrated with my own thick-tongued slow-wittedness. "I guess I'm still kind of trying to figure that out."

Eliza didn't seem to be bothered. "Well," she said, bumping her knee gently against mine, "guess you'd better get figuring, then."

I was still trying to decide exactly how to respond to that when all at once I spotted Holiday hurtling toward us, her hair a wild corona around her face as she darted through the crowd. "Um, hey," I said, surprised. For as long as I'd been sitting here with Eliza, I'd forgotten about Holiday completely, and about Wells and the sweatshirt; the sight of her struck me with the same strange, disorienting cognitive dissonance of bumping into your teacher at the public pool. "You came."

"Of course I came," she said, sounding a little breathless. When I looked at her more closely, I realized her cheeks were flushed, like possibly she'd been running around for a while trying to find me. "Sorry," she said, waving shortly at Eliza. "Hi. Linden, can I just borrow you for a second?"

I frowned. I knew she had suggested using tonight to try to

figure out what was going on with Wells, but in that particular moment, abandoning what was happening with Eliza to go snoop around playing detective was the absolute last thing I wanted to do. "I mean . . ." I hedged. "Can it wait?"

I saw a flash of temper in Holiday's eyes just then, though nothing about her tone or body language changed at all. "Totally," she said, all smiles. "I was actually just about to take off, so. I'll catch you around."

Right away I felt like a massive, swinging boner. "You know what? Now's good." I turned to Eliza. "I'm sorry," I said, and I meant it. "I'll be right back."

Now it was Eliza's turn to smile tightly. "Sure thing," she said, and I winced. *It's not that I don't really like you and want to get to know you better,* I imagined myself telling her. *It's just that my friend and I think your older brother might have committed a violent felony, and I need a little bit more proof.*

Once we were alone, I turned to Holiday, eyebrows raised. "What's up?" I didn't quite say *This better be good,* but I was 100 percent thinking it, and from the look on Holiday's face, she could definitely tell. For a second I thought she was going to give me hell about my piss-poor attitude, but in the end she just turned on her heel and motioned for me to follow her through the teeming crowd, curling her hand around my wrist and yanking when I wasn't fast enough. At last she tugged me around the side of one of the artfully lit-up cottages, gesturing with her chin.

"There," she announced curtly. "Look."

I squinted across the street in the deepening twilight, following her gaze until I spotted them: Wells was standing beside a dark blue Jeep, talking to a middle-aged woman I didn't recognize. "Okay . . . ," I said slowly, trying not to sound too obviously irritated. This was what Holiday had dragged me away from Eliza to see? Wells talking to some random rich lady? "Who's that?"

"You don't *know*?" Holiday was disbelieving. "Are you seriously telling me you didn't do even a cursory Google of any of these people?" She shook her head. "That's Greg's mom."

"Oh." I stared, suddenly a hell of a lot more interested. "Holy shit." Mrs. Holliman had the same slightly bland, well-groomed look that all the moms on the Vineyard seemed to have; she was wearing a lightweight maxi dress and a denim jacket, the sleeves rolled up to reveal a pair of tasteful gold bangles around her wrist. "What's she doing here?" I asked. "Shouldn't she be at the hospital?"

"Greg has a little sister," Holiday informed me. "Maybe they came here to try to keep things normal for her?"

"Maybe," I said. But something about the way Mrs. Holliman was standing—the specific, almost intimate way her body was angled toward Wells's—made me think that wasn't the full story. I watched them for another moment: their heads close together, their hands brushing down at their sides. Then, so quickly I would have missed it if I hadn't been actively staring at them like a giant weirdo, Wells laced his fingers through hers and squeezed.

"Holiday," I began, even as Mrs. Holliman was pulling away and shooting Wells a warning look. It took a second for the realization to become clear in my head, like waiting for a hi-res picture to load on slow, shitty Wi-Fi. "Doesn't it kind of look like they're—"

"Uh, yup," Holiday agreed. "More than kind of."

I nodded grimly. "So, not a Hello Kitty collection, then."

"I mean, could always be both." She made a face. "How old is Wells again?"

"He's twenty," I reminded her, "so it's not illegal. It's just . . . gross."

"But also weirdly compelling?"

I snorted. "Keep it in your pants, Proctor."

"I'm just saying!" Holiday laughed a little hysterically. "Good for Mrs. Holliman, I guess? Unless he's only doing it to get some kind of horrifying revenge against Greg and his dad."

"You think?" I asked, though truthfully, I'd been wondering something similar. "I mean, Wells is a creep, but retaliatory mom-banging feels extreme even for him."

"More extreme than pushing Greg into the pool?" She fell quiet, tugging on a strand of her hair. "It does make me wonder if Greg found out somehow, though."

"He might have," I said thoughtfully. "If anything would have given him a reason to go back to August House the night of the party, telling Wells to stop screwing his mom would probably be it."

"You should write Hallmark cards, you know that?" Holiday observed flatly. "You truly have a way with words." She took my arm again, making to steer me back around the cottages. "Come with me," she instructed. "I need to go scope out Greg's house."

"Wait, what?" I pulled away, planting my feet like an instinct. "Why? Now?"

"It's the perfect time to do it," she pointed out, impatient. "We know there's nobody there."

"What about Greg's dad?"

Holiday shook her head. "He only comes to the Vineyard like, every other weekend," she told me. "He stays in Boston most of the time to work."

"Seriously? Even now that Greg's in the ICU?" I tried to imagine my mom being anywhere but in my hospital room if I somehow wound up in a coma, and couldn't; granted, thankfully, I also couldn't imagine her carrying on a clandestine affair with one of my former best friends. The whole thing made me feel a little sad for Greg, and also made me wonder if possibly he hadn't earned his reputation for copious douchebaggery entirely on his own. "How do you even know that?"

Holiday rolled her eyes, all exaggerated exasperation. "Cursory! Research!" She nodded again at the edge of the campground. "Come on," she said, "I'm parked a couple of blocks over."

I hesitated, glancing back in the direction of the bandstand. I was worried it was going to start looking suspicious if I kept blowing the Kendricks off to creep around on secret investigative missions, but that wasn't the only reason I didn't want to bail. Mostly I just felt torn: between wanting to know what had happened to Greg and wanting an actual vacation. Between Holiday and the Kendricks. Between who I wanted to be—how I wanted to look to other people—and who, I suspected, I actually was.

I almost told Holiday to forget it, or to go on without me. I wanted to; I probably would have, if she'd been anyone else. But then I thought of what she'd said about Greg having a little sister. I thought of my mom at home back in Eastie, and the person she thought she'd raised. I thought, a little shamefully, about Wells calling me a freeloader, and barely managed to hold back a growl of frustration.

"Fuck Tom Brady," I mumbled finally, nodding toward the parking lot. "Let's go."

Holiday frowned. "What?"

"Nothing. Lead the way."

I had half expected Holiday to drive a lime-green Mini Cooper or a vintage Volkswagen Beetle with a flower on the dashboard, but in fact, her car was a nondescript gray sedan that smelled strongly of palo santo and was full, nearly to bursting, with trash. She apologized as I climbed into the passenger side, reaching across my lap and grabbing a handful of granola bar wrappers and empty coffee cups off the floor before tossing them half-heartedly into the backseat. "I keep saying I'm going to clean it out."

"I mean, why would you?" I asked teasingly, reaching down and pulling what I realized one second too late was a satin bra out of the center console. "Uh." I felt my face redden. "Never know when this is going to come in handy."

"Give me that." Holiday snatched it out of my hand and chucked it over her shoulder. "You try wearing an underwire for twelve hours a day, see if you never need to yank it off at a red light on the way home."

I cleared my throat. "I . . . will be sure to do that."

Greg's house hulked a ways down the beach from the Kendricks'; the windows were dark when we pulled up in front, the whole place empty and deserted-looking. It was more modern than August House, all severe angles and huge panes of glass; the back end of it cantilevered out over the ocean in a dramatic feat of architectural excess. "It looks like the house where a corporate supervillain would live in a Marvel movie," Holiday observed, letting out a low whistle.

I hummed my distracted agreement, glancing uneasily down at my phone. I'd texted Eliza to apologize and tell her I'd meet up with the rest of them back at the house later, but so far she hadn't replied. "Remind me what we're looking for, exactly?"

"Just getting the lay of the land." Holiday unbuckled her seat belt and climbed halfway into the backseat, rooting around like a raccoon in a dumpster until she came up with a pair of binoculars. "They're my dad's," she explained off my gobsmacked expression. "He went through a thing with birds when he turned fifty. My mom was like, *Better birds than graduate students,* et cetera. I threw them in here a couple of days ago just in case."

"Of course you did," I agreed. "By all means, proceed."

Holiday lifted the binoculars to her eyes and leaned across me to peer out the passenger side window at the dark specter of Greg's house. "Do you want me to do that?" I asked, reaching for the glasses even as I squished myself back against the seat to give her room.

"Shh," she said distractedly, swatting my hand away. She stared for another long minute, her thick hair tickling my nose, before finally retreating to the driver's side and dropping the binoculars—which had to have cost hundreds of dollars—into the backseat with such carelessness that I cringed.

We didn't talk much as she drove me back toward August House. I could tell by the satisfied expression on her face that there was a plan coming together in the madcap tinkerer's workshop of her brain, though I didn't bother to ask what it might be. I knew from experience that she'd tell me when and only when she was good and ready—or possibly not at all.

Still, my curiosity got the better of me as we pulled into the driveway. "Did you get what you came for back there, at least?" I couldn't help but ask her. "The lay of the land, or whatever?"

"Something like that." Holiday grinned, teeth flashing white in the darkness. I was almost up the front steps when she called my name. "Meet me at the beach tomorrow morning," she instructed through the open window, turning the key in the ignition and putting the car into drive. "And wear your running shoes."

August House was still and quiet when I let myself inside, Whimsy's contented snores faintly audible from the kitchen and the cloying smell of the late-summer flowers on the front hall table hanging in the air. Mr. and Mrs. Kendrick always went out with friends after Illumination Night, I knew, and though Wells had mentioned something about going to Doc's, so far neither Jasper nor Eliza had answered my texts and I felt weird about just showing up unannounced. Holiday probably would have wanted me to use the opportunity to do a little digging—in fact, if I'd let her know the house was empty, she probably would have left skid marks on the pavement in her hurry to turn around and come back—but I'd had about all I could stomach of the investigative life for one evening. Instead I headed upstairs to the turret room with a vague plan to either watch a movie on Netflix or jerk off in the shower, but as I turned the corner on the landing, I glanced out the window into the backyard, panic closing sharp and sudden around my throat:

There was another body in the pool.

It was floating facedown in the deep end: arms and legs akimbo, swim trunks ballooned around its pale, skinny legs. It was perfectly, preternaturally still, like possibly it had always been there—part of the landscape architecture, maybe, or an art installation I wasn't sophisticated enough to understand.

I couldn't breathe. I couldn't yell for help. I couldn't make sense of anything but the pure white fear ricocheting through every vein and synapse, the animal urge to get as far as humanly possible from this fucked-up place. What had I done, by coming here? What in the holy hell was going on?

That was when the body stood upright.

It wasn't a body at all, I realized belatedly, fingers curling around the windowsill even as my knees threatened to give: it had only been Jasper, doing the Dead Man's Float in the pool. I watched as he tossed his head to get his hair out of his face, water spraying off him like a dog shaking himself dry after a bath. He made his way over to the ladder, pulling himself up and out of the pool in one smooth motion; if he sensed that I was watching, or that anyone was, he gave no indication.

I sat down on the delicate antique bench on the landing, my heart still slamming wildly away as relief and embarrassment battled it out in my chest cavity. I forced myself to take a deep breath, glancing warily in both directions to make sure nobody had caught me making a fool of myself and trying not to notice the way the walls felt just a little bit closer than they had a moment before. Downstairs I could hear Jasper letting himself into the kitchen, his wet feet slapping against the tile; I thought about calling out to him and telling him he'd scared the shit out of me, turning the whole thing into a funny story about what a dumbass I was, but when I opened my mouth, I found I didn't quite have the heart to do it. I thought again about how he'd kept the truth about his dad from me, even though I would have called him my best friend back at Bartley. I wondered again what else there was about him that I didn't know.

I glanced out the window one more time, watching the patio lights as they reflected off the still, peaceful surface of the swimming pool. Then I got up and climbed the steps to my room.

12

I FOUND HOLIDAY WAITING FOR ME A FEW HUNDRED yards down the beach from August House the following morning, dressed in jogging shorts and a T-shirt from someone named Alina's Bat Mitzvah, which, based on the hot-pink date screenprinted on the back, had occurred four years earlier. "Wait," I said, confusion briefly muddying my baseline crankiness; I'd had to turn down a brunch invitation from the Kendricks to be here, and Eliza hadn't even spared me a glance as they walked out the door. Between that and last night—she'd never answered the text I'd sent her—I was pretty sure I'd blown it. "Are we actually running?"

"What?" Holiday looked appalled. "God, no. I make it a personal policy not to run unless someone is actively chasing me. Or *I'm* actively chasing *someone,* I guess, though honestly, I can't imagine wanting to pursue another human being that badly." She gestured down at her clothes. "This is a costume."

"Very Method of you," I said.

"If we're going to do this, we're damn sure going to do it right."

"I'm sorry," I said—thinking longingly of the brunch I was

missing at this very moment, whether or not Doc might be attending, and, if he was, where he might be sitting at the table in relation to Eliza. "If we're going to do *what*, exactly?"

"You'll see," Holiday promised mysteriously. "These beaches are private, aren't they?"

I sighed, scrubbing a hand across my face. "They are," I confirmed, "so probably we should try not to look *quite* so much like rabble."

"I'll do my best," Holiday promised, and set off along the shoreline. I trailed reluctantly after her, neither one of us talking as we followed the water for what felt like miles. I assumed we were headed for Greg's house, though I had no idea what we might do when we got there. I could feel the sun burning the back of my neck. My ankle protested, then complained, then hollered; I was just about to tell Holiday I wasn't going to go another step without an explanation when all at once she stopped. "That's it, right?" she asked, nodding up the beach.

I followed her gaze. In daylight the Hollimans' stark, modern house looked even more like an alien aircraft, squatting at the edge of the sand like it might have abruptly fallen from space in the moments just before we strolled up. "Yup," I agreed. "That's it."

Holiday nodded. She closed her eyes, breathing deeply; when she opened them again, I was shocked to see they were filled with actual, bona fide tears. "Holy shit," I said, alarmed. "Are you—" But Holiday was gone before I could get the question out, rushing through the back gate of the Hollimans' house and ringing the doorbell over and over.

Greg's mom answered a minute later, hassled and harried in head-to-toe luxury athleisure. "You haven't seen a dog, have you?" Holiday wailed before Mrs. Holliman could say anything. "A Havanese? Her name is Bunny and she looks like—well, she looks like a *bunny*, and she never runs away but she just ran away, and for all I know, a coyote is already tearing her into a thousand pieces. Are there coyotes here, do you know?"

"I—no," I heard Mrs. Holliman say, peering out the door behind her; instinctively I dove behind a dune. "I'm sorry, sweetheart, but this is a private—"

"I didn't bring my phone because I've been trying to practice mindfulness," Holiday interrupted tearfully. "You know, being present in the moment and all of that? Have you tried it? It's supposed to be very good for anxiety, which I have, but now I need to get in touch with my mom to tell her what's going on and I might as well be a farmer in 1826, I might as well send her a message by *carrier* pigeon, and—"

"All right, hang on just one second." Mrs. Holliman looked emphatically underwhelmed by the prospect of having to comfort the hysterical girl on her doorstep, and I couldn't help but feel a little bit shitty for manipulating a woman who'd clearly already been through so much. On the other hand, I reminded myself, we *were* trying to help her, in a roundabout kind of way. More than that, we were trying to help Greg—at least, I thought we were. I still had no idea what Holiday was doing.

"Here," Mrs. Holliman was saying, fishing an iPhone out of the pocket of her leggings and keying in her password before handing it over. "Go ahead and use mine."

Holiday gasped theatrically. "Thank you so, so much!" she cooed, snatching it out of Mrs. Holliman's hand and darting away from the doorway. "I'll bring it right back."

She paced back and forth across the yard as she pretended to dial, covering more and more distance with each turn until eventually she made it back down to my hiding spot on the beach. "Mom?" she called, loud enough that Mrs. Holliman would be able to hear her back up at the house. "Mom, I lost Bunny!" She let out another noisy, guttural sob for good measure, then immediately composed herself. "Okay," she said quietly, clicking frantically at the screen with both thumbs and muttering like a contestant on *Wheel of Fortune* hoping to win a trip to a Jimmy Buffett–themed resort and casino. "Big money, big money."

"What are you *doing*?" I reached for the phone, trying to see what she was looking at, but Holiday batted my hand away.

"Shh," she said urgently. "I figure we've got like a minute, tops, so we have to make this count."

"Make what count, exactly?"

Holiday didn't answer, so I had no choice but to wait, flopping around like a beached fish while she frowned stonily at whatever she was watching. Finally she sighed, her shoulders slumping; she was silent for a moment, yanking at a strand of her hair.

"I still think somebody pushed Greg into the pool," she announced after a moment. "But it wasn't Wells."

"I— *What?*" I blinked at her, completely bewildered. "Okay," I said, "enough. What the hell is going on?"

"See for yourself," Holiday said, handing me the phone at long last.

I looked down at the screen, squinting in the midmorning glare. "Oh, damn," I said after a moment, "is this—"

"Yep." Holiday had opened up the security camera app on Mrs. Holliman's phone, flicking backward through the digital files until she got to the night of the party. Sure enough, there was Wells pulling up in front of Greg's house in the little car just before one in the morning, glancing around to make sure nobody was watching as he made his way up the front walk.

"I saw the cameras on the house when we were here last night," Holiday reported as I looked at the phone, watching Mrs. Holliman usher Wells inside. "I was pretty sure they were the kind that link directly to a mobile app, but I wasn't sure if we'd be able to get our hands on the footage."

"And you couldn't have just explained that to me in real time?"

"I mean, I *could* have," Holiday allowed. "But where's the fun in that?"

I shook my head, a soup of admiration and annoyance and disappointment coming to a slow simmer inside me. "Wells coming over here that night doesn't necessarily clear him, does it?" I asked hopefully. "I mean, he could have gone back to August House, run into Greg, and—"

"I thought of that," Holiday interrupted, "but the timing doesn't work. Look." She reached over and dragged her thumb along the scroll bar to move the footage forward, the on-screen sky changing slowly from black to navy as the hours passed. According to the time stamp, it was just before four-thirty when the front door opened again and Wells stepped out onto the porch—only this time, he was wearing the same striped rugby shirt we'd found in his bedroom yesterday afternoon. He wrapped his hand around Mrs. Holliman's waist, pulled her close, and—

"Anyway," Holiday said, closing the app so fast I was surprised she didn't sprain her wrist. "I've officially seen enough." When she looked up at me, her cheeks were pink, though I wasn't sure if it was embarrassment or sunstroke. She jogged up in the direction of the house, returning the phone with a fresh deluge of grateful tears.

"How the fuck do you keep doing that?" I asked when she got back.

Holiday looked at me curiously. "What," she asked, "the fake crying? I played Emily in a steampunk version of *Our Town* at Greenleaf last spring." Then, before I could ask what any of those things were: "You'll be happy to know, meanwhile, that Bunny the wayward Havanese has made her way home safe and sound."

I blinked. "That's great," I managed, though in truth I didn't really feel like joking around at this particular moment. I felt like someone had hit me over the head with an oar. "Glad to hear it."

"So, okay," Holiday said as we turned back toward August House, tucking her wild hair behind her ears; right away it flew into her face again, the ocean breeze blowing it in a million different directions. "Let's review. Wells left the Kendricks' after the party and came here. He must have had his own blood on him from the fight, so after they were done doing . . . whatever they were doing, Greg's mom gave him one of Greg's shirts to change into?"

"And the blood that we saw on it yesterday in his bedroom—"

"Must have been Wells's own from a cut opening up again or something, not Greg's."

"Either way," I mused, "this means Wells has an alibi. Even if he sped, he would have just been getting back to the house when Eliza found Greg in the pool—which tracks, actually, since he was the first one out there on the patio after me." As much as I didn't want to admit it, Holiday was right. "It couldn't have been him."

We were quiet as we trudged back toward August House, the heat from the sand seeping up through the soles of my sneakers and the faintly fishy smell of low tide hanging in the air. The longer we walked, the darker my mood got—and the more ridiculous and humiliated I started to feel. What did I think I'd been doing, running around the island like a little kid playing pretend? Fuck, we'd been this close to accusing Wells of attempted freaking *murder*—and over what? Some dopey middle-school hunch? I should have been sitting on an overpriced restaurant patio with Jasper and Eliza and tucking into a giant plate of stuffed French toast right now, not looking for new and creative ways to alienate a family that had been nice enough to welcome me into their house in the first place. The last few days I hadn't been able to get over the sneaking suspicion that something about the way the Kendricks were acting wasn't totally aboveboard. But all at once it seemed pretty clear that the only slimy one here was me.

"Look," I said once we finally made it back to Holiday's car, which she'd parked on the side of the road not far from August House. I'd sweat through my T-shirt, the damp cotton sticking to my skin. "Maybe we've been taking this whole thing a little bit too far."

All at once, Holiday got very still. "This whole thing, like—"

"The whole thing like, the whole thing." I shrugged. "Our little *investigation,* or whatever. I just think maybe we should cool it, that's all."

"Cool it?" she asked, looking at me carefully. "Or call it off?"

"I mean, the whole Wells thing was clearly a nonstarter, right? And it's not like we've got a ton of other leads. Not to mention the fact that for all we know, this whole thing really was just an accident." I was talking fast and loud now, not entirely sure which one of us I was trying to convince. "I just feel like maybe we're putting all this energy into trying to solve a mystery that doesn't actually exist, you know?"

Holiday nodded slowly. "Sure," she said, her voice perfectly even. "I hear you."

"We should still hang out, though," I said quickly, though even to my ears the offer sounded hollow. "I'm here for a couple more days."

I stood on the side of the road for a long moment after we'd said our goodbyes, watching her taillights disappear before turning back toward August House. I wasn't sure why I felt weirdly bereft. After all, until this week I hadn't given Holiday a second thought in years, on top of which it wasn't like we needed to be LARPing an attempted murder in order to spend time together. If I wanted to see her, I could text her. And she could do the same.

Still: it had been kind of nice to have an excuse.

Back at the house I headed out onto the patio, where Jasper was floating around the pool on the flamingo raft, beer in hand. "There he is!" he called, grinning as I hopped barefoot across the hot stones like a cartoon character doing a coal walk. "I was just saying I thought maybe you'd gotten on the fucking ferry and gone home."

"And miss out on the opportunity to get pelted with some more organic citrus?" I asked. "Not a chance." I made my way over to the lounge chair where Eliza was lying on her stomach reading, knees bent and ankles crossed. "Hey," I said quietly. "I was thinking we could take one of the cars into town later, maybe get something to eat?"

Eliza lifted her chin to look at me from behind her sunglasses, offered me a dazzling smile. "We could," she allowed brightly. "Or I could wander down to the beach, catch a fish with my bare hands, and rip its spine out with my teeth like a dog." With that, she got up off the lounge chair and strolled across the patio and into the kitchen, index finger still marking her place in her book.

"Oh yeah," Jasper said once she was gone, in a voice like he'd meant to pass along a message but that it had somehow slipped his mind, "Eliza thinks you're a giant asshole."

I looked behind me at where she'd been, watching as one lonely dragonfly buzzed idly across the patio. "I mean, she's not wrong," I admitted grimly, then belly-flopped into the pool.

13

I FLOATED AROUND IN THE WATER WITH JAS FOR A while, but my heart wasn't in it, and finally I trudged up the stairs to the third floor, shutting the creaking door of the turret room behind me. I was about to pull my shirt over my head—I needed a shower after my little beachfront excursion with Holiday—when all at once I straightened up, my hands getting suddenly clammy and my gaze darting wildly around the room.

It almost seemed like—

I mean, if I didn't know better—

"Don't be an idiot," I said out loud, the sound of my own voice reedy and unfamiliar. With some effort I forced myself to keep getting undressed, tossing my shirt in the corner and fumbling at the drawstring on my still-wet basketball shorts. Still, the more I stared at the scene before me, the more undeniable it was: the face wash and loose change slightly askew on the dresser. The T-shirts neatly stacked inside my open duffel, even though I was pretty sure they'd been spilling out onto the floor when I left. The door of the empty closet cracked just a few inches, the slice of darkness inside a sharp contrast to the bright white trim.

Someone had been through my stuff.

I sat down hard on the edge of the mattress, trying to think clearly even as my vision started to spot. It was possible Birdie had come upstairs to put laundry away—the Kendricks insisted it was fine, that she did everyone's, and though the idea of her washing my dirty socks made me deeply uncomfortable, eventually I'd given in—but even as I tried to talk myself into the thought, I knew in my gut that wasn't what had happened here.

So who, then? Jasper, dicking around harmlessly in search of a lighter or a pocketknife? Eliza, annoyed that I'd blown her off and wanting answers?

Or someone else altogether?

I stood up again and dug my phone out of my pocket, snapping quick pictures of everything that looked even remotely out of place. I'd already opened up my messages to send the photos to Holiday—sure, I'd literally just told her there was nothing to investigate, but clearly, I'd been wrong—when all at once I stopped, setting my phone back down on the nightstand. What good could possibly come out of me texting her right now? The whole thing made me feel paranoid, first of all, on top of which, knowing Holiday, she'd blow it completely out of proportion. She'd probably have me spending the rest of the day combing through the rug with tweezers looking for evidentiary fibers, and for what? Even if somebody *had* been poking around up here—and that was a big *if*—what did it matter? It's not like there'd been anything to find.

Everything matters, I remembered Holiday saying, then pushed the thought out of my mind. All at once I felt exhausted, the heaviness of the last few days weighing down on me like a beach bag full of wet sand. I didn't want to deal with it. More to the point, I didn't want to deal with Holiday.

Shower momentarily abandoned, I crawled under the covers, doing my best to ignore the creeping feeling of being watched. I didn't think I'd sleep—I was way too edgy—but sure enough, the sound of my phone ringing woke me a couple of hours later. "Hi there," my mom said when I picked up. "This is Suzie Linden. I think this used to be my son's phone number? Tall kid, kind of handsome if you squint. If you happen to run into him, could you possibly tell him to call home?"

"I'm sorry," I told her groggily, laughing in spite of myself. I'd been ignoring her calls and answering her texts as vaguely as possible for the last few days, not for the sake of being an asshole who was too cool to talk to his mother but because I honestly didn't know what to tell her about what had happened with Greg. I didn't want to lie, but somehow I couldn't imagine explaining it to her: the details of what had happened, yeah, but also the fact that I was still here at all—and that everything at August House, down to an elaborate picnic at Illumination Night, was still proceeding as normal. "I'm a jerk."

"Oh, you're not," she said easily. "I'm just teasing you." She wasn't the type to get worked up about stuff like that; she wasn't the type to get worked up over much, really, with the notable exceptions of social justice and bad TV. "I'm glad you're having fun with your friends. The only reason I'm calling again is because I wanted to see what your plan was for this hurricane."

"Oh," I said, slightly taken aback. For a second I wasn't sure what she was talking about, but as my sleepy head cleared, I vaguely remembered there being something on the radio yesterday about a storm rolling up the coast from the Bahamas, and I thought I'd heard Birdie mention a run into town to stock up on supplies. Still, for some reason I hadn't actually made the connection that an impending storm might be something that had any bearing on my plans. "It's not going to hit until this weekend, right? I'll be back by then." Even as I said the words, they sent a little shock through me. It felt like I'd just arrived at August House, though when I thought about everything that had gone on since I'd been here, time seemed to take on a warped, fluid quality, stretching in some places and contracting in others.

"Okay," my mom said, though she didn't sound satisfied; it was the same tone she got sometimes when I called from Bartley, like there was a part of her that was worried I might be swallowed up entirely into some new life at any given moment, never to return. "Just let me know if you want me to grab you at South Station." Then, her voice just a little too casual not to be put on, she continued: "Hey, have you run into Holiday at all?"

"Uh, yeah," I admitted, not sure why my impulse was to be vague about it. Well, no, that's not true, I knew exactly why my impulse was to be vague about it: first, because my mom had always cared way too much about whether or not I was still friends with Holiday, and second, because what the fuck was I going to say? *Oh, totally, we spent a little time poking around an attempted murder together, it was a real warm and fuzzy reunion?* "A couple of times. She says hi."

"Oh good," my mom said, seeming to know better than to ask any follow-up questions. "I'm glad." She paused for a moment, like she was debating her next move. "There's one more thing, Michael," she admitted, and for the first time in our entire conversation, I thought she sounded uncertain. "I got a call from Coach Lydell yesterday."

Right away, I sat upright on the mattress. "He called you?" I asked, my temper flaring. "Why didn't he call me?"

"I mean, I *am* still your mother," she pointed out reasonably. "He just wanted to see how your ankle was holding up, how your physical therapy was going. If I thought you'd be ready when practice starts."

I looked down like an instinct, though my legs were still under the covers; I had a sudden mental image of myself as a doddering old man in a nursing home, a knitted afghan covering my withered knees. "Of course," I insisted. "I'm good to go."

"That's what I told him," my mom said quickly. Then, after a moment, "Did I lie?"

"I'm *fine*, Mom."

She was quiet for a moment. "Okay," she said finally. "Well, you're the boss. Let me know what you decide to do about that hurricane."

"I will," I promised. "Don't worry."

My mom hummed, noncommittal. "I love you," she finally said.

"I know." I flopped back onto the pillows, a feeling like a hang-over beginning to thump behind my eyeballs even though I hadn't had anything to drink last night. My ankle ached underneath the sheets. "I love you too."

Jasper had left a note to say he'd gone out to see Aidy, so I borrowed a bike and rode into town to clear my head. I took my time, dawdling in the coffee shop and the bookstore and the pharmacy to pick up some more ibuprofen for my swollen ankle; by the time I got back to August House, it was almost cocktail hour and Eliza was lying on the porch swing with her legs crossed, her hair golden in the late-afternoon sun. She was a third of the way through a different novel than I'd seen her reading this morning, something thick with yellowing pages and a serious-looking cover. She didn't look up as I approached.

I leaned against the railing with my hands in my pockets, waiting to see if she'd acknowledge me. My ankle was still throbbing quietly, a dull constant ache. "You go through books really fast," I finally observed.

"Oh, I don't read them," Eliza deadpanned, eyes still fixed on the page in front of her. "I just like to gaze at the words."

"Like a Magic Eye?"

"Exactly," she said, lips quirking faintly. "Eventually, once I relax and stop trying so hard, a hidden picture appears."

I smiled back, a little uncertain. Sometimes it felt like Eliza was speaking a language I wasn't entirely fluent in, like I kept missing the idioms and the nuance. "How was your day?"

"It was nice," she reported lightly, rubbing her shin with the sole of her opposite foot as she idly turned a page. "I went to the beach with Doc."

I wasn't sure if she was trying to make me jealous or not, but if she was, it was working. "How was that?"

"It was hot," she said, and at last she put her book down. "Did you need something, Linden?"

"No," I said, too quickly. "Well, yes? I, uh, brought you something."

Her eyebrows lifted at that, just slightly. "Did you now?"

I nodded, pulling a book out of my back pocket—David Foster Wallace, *Consider the Lobster*—and handing it over. "Have you read it?" I asked her. "The guy at the bookstore said this was his favorite collection of essays."

Eliza nodded, turning it over to look at the back with a smile that seemed to be mostly to herself. "I'm sure he did," she agreed. "Let me guess—plaid button-down, hipster glasses?"

"Uh, yeah," I said in surprise. "Friend of yours?"

"Not exactly," Eliza said, pushing her sunglasses up onto the top of her head. "He once told me that he couldn't recommend any novels by female authors because he, and I quote, didn't really do books about *romantic shit*."

"Whoops," I said with a wince, tucking my hands into my pockets. "What did you say?"

"I told him that Mary Shelley wrote *Frankenstein,* and that it was clear he'd never given a woman an orgasm," Eliza said lightly.

"Then I slashed the tires on his recumbent bike." She grinned in a way that made it extremely unclear to me whether or not she was kidding. "Anyway, now I mostly use the library."

I nodded. "So I'm totally striking out here, huh?"

But Eliza shook her head. "I wouldn't go *that* far," she said, waggling the book in my direction. "This was very sweet, Linden."

"I was an asshole last night," I told her ruefully. "And this morning too, when I blew off your brunch invitation. I've known Holiday a long time, and we had some stuff to work out—friendship shit," I clarified quickly, "not romantic shit—but that's taken care of now. I only have a few more days here, and I want to make them count."

"Oh yeah?" Eliza bit her lip—to hide a smile, I was pretty sure. "And how do you plan to do that, exactly?"

"I don't know," I told her honestly. "But I was kind of hoping you might help me out."

Eliza tilted her head to the side like she was considering it; my rib cage expanded with anticipation and hope. "You know what, Linden?" she decided, curling her legs up on the swing to make room for me to sit beside her. "I just might."

14

THE NEXT COUPLE OF DAYS WERE EXACTLY WHAT I'D been picturing when I accepted Jasper's invitation to the Vineyard to begin with: We swam. We drank. We dicked around. Dean dug a pit down on the beach and we did a clambake at dusk, the sun oozing down below the horizon while we sat in the sand and stuffed ourselves silly; we made s'mores over the bonfire, Eliza kissing the melted marshmallow from my bottom lip when nobody was paying attention.

My tan deepened. My ankle didn't hurt. In fact, I didn't think about my ankle at all, or what might happen in a few short weeks when Coach Lydell realized I couldn't actually run worth a damn, let alone run and play championship-worthy offense at the same time. I didn't want to go back to Boston. I didn't want to go back to school. I wanted to stay here, blissfully relaxed, only planning as far ahead as the next meal that Birdie might bring out to the patio table or the next bathing suit that Eliza might wear.

Eliza thought Meredith needed to blow off some steam— "You've been living at that hospital," she pointed out with a frown, "and it isn't healthy"—and convinced her to come to Doc's birthday party with us the following evening, a formal affair under a tent in Doc's parents' sizable backyard that necessitated borrowing a jacket from Jasper's well-stocked closet. "Who the fuck brings six different ties on vacation?" I asked, staring into his closet with equal parts horror and fascination.

"Gentlemen, obviously." Jasper grinned, handing one over with a flourish. "Here you go, princess. This'll bring out your eyes."

I was expecting the whole thing to be a country-club drag, but it was actually pretty impressive in a throwback sort of way, with an old-fashioned band in spotless white dinner jackets and tuxedoed cater waiters passing signature cocktails off silver trays. "I'm sorry, this is his *birthday* party?" I asked Eliza, trying not to sound too outwardly wowed; for my last birthday, back at the beginning of the summer, my mom had picked up a two-person ice cream cake at J.P. Licks on her way home from work and called it done. "Or his debutante ball?"

"Be nice," Eliza chided, poking me in the ribs with one manicured finger before heading across the parquet dance floor to kiss Doc hello. I tried not to scowl as I watched them with their heads bent close together, unable to shake the feeling that, no matter what she said about the status of their relationship, he was a way better match for her than I ever could be: Rich. Taller, frankly. And sophisticated in a way I could only ever try to fake.

I got myself a drink and looked around at the party, trying not to think about how much Holiday would love this—the pomp and theater of it, all the potential for glamorous intrigue. I hadn't talked to her since our awkward goodbye on the side of the road the other day; I'd figured she might reach out, but she hadn't, so I hadn't either. Not that it mattered, I reminded myself. There was nothing left here to investigate.

Meanwhile, Eliza had been right: Being out around other people did seem good for Meredith. She was more animated than I'd seen her since the night of the party at August House, sipping an Aperol Spritz through a whimsical paper straw as she turned circles on the dance floor with some girls she and Eliza knew from the beach. "Is it just me?" I asked Jasper, popping a crab puff into my mouth. "Or is Meredith, like . . . actually kind of fun?"

"It's you," Jasper assured me, stealing a cocktail shrimp off Aidy's appetizer plate. He'd asked Doc if he could bring her at the last minute, and I couldn't help but notice that she looked as out of place as I felt, in a dress that was one click too tight and skinny heels that sank into the grass when she walked; on her face was the expression of a person who would have been more comfortable eating a burger and fries alone in the Harvard Square T station.

"Don't listen to him," Eliza said, sidling up beside me with a flute of champagne, a fat pink raspberry bobbing merrily at the bottom of the glass. She was wearing a floor-length dress in a silky midnight blue, delicate straps crisscrossing up the back; all I had been able to think about all night was how it would feel to wrinkle the cool, smooth fabric in my hands. "You should go dance with her."

"With Meredith?" I shook my head. "I . . . don't dance."

"You don't, huh?" Eliza's lips twisted. "Shocking."

In the end Doc was the one who joined her, the man of the hour in a bespoke seersucker suit that should have been deeply ridiculous but somehow wasn't. I watched as the two of them twirled around in dizzy circles, Meredith smiling the wide, genuine smile of someone who'd managed, just for a moment, to forget how bad things were outside the gilded universe of this party tent. Greg's condition still hadn't improved, Eliza had told me earlier; he was breathing with the help of a ventilator, hooked up to a million different machines. Imagining him lying there while the rest of us joked around eating crab legs made me feel a little sick to my stomach, so I tried not to imagine it at all.

Still, I think Eliza could sense I was distracted; she reached out and slid one finger into the belt loop of my khakis, yanking hard enough that I stumbled into her. "You *sure* you don't dance?" she asked, stepping even closer.

"Tell you what," I said—collecting both her hands and squeezing gently, reaching up and winding her arms around my neck. "Just this once, I might make an exception to the rule."

I was lying on the flamingo raft the following morning, waiting for the morning sun to bleach the hangover out of me, when Eliza crept up behind me and shoved the float over with both hands, sending me sputtering into the deep end. "Sorry," she said when I surfaced, grinning as I pushed my wet hair back off my forehead. "Just making sure you were paying attention."

"I mean, I am *now*," I said with a laugh—taking a step closer, backing her up against the side of the pool. Over on the patio the dark, juicy stain from our game of Orange was still faintly visible, though I knew for a fact that Dean had power washed the stones twice since the day we'd played. Just for a second I thought of Macbeth, which we'd read in my English class at Bartley last semester—*Out, damned spot.* "I think I was sleeping."

"I think you were too." Eliza ducked under my arm and commandeered the raft, hopping up onto it with practiced ease and stretching her long legs out in front of her. "See?" she asked teasingly. "It's not so bad here, once you unclench."

"I am . . . definitely unclenched," I admitted. "I can't believe I have to leave tomorrow."

She hummed quietly, then: "What if you didn't?"

That got my attention; still, I tried to play it cool. "I mean," I said with a smirk, "I think eventually when Birdie and Dean closed the pool up, it would get a little hard to breathe."

"Cute," Eliza said. She rolled over onto her stomach, gazing at me over the tops of her sunglasses. "You know what I mean. A couple of extra days, that's all. You've got time before school starts, don't you? And your internship is done?"

"My what? Oh yeah," I said, catching myself just in time. "It is." She was right, I realized as I thought about it—there *wasn't* anything particularly urgent for me to get back to, at least not yet.

"So then?" Eliza raised her eyebrows. "Besides," she pointed out, "the hurricane is supposed to hit in a couple of days."

I frowned. "Don't people usually try to get *off* the island when a hurricane is coming?"

"Patsies, maybe." Eliza grinned. "Not real islanders. We've ridden out storms here a bunch of times before. It's fun, actually—we board up all the windows and stock up on food and have a fire in the fireplace."

I was pretty sure that what she actually meant was that Birdie and Dean did all those things for them, though I had to admit it did sound kind of cozy. Still, I shook my head. "I don't know. I feel like I should get out of your hair, with everything going on. What's that old quote? Fish and visitors start to stink after a few days, or something?"

"You smell okay to me," Eliza said, then surprised me by leaning down and pressing her mouth to mine. "Convinced yet?" she asked.

"Getting there," I admitted, reaching out and running a finger along the strap of her bathing suit. "Maybe you should try again."

Eliza laughed. "In your dreams, maybe," she said, then slipped off the raft and boosted herself up out of the pool.

"Dude, you should totally stay," Jasper said when I mentioned it to him out on the porch after dinner later that night. He and Aidy were sitting side by side on the swing while I stretched out cross-legged at the top of the steps with my back against one of the support beams. The night was cool, the hoot of an owl audible from high up in the trees; I hadn't gotten a single mosquito bite since I'd been here, like possibly there was some kind of invisible rich-person net that kept them all away.

"I'm thinking about it," I admitted. Something about this

place reminded me of the poppy field in *The Wizard of Oz,* like if I wasn't careful, I might look up one day and realize that years had passed and I'd forgotten to do something extremely important. Still, I could feel the urge to stay tugging languidly at my limbs. "You think it'll be cool with your mom and dad?"

"I can assure you, they absolutely will not care," Jasper said with confidence. "Meredith has been here all summer, remember? And they like having a lot of people in the house. It helps them forget that they don't actually like each other that much."

I looked at him with curious surprise, not entirely sure what to say to that. Mr. and Mrs. Kendrick had seemed pretty solid to me, but what the hell did I know? They weren't my parents. The truth was, I barely knew them. Sometimes it felt like Jasper's entire family kept shape-shifting in front of my eyes, like I couldn't tell what was real and what was fake.

Only one way to find out, reminded a voice in my head that sounded suspiciously like Holiday's; I ignored it as studiously as possible, reminding myself to get a grip. So whatever, it had been fun to randomly run around with an old friend for a couple of days on vacation. But it wasn't like we were suddenly going to go back to having sleepovers and eating tuna fish sandwiches on her front steps. We'd grown up. We'd moved on. We had better things to do.

"Okay then," I said. "I'll stay."

"There you go," Aidy said, lacing her fingers through Jasper's like she was worried he was going to escape. The two of them had spent the last few days joined at the hip every second she wasn't working at Red's, gazing adoringly at each other and sharing the same piece of chewing gum and generally nauseating the rest of us with their unceasing PDA. "Bro, I'm in love," Jasper had announced to me that morning, watching Aidy make her way up the beach in a vintage-looking bathing suit and a pair of heart-shaped sunglasses. And yeah, I'd heard him say it before, about his SAT tutor and the bagel shop barista and the girls' swim coach back at Bartley; still, something about the way he was looking at Aidy now made me wonder if maybe this time he was telling the truth.

Eliza came out through the front door just then, Whimsy at her heels. "Linden's staying for the hurricane party," Jasper announced with a grin.

Eliza hopped delicately up onto the deck rail, perching herself there like a rare island bird. "Of course he is," she said lightly, like as far as she was concerned, we'd settled the matter hours ago. Come to think of it, we probably had.

The four of us sat on the porch for a long time—chatting idly as we listened to the wind rustle, breathing the end-of-summer air. One thing I liked about August House—a thing I liked about the Kendricks—was that nobody ever seemed to be worried about wasting time. Back at Bartley there was always something I was supposed to be doing: lacrosse practice or time in the weight room or my job at the library; homework to keep my grades up so I wouldn't put my scholarship in danger. And all summer I'd been hustling to bank as much money as I possibly could. But here it was like nobody expected me to do anything. There was nothing *to* do except . . . be.

I leaned my head back, only half listening as the conversation swirled around me: an article that Eliza had seen in the *Vineyard Gazette* about a family of possums drunk on Cheez-Its caught having a bacchanal in someone's pantry; Jasper's thoughtful musings on which members of our class at Bartley were most likely to have experimented with bestiality. A story that Aidy knew about the Crying Swamp, a patch of woods turned cranberry bog in West Tisbury where people used to swear they could hear someone wailing all night long, their heartbroken cries echoing endlessly out into the darkness.

"Someone?" Eliza asked, lips quirking. "Like what, a ghost?"

"Or something," Aidy said with an ominous shrug.

"Seriously?" Jasper looked over at her with some interest. "You don't actually believe in that, do you?"

"Of course not," Aidy said, a whisper of defensiveness audible in her voice. "But that doesn't mean it didn't happen." She shrugged almost violently. "I've lived on this island my entire life, and I can tell you that more than enough extremely fucked-up stuff happens here without dragging the supernatural into it."

Something about the way she said it caught my attention, like possibly she was talking in specifics and not generalities, but before I could figure out a low-key way to ask what she meant, Eliza and Jasper had already moved on, launching into yet another arcane Kendrick family parlor game. Tonight's was called Pervy Congressman, the object of which, so far as I understood it, was to come up with mean campaign slogans for people Jasper and Eliza didn't like, including their father's attorney, members of several prominent Vineyard families, and Wells. "You realize you both sound completely stoned," I told them, laughing in spite of myself.

"I *wish* I was stoned," Aidy said longingly. Pervy Congressman hadn't seemed to hold her attention, and I thought again of how uncomfortable she'd looked at Doc's party. I wondered if she sometimes felt like an outsider with the Kendricks the same way I did, always half a beat behind, or if possibly she was still thinking about the Crying Swamp and whatever—or whoever—might be grieving deep inside it.

"I wish I was stoned too, actually," Eliza admitted, then poked Jasper with one bare foot. "Go get your Black Box, will you?" I knew from our years of living together that the Black Box was where Jasper kept his weed, an old Utz Cheese Balls canister he'd named after the box where Winston Churchill kept his official correspondence during World War II. It always seemed to me like the first place anyone would look if the administration at Bartley ever went through with the room checks they were always threatening whenever somebody got caught with drugs in the dorms, but Jasper felt confident his Fourth Amendment rights would hold if it ever came to that, and I suspected he was probably correct.

But now he shook his head. "Cupboard is bare," he reported sadly. "We went through the last of it the other night."

"So?" Eliza asked with a shrug. "Go get more."

Jasper snorted. "Oh, I'm sorry. Have I not been paying enough attention to your personal pharmacological needs while the cops are strolling around our backyard and your houseguest's boyfriend is comatose in the hospital from partying too much?"

I glanced over at him, surprised—it was the first time he'd said anything to suggest what had happened with Greg was still on his mind—but Eliza looked patently unimpressed. "Oh, please," she said, "the cops know exactly what happened, which is that Greg was a dirtbag who shouldn't have been creeping around our house in the first place. They could give a shit about my *personal pharmacological needs.*"

I couldn't help but wince at the callousness in her voice, even though I knew she was right: in fact, Eliza probably could have gotten stoned on whippets, crashed the big car into the Flying Horses Carousel, and still made it back to August House by dinner. I thought again of how the Kendricks seemed to play by an entirely different set of rules than the rest of us, swallowing down a sudden storm swell of resentment.

"One thing I'll say about Holliman," Jasper continued, seeming to concede his sister's point, "is that if he was here, he could definitely hook us up."

"There's *his* campaign slogan," Eliza joked. "Excellent weed in every bowl."

"And oxy," Jasper pointed out. "And coke, actually. A man of many talents."

"What about you, Aidy?" Eliza suggested, crossing her delicate ankles, and it took me a second to realize she was still on the hunt for something to take the edge off. "You must know somebody who could help us out."

"Why, because I'm a townie?" Aidy's lips twisted. "Classist."

"Oh, right, because whoever Greg was working with was definitely the president of the Greenwich chapter of the Daughters of the American Revolution." Eliza shook her head, though I thought

I saw her cheeks pink up a bit at the callout. "Aren't you the one who said he was dealing for some total sketchballs from Southie?"

That got my attention, first because from the way she said *Southie,* I could tell she was picturing the set of *Good Will Hunting* rather than the fratty, gentrified neighborhood full of condos and swanky bars that I knew South Boston to be these days, and second because, gentrification or not, *dealing for some total sketchballs from Southie* sounded suspiciously like a lead. *You're not looking for leads anymore, dickhead,* I reminded myself firmly.

"Honestly, I don't know what that guy was up to," Aidy said, shooting a cautious look at Jasper, "and I don't care. I wish him a speedy recovery and everything, but as far as I'm concerned, he and I are kind of ancient history at this point." She quirked an eyebrow. "I mean, I also had a scoliosis brace and orthodontic headgear, but that doesn't mean it's a part of my life I particularly want to relive."

"You had *headgear?*" Jasper asked with a smile.

"And rubber bands," Aidy reported grimly.

Jasper shook his head. "I can't help it," he said. "I still think you're cute."

The two of them took off not long after that—to go for a walk, they said, which I assumed was code for *fool around down at the beach.* Once they were gone, Eliza stood up, holding her hand out. "Come with me," she instructed, leaving no room for argument. "I want to show you something."

"Oh yeah?" I asked, unable to keep the implication out of my voice. "What's that, exactly?"

Eliza rolled her eyes. "Don't be basic, Linden," she scolded. "Come on."

"Sorry, sorry." I let her lead me inside the house and up the back staircase, past her room, then up another flight of stairs and past mine. She opened a door I'd thought this whole time was a closet, scuttling up a narrow wooden ladder before finally unlocking a hatch that led to the roof. I followed her up and out onto the widow's walk, where the air was cool and salty, the endless sky cluttered with stars—thousands of them packed densely all the way out to the horizon, stars like I'd never seen in my life. I spent a lot of time back then trying not to seem impressed by things, but this time I couldn't hold back my awe. "Holy shit," I said quietly—turning a slow circle, taking it all in.

Eliza smiled. "View's not bad," she said, coming to stand beside me at the railing.

"No," I agreed, looking at her pointedly, "view's not bad."

Eliza burst out laughing, the sound of it echoing baldly out over the water. "Shit, Linden," she said once she'd finally composed herself, propping her elbows up on the railing, "I like you, so I'm going to pretend for both our sakes that you did not just say that."

"Fuck you!" I said, laughing myself even as I felt my cheeks flush. "That was romantic as all hell."

Eliza wrinkled her nose. "Is that what you'd call it?" she asked. "Really now?"

"It is," I told her, hoping I sounded more confident than I felt. "Not to mention the fact that you're talking a pretty big game for a person who just brought me up onto the roof to look at the fucking stars."

Eliza tilted her head to the side like, *Fair point.* "I did do that," she admitted. "That was a tip of my hand."

"Say more about how much you like me, why don't you."

"No, I don't believe I will."

"Uh-huh." I nodded, smirking at her in the moonlight. "That's what I thought."

"Can't let you get too confident, bro," she said, doing a pretty good impression of Jasper. "Gotta keep the mystery alive."

"Yeah, yeah." We were quiet for a moment, both of us gazing out at the endless blackness of the ocean. The waves sounded louder from up here, slamming against the rocks with body-breaking force. I thought of the hurricane swirling its way up the coast at this very moment, of squalls and shipwrecks and lives lost forever at sea.

"I used to come up here every night of the summer when I was like ten and eleven to look for ghosts," Eliza told me quietly, as if possibly she could read my mind. "You know that age when little girls are like half-feral and really into like, ancient Egypt?"

"Not really," I confessed, though now that she mentioned it, I did faintly remember Holiday going through a phase with scarabs. "Is that a thing?"

"It's a thing," Eliza assured me. She frowned out at the smudgy horizon, the wind whipping her hair around her face. "This used to be an actual fishing island, you know. The women who lived in this house when it was first built used to climb up here to wait for their husbands to come back from these long, dangerous voyages, knowing the whole time that the odds were they probably wouldn't."

I glanced over at her, teasing. "Did you used to pretend you were one of them?"

"Fuck no!" Eliza said, whirling on me in faux outrage. "I used to pretend I was an eighteenth-century lobsterman. I was like, really into sea shanties." She made a face at the memory. "I was a weird kid."

"It sounds like you were great."

That made her smile, ducking her blond head almost bashfully. "I had my moments," she allowed. "I definitely had an overactive imagination, though. Wells used to stand at the hatch when I was up here and make ghost sounds to torture me."

"Sounds about right," I said with a laugh. "What'd you do when you realized it was him and not the creature from the Crying Swamp?"

"Well, one time I ran over there and shoved him clean down the ladder. Broke his arm in three places."

I blinked, startled by the starkness of the confession. Something about the self-satisfied tone in her voice made me uneasy, and I had the uncomfortable sense I'd had around her a couple of times before—the sneaking suspicion that she was leaving me a trail of bread crumbs in the hope that eventually I'd follow them to . . . what, exactly? There was a tiny voice at the back of my head that wondered if maybe I didn't actually want to know.

I kissed her instead of asking, the combination of her warm body and the chilly wind setting all my nerve endings humming. Eliza wound her arms around my neck. I walked her backward until she was pressed against the railing, wanting to get as close to her as humanly possible; she slid one curious knee between mine, and I groaned.

Eliza smiled at that, the curve of it like a brand against my jaw. "I *do* like you, you know," she murmured—voice muffled and mouth hot against my skin, so quiet that I almost didn't hear her over the whine of the water. "I like you a lot, Linden."

I grinned, slipping a thumb beneath the strap of her sundress, drawing circles over the smooth skin of her shoulder. The truth was, I liked her too; I *more* than liked her, potentially, though part of me knew it was way too soon. I thought of what I'd felt for Greer, how hard and fast I'd fallen. I thought of what it had cost, in the end.

"Let me take you out," I said—pulling back, straightening up a little. We could get to know each other for real, I figured; have an actual conversation, far from August House with its secrets and its history and its ghosts. "Tomorrow night?"

But Eliza shook her head. "I'm gone tomorrow night," she said, looking sincerely disappointed. "My friend Pearl is in town, who I used to ride with. Her parents have a place out on Chappie— Chappaquiddick, I mean."

My lips twisted. Chappie was smaller and way more remote than the Vineyard, studded with a handful of secluded old-money mansions and not much else. The thought of being out there overnight—even in what I was sure would be the most luxurious of accommodations—gave me the creeps, though I wasn't about to admit that to Eliza. "I've heard of it, thank you."

"I mean, *I* don't know what they teach you at Bartley." She traced her index finger along the underside of my arm. "Anyway, I'll be back before the storm hits. You can take me out when the weather clears, how about. *Or*"—she popped up on her tiptoes and kissed me again, tugging gently at the hair at the nape of my neck—"who knows? Maybe we can stay inside."

I made a helpless sound, pulling her even closer in the moonlight. There was more than one way to get to know someone, I reminded myself. "Eliza," I muttered against her neck, my mouth moving slowly across her collarbone, "come downstairs with me."

Eliza pulled back and grinned, her face full of promise, then gestured up at the sky. "Stars are for wishing on," she announced, all finishing-school polish. She kissed me one more time before she slipped away down the ladder.

15

I WOKE UP EARLY THE NEXT MORNING—OR, MORE AC-
curately, I didn't actually sleep at all, tossing and turning and
sweating through my sheets for most of the night. I thought about
Eliza. I thought about Greg. I thought about Greer, who I'd more
or less made myself forget for the better part of the last six months.
We hadn't talked all summer—or, more accurately, we hadn't
talked since that night in the library a few days after the accident
last spring. I winced at the memory: the precarious, off-balance
sensation of hobbling around Bartley's still-snowy campus with a
cast and crutches, the makeup-covered cuts just visible on Greer's
sharp cheekbone. "Can I trust you?" she'd asked, and her eyes were
so serious. It wasn't until later that I realized what she'd meant.

A little after three a.m. I reached over and picked my phone
up off the dresser, opening Instagram and typing in the first few
letters of her handle. She didn't post much—Greer was too cool
for that, or at the very least I knew she wanted people to think she
was—but there was a shot from the Fourth of July of her standing

on a wide, green swath of lawn, drawing a long line of light behind her with a sparkler. *Glow up, as the kids say,* the caption read.

I flopped back against the pillows, trying to tell myself I didn't feel anything for her anymore and knowing that was mostly bullshit. We'd gotten together back in the fall of my junior year: At Bartley I had a job shelving books at the library three nights a week after dinner, which wasn't *quite* as overtly embarrassing as washing dishes in the dining hall after meals, but still I kept my head down while I was there, slinking through the stacks while I ran my fingers along the spines of novels and biographies, making sure everything was in order. I'd seen Greer around campus sometimes—getting coffee at the kiosk with the other seniors in her cohort, lying on a quilt out on the green—but I didn't think I'd ever registered for her one way or the other until one night a few days before Halloween when I looked up from the transcendentalist poets and there she was, leaning against the shelves with her arms and ankles crossed.

"Tell me this, Linden," she said, gazing at me from behind a pair of round tortoiseshell glasses; she was wearing flannel pants and Bean boots, her soft-looking hair catching the overhead light. "How long is it going to take for you to pull your head out of your ass and ask me to hang out?"

We were inseparable after that.

Until we weren't.

Now I dropped my phone back onto the dresser with more force than I meant to, a clatter that had me wincing and listening for movement in the house. Thinking about Greer made me feel sick and overserved in a way that I usually associated with drinking too much or eating an entire bag of Doritos in one sitting. I wanted to get up and run—and I would have, if not for the pain in my busted ankle. Instead I threw back the covers and padded downstairs as quietly as I could. Birdie had made a plum cake with dinner, and I was headed for the kitchen to see if there was any left when a quiet, knowing voice shattered the silence: "Couldn't sleep?"

I sucked in a breath, my gaze skittering toward the darkened dining room. It was a polished, formal space, and the Kendricks hardly ever used it—they ate out on the patio, or otherwise clustered around the island in the kitchen, everyone talking at once—but Mrs. Kendrick was sitting in her bathrobe at the far end of the long oak table, a half-full wineglass in front of her and the nearly empty bottle at her side. I was startled, though I probably shouldn't have been: A thing I was starting to realize was that even in the middle of the night, August House was never entirely still. There was always someone awake, someone restless. Someone watching or listening in.

"Um, yeah," I said—slightly befuddled, not wanting to let her know she'd rattled me. I stepped closer to where she was sitting, "Or—no, rather. Couldn't sleep."

"Me neither." She held up her wineglass in a girlish little toast. "Did you kids have fun tonight?"

"We did," I said, aiming for politeness but also not particularly wanting to settle in for an impromptu heart-to-heart. There was something slightly creepy about finding her here by herself in the dark like this, without so much as an up-in-arms Facebook group or a book of Sudoku puzzles to keep her occupied. It felt almost like she'd been waiting for me, though I knew that was impossible. "Thank you again for having me."

"Oh, Linden, don't be ridiculous." She waved a hand to bat away the gratitude, lifting one thin eyebrow. "You and my daughter seem to be getting along."

I almost choked on my own tongue. "I . . . yeah," I said; then, realizing that didn't sound particularly gentlemanly: "I mean, I like her very much. I think you'd have to ask her if she feels the same."

Mrs. Kendrick liked that: "Oh, that's clever," she replied softly, lips quirking. There was a detached, almost floaty quality to her voice, like she was here in the room with me but also not all the way. She was a little drunk—more than a little—but I didn't think that was it, entirely. I remembered what Eliza had said when I'd first gotten here, about needing to count her mom's Xanax; it hadn't fit with the image I had in my head of tennis-playing, gala-attending Mrs. Kendrick, and I'd dismissed it as hyperbole. But now suddenly I wasn't so sure. "How would you say she's doing?"

"Eliza?" I asked—surprised by the question, wondering why she wanted to know. I thought uneasily of the story Eliza had told me earlier, about Wells and the staircase to the widow's walk, then pushed it resolutely out of my mind. "She's great."

Mrs. Kendrick smiled to herself. "She is, isn't she." She took a sip of wine, the glass wobbling dangerously as she set it back down.

"Whoops," I said, reaching out and steadying it with one hand just before it tipped.

Mrs. Kendrick eyed me across the table. "You don't miss a trick, do you, Linden?" she asked, lifting it to her lips one more time.

"I . . . guess not?" I said uncertainly, watching as she drained its ruby-colored contents. "Quick reflexes, I guess."

"No, I don't just mean that. You're observant." She lifted her chin. "I see you when you're with my children. They're chatterboxes, all three of them. It drove me up a wall, when they were young: all that *talking*. All those *questions*. But not you. You're quiet. You"—she gestured with the empty glass—"take it all in."

". . . Maybe," I agreed slowly, not sure what she was driving at. "I think I'm mostly just trying not to say anything dumb."

Mrs. Kendrick didn't laugh. "I used to be the same way," she said, reaching for the wine bottle and pouring herself a refill. "Noticing everything. But it's not always such a good trait, in a person. As you get older, you'll find sometimes it's better not to notice some things at all."

My pulse sped up at that, a feeling like someone had reached inside my chest and started pumping my heart like a stress ball. Was that a warning? Did she know somehow that Holiday and I were trying to figure out what had happened the night of the party?

More to the point: Did *she* know how Greg had wound up in the pool?

All at once I was struck by the urge to get out of this room— and this conversation—as quickly as possible. "That's . . . good advice," I said, trying to put some distance between us in a way that wasn't too painfully obvious. "I should probably try to get some rest. Have a good night, Mrs. Kendrick."

Birdie's plum cake forgotten, I headed back up to the third floor at a pace that could only be called a scamper, shutting the door firmly behind me and flicking the tiny antique lock. I spent the dregs of the night sitting upright in bed and staring darkly at the botanical prints on the wall, the outlines of the plants just barely visible in the moonlight seeping in through the window, and the moment the sun finally dripped up over the horizon, I was out of bed and pulling a pair of shorts out of the creaking chest of drawers. I crept back down the stairs as quietly as I could, not wanting Mr. Kendrick to conscript me for an early-morning polar plunge, then hopped on one of the bikes that was leaning against the porch and pedaled furiously down the drive. It was warmer than I had bargained for, and I was covered in sweat by the time I got to Holiday's house, wiping my forehead with the back of my arm as I climbed the steps to the porch.

"Um," she said, eyes widening when she answered the door. *"Hi."* She was still wearing her pajamas, a pair of ratty sweatpants and a Greenleaf T-shirt. It occurred to me, though I was trying very hard not to notice, that she wasn't wearing a bra. "You're up early."

I'd told myself I was just stopping by to say hi, maybe ask if she wanted to go get an iced coffee, but before I knew it, I was blurting out everything that had happened since the last time we'd talked in one long, punctuationless sentence: Greg and the drugs and *some total sketchballs from Southie,* Mrs. Kendrick at the dining room table, and somebody going through my stuff. "I fucked up," I admitted when I was finished, my chest heaving a little with exertion. "I was wrong."

Holiday gazed at me for a long moment with an expression I didn't entirely recognize. Then she sighed. "Okay," she said, holding one hand up. "I need a minute."

She held the screen open and waved me into the front hall, where it was cool and dark and quiet. "Wait here," she instructed, then disappeared upstairs. I stood on the brightly colored rag rug with my hands in my pockets, trying not to look like I was casing the house for a possible robbery. Holiday's parents' place was more in line with what I had always pictured beach houses to be like—weathered shingles and a slightly saggy front porch, a living room full of comfy-looking but decidedly mismatched furniture, and a bookshelf stuffed with ancient board games as well as what appeared to be every novel that Danielle Steel had ever written.

"Big fan?" I asked when Holiday thundered back downstairs.

Holiday shook her head. "They were my grandma's," she explained. She'd gotten dressed in denim shorts and an army-green button-down, notebook and laptop tucked under her arm. "My mom used to be, like, extremely anti–romance novel, but then like five years ago she wound up reading one while we were here and had this big feminist reawakening, and now she teaches a class about them at the Extension School."

She thrust the laptop and notebook into my arms, then turned and headed into the kitchen. I wasn't sure if I should follow, so I stayed where I was, and a moment later she returned again, this time clutching a plastic tumbler of cold brew in each hand. "Out," she said officiously, shooing me back onto the porch.

I sat down across from her at the tiny iron bistro table, where she took her time organizing and arranging her various supplies without bothering to spare me a second glance. "Okay," she finally repeated, her tone all business as she opened her notebook to a fresh, blank page. "Say all that again." Then—and only then—she smiled. "Up to and including, obviously, the part about what a horse's ass you are."

I grinned, pure narcotic relief flooding through me; it wasn't until that moment that I suddenly realized I'd been terrified she was going to tell me to fuck off once and for all. "Did I say I was a horse's ass?" I asked.

Holiday put pen to paper, glancing up at me through her eyelashes. "I think it was implied," she said crisply. "Now go."

I relayed the events of last night as clearly as possible, right up until the part about Eliza breaking Wells's arm when they were kids—which, I reminded myself firmly, didn't actually have anything to do with our current investigation. When I was finished, Holiday frowned. "First of all," she began, "Southie is like, extremely gentrified now."

"I mean, *I* know that," I said, "but—"

"No, no, I take your point." Holiday held a hand up. "And you're right. As a matter of fact . . ." She trailed off, pecking away at her laptop for a moment before turning the screen to face me.

I squinted, the glare of the early-morning sun making it difficult to see what looked like the results of some kind of records request. "What am I looking at?" I asked.

Holiday's dark eyes were shining. "The security footage from Greg's house didn't give us Wells," she reminded me, "but it might have given us someone even better."

I shook my head, not understanding. "Okay . . . ?"

"About an hour before the Kendricks' party, some guy in a red Honda showed up in front of the Hollimans'," she explained, tapping the make and model of the car listed on the screen. "Greg came out to talk to him, and I obviously couldn't hear what they were saying, but from their body language it looked like things got pretty heated."

I felt my eyes widen. "And you didn't think to mention that to me at all?"

Holiday was unmoved. "First of all, there are a lot of things I don't tell you," she fired back, "and second of all, I didn't know if it mattered or not. But then when I looked up the license plate—"

"You memorized the *license* plate?" I interrupted. "In the thirty seconds you were watching that tape?"

"I mean, I also got a cool sixteen hundred on my SATs," she informed me. "My brain is weird, Michael. I would think you of all people would know that by now."

It did seem on-brand for her, now that I thought about it. "I didn't even know you could look up license plates if you weren't the police."

"There's a bunch of stuff like that you can do if you're willing to pay a fee," Holiday said with a shrug. "I mean, let's be real, the site was totally questionable and they probably have my credit card information on file at the Kremlin or whatever, but we can solve that problem next." She grinned. "The point is, the car is owned by some guy named Topher Leal. Who just happens to be . . ." She drummed a nerdy little tattoo on the table.

"Shut the fuck up."

"A drug dealer," Holiday said happily. "From Southie."

I shook my head. "Is it weird that I kind of want to kiss you right now?"

The words were out before I could think better of them; right away I felt myself blush, but Holiday only preened. "I mean," she said breezily, "when don't you?"

"Cute." Then, wanting to course-correct the conversation as quickly as possible: "How do you know he's a drug dealer?"

"Oh, just a little trick of the trade I like to call Google dot com," Holiday said with a toss of her hair. "He's been arrested a couple of times, and his name popped up on some local blog about how crime and yuppie coffee shops are equally responsible for ruining the neighborhood. I also found his relay times from when he used to run track in high school and the website for his now-defunct ska band."

"Thorough," I admitted appreciatively. "Say Greg really did owe this Topher guy a buttload of money, though. Why would Topher want to kill him? How's Greg going to pay him back if he's at the bottom of the Kendricks' pool?"

"Maybe he just meant to rough him up a little," Holiday said, and I snorted.

"*Rough him up?*" I echoed. "Who are you, Sammy the Bull?"

"I'm just saying!" Holiday made a face. "Maybe Greg is dealing for Topher, but he gets in over his head somehow, so he comes out here for the summer thinking he's bought himself some time to come up with the cash—except for the part where whatever Greg owes to Topher, Topher probably owes somebody else. I'm thinking Topher showed up at Greg's house to collect, and they argued—that much, at least, is clear from the video. What I'm less sure about is how we get from there to the bottom of the Kendricks' pool."

"Topher might have followed Greg back to August House after the party," I hypothesized. "Jasper said something about catching Greg and Meredith in the outdoor shower one night a few weeks ago; he was making a big stink about having to burn the whole thing down and have Dean rebuild it. It's possible Greg headed back over there for a hookup—"

"And got a lot more than a hand job for his trouble?"

I snorted, reaching for my iced coffee and stretching out in the rickety patio chair. "Not to put too fine a point on it, but yes." I frowned. "What do we think about Mrs. Kendrick?"

Holiday shrugged. "I mean, we should definitely keep it in mind, but honestly, it sounds like standard late-night wine-mom talk. You said Jasper mentioned his parents were unhappy, right?" She grinned wickedly. "The way things are going with those people, you should probably be thankful she didn't ask you to wait a minute while she slipped into something a little more comfortable."

"Oh my god, fuck you," I said, but I was laughing. It felt good to be in her company again—coming up with theories, joking around. I'd enjoyed myself the last couple of days, tooling around with Jasper and Eliza. But the truth was I'd missed Holiday too. "So what's our play here?" I asked, tipping the chair back on two legs.

"Listen to you, Bold Assumptions!" Holiday cocked an eyebrow. "What exactly do you think I've been doing for the last three days, just sitting around coming up with various investigative plans on the off chance you happened to pull your head out of your own ass before you left town?"

"I mean," I said sheepishly, "yes, kind of."

Holiday's eyes narrowed. "You're very annoying, do you know that? But you're also not *entirely* wrong." She sighed. "I think we should stake out the hospital," she told me. "See if Topher Leal— or anybody else—shows up."

"At the *hospital*?" I shook my head. "What's he going to be doing, waiting to see if Greg jumps out of bed like Lazarus and does the Wobble out the front door? It's not like he can just stroll on in there and introduce himself, camp out by the vending machines next to Meredith."

"Aw, I think they'd have a lot in common if they just got to know each other a little," Holiday deadpanned, then grew serious. "Chances are, Topher can't show his face back in Boston until he gets the money. If I were him, I'd be sitting on that hospital like a mother duck waiting for her eggs to hatch."

We made a plan to meet up later that night. Eliza had taken the tiny, janky-looking ferry out to Chappaquiddick to see her friend, so I spent the day at the beach with Jasper and Doc, the three of us wave jumping and playing can jam and goofing around on paddleboards. Birdie brought lunch down in a giant basket, tomato-and-mozzarella sandwiches slathered with pesto made from basil she'd grown in a garden at the side of the house. "I made one for your brother," she said to Jasper, then—I thought—flicking her gaze ever so quickly to me. "Is he not here with you all?"

Doc shook his head. Wells seemed to be keeping his distance the last few days, drifting in and out of the house at odd hours:

"He's probably got some secret girlfriend he doesn't want any of us to know about," Jasper hypothesized, and I shoved a fistful of chips into my mouth.

Holiday picked me up just as the sun was setting. "I brought snacks," she announced, nodding at a tote bag on the crowded floor of the passenger side, "but no drinks because I didn't want us to have to pee in a coffee cup halfway through."

"Very forward-thinking of you," I said.

"Not my first stakeout," she said with a shrug.

The hospital was on the other side of the island, twenty minutes from August House. I was accustomed to Boston hospitals, sprawling medical campuses crammed with tall, interconnected buildings that towered against the skyline, but this was a smallish, squat structure that looked like it belonged in a suburban office park. "I think they mostly treat like, tourists with heatstroke," Holiday explained as we pulled into the parking lot. Life-threatening injuries were usually helicoptered back to the mainland.

"So Greg's condition can't be too bad, then," I pointed out hopefully.

"Maybe," Holiday agreed, pulling into a spot at the far end of the lot and killing the engine. "Or they don't think more sophisticated treatment would help enough to be worth it."

I didn't know what to say to that, so I didn't say anything, unbuckling my seat belt and settling in. The two of us were quiet for a while, watching the emergency room doors whoosh open and shut and keeping track of the cars coming and going in the mostly empty lot. It reminded me of when we were little kids, the two of us lying on our stomachs side by side on the fancy rug in her parents' living room, working on opposite pages of a coloring book. We chatted on and off now, idle: a music festival she'd been to earlier in the summer, a comedian both of us liked. Holiday's school, which started up again in two weeks. "What about next year?" I asked. We were both about to be seniors, though we hadn't talked much about it. "What happens then?"

Holiday sighed. "That's a great question." She leaned back against the driver's side window, pulling one leg up onto the seat and resting her chin on her knee. She was wearing leggings and a hoodie from some performing arts camp up in Maine, her hair in a giant knot on top of her head. "I don't know. College, conceivably. Grad school. But there's also a part of me that wants to say fuck it and move out to Lenox to live in a commune with a bunch of other ladies and knit socks in Fair Isle patterns all day."

I grinned—not because I couldn't picture it but because I kind of could, right down to the loaves of sourdough bread cooling on their butcher-block counters and the low drone of NPR on the radio. "Can I ask you something personal?" I blurted. "Are you . . ." I trailed off, immediately rethinking the sagacity of this line of questioning and filled with searing regret, but Holiday burst out laughing.

"A lesbian?" she prodded, lifting one thick eyebrow. "No,

Michael. Despite my admittedly impressive ability to quote Mary Oliver and love of an ethically made garment, I regret to inform you I am not a lesbian."

My entire body prickled hot and red, though it's not like that wasn't what I'd been trying to ask her. "It would be fine if you were, obviously!" I backpedaled.

Holiday snorted. "Thank you for your blessing."

"No no," I said quickly, "I didn't mean it like that, I just—"

Holiday held up a hand to save me from myself, though to my relief, she looked more amused than offended. "What about you?" she asked.

"Oh, I'm not a lesbian either."

She pressed her lips together, but I saw her smile anyway. "What are you going to do about next year, smartass?" she amended. "Actually, forget next year. What are you going to do about Bartley?"

I shrugged, leaning my head back against the seat. I didn't particularly want to talk about it, though I supposed that at this particular moment I didn't really have a leg to stand on when it came to invasive questions. "I have no idea," I confessed. "Show up at practice and hope nobody notices I suck, I guess. Go back to Boston if I lose my scholarship."

"You really think they'll pull it if you're injured?"

"They've done it to other guys before," I told her; I knew because I'd checked. "And then there's like, college to think about. My grades are fine, but without lacrosse there's nothing super impressive about me."

"I wouldn't go *that* far," Holiday protested.

That made me smile. "Oh no?" I asked reflexively. "How far would you go?"

There was a distinctly flirtatious undertone in my voice that I hadn't consciously intended, and I saw the look in Holiday's eyes change as we both heard it. Right away I sat up straight, clearing my throat a little. Fuck, what was *wrong* with me today? First that thing about wanting to kiss her, and now this. Was this the only way I knew how to talk to girls all of a sudden? Or was there a part of me that just . . . wanted to flirt with Holiday?

"I mean," I started, not at all sure how I was going to follow it up, but all at once Holiday grabbed my arm to stop me.

"There he is," she said, her short nails digging into my arm.

I followed her gaze. Sure enough, a shiny red Honda was pulling into the hospital parking lot, cruising slowly across the blacktop before coming to a stop beneath a copse of pine trees near the side entrance.

"Holy shit," Holiday breathed, her eyes glowing with excitement and satisfaction. "I . . . definitely did not think he was actually going to show up."

"Wait, seriously?" I asked, turning to look at her. "Then why did you drag me out here in the first place?"

"To be alone with you, obviously," Holiday deadpanned, but before I could even begin the process of figuring out how to respond to *that,* the driver's side door of the Honda swung open and a pale, lanky guy climbed out. Holiday and I watched raptly as he crossed the parking lot, his gait slow and the tiniest bit bowlegged. He made his way through the sliding glass doors and up to the reception desk, where, Holiday reported once she'd dug her father's trusty bird-watching binoculars out of the rat's nest in her backseat, he chatted with the clerk for a moment before turning around and coming back outside.

"Checking to see if Greg's still on the admitted list, I'm guessing," Holiday hypothesized, lowering the binoculars, "but it feels like it would be risky to do that every night."

"Why not just call?" I wondered out loud.

"They don't give out patient information over the phone," she explained absently. "I tried."

"Of course you did."

We watched as Topher headed back in the direction of the Honda, head ducked and hands shoved deep into the pockets of his hoodie. He pulled out a pack of cigarettes as he approached, then leaned against the hood of the Honda and lit one up, the tip of it glowing orange as the smoke billowed around his face in the purple night.

"He looks so . . . regular." Topher was probably four or five years older than us, dressed in dark jeans and hipster sneakers. His haircut, I couldn't help but notice, was definitely way closer to a Macklemore than mine.

Holiday laughed. "I'm sorry, when you heard *Southie drug dealer,* what were you expecting? Matt Damon wearing a fur coat and carrying a shotgun?"

". . . No," I said, though I knew I sounded just a hair too defensive for her to believe me. I watched as Topher ground his cigarette butt out on the asphalt before climbing back into the car and revving the engine, pulling out of the lot so fast I was surprised he didn't leave skid marks on the ground.

"Where do we think he's going?" I asked.

Holiday shrugged. "Only one way to find out."

I had never tailed anyone before in my life, but Holiday seemed to know what she was doing—keeping her distance from the Honda, hanging back a car or two as we followed Topher along the winding night roads of the Vineyard. Eventually he pulled into the lot of a motel in Oak Bluffs. "Well, that answers the question of where he's staying," Holiday pointed out, cruising to a stop at the scrubby curb across the street.

"Not exactly Martha's Vineyard's most exciting hotel experience." I twisted to peer out the window. The motel was run-down and just this side of grimy-looking, a double-decker U-shaped structure arranged around a parking lot with an office at one end and a scummy, dilapidated pool at the other. It was the kind of place where I imagined you could bring your mistress and rent by the hour, assuming renting by the hour was even a real thing and not just something I'd heard about on television. I thought about asking Holiday, then didn't.

"Pretty deserted, though." She glanced over her shoulder. The motel was the only business on this stretch of road, surrounded by dense patches of overgrown woods on either side. "If you were hoping to fly under the radar while you were here, this would be a pretty good way to do it."

We sat there in pregnant silence for what felt like ages, waiting for Topher to get out of the car. "The hell is he doing in there?"

I finally asked, my shoulders dropping. "Working the mini cross-word?"

"Taking care of a little mobile banking," Holiday suggested.

"Waiting to see if they play his After Hours song request on the radio."

Finally the driver's side door opened and Topher climbed out. He looked taller than he had back at the hospital, more physically imposing—a better match for Greg, I noted with some interest. In fact, I was so busy thinking it that it took me a moment to register the fact that he wasn't headed for the door to one of the motel rooms. In fact, he wasn't headed into the motel at all.

He was headed straight for our car.

All at once Holiday's face got very, very pale. "Michael," she said softly, just as Topher Leal rapped hard on the passenger side window.

"Get out of the car," he ordered. "Both of you."

We should have floored it. To this day, I don't know why we didn't except that, apparently, deep in our hearts the two of us were a couple of spineless order-followers, unbuckling our seat belts and climbing out onto the asphalt as obediently as a pair of well-trained dogs. Topher looked back and forth between us, wild-eyed.

"Who the fuck do you work for?" he demanded.

I opened my mouth, then shut it again, racking my brain for the answer that was least likely to wind up with Holiday and me splattered all over the pavement. All at once the utter recklessness of this entire outing crashed into me like a riptide: going on a *stakeout*? Tailing a *drug* dealer? What the fuck had we thought we were doing? If Topher really was the person who'd hurt Greg, there was no reason to assume he wouldn't be just as willing to hurt us.

There was also no reason to assume, I realized as my heart turned to vapor inside my chest, that he didn't have a gun.

"We're nobody," Holiday assured him quickly. "We were just—" She gestured back and forth between us, wiggling her eyebrows in what I assumed was some pathetic attempt to indicate *fooling around in the car.* "You know how it is."

But Topher wasn't buying. "Don't fuck around with me," he said. Up close his mannerisms were twitchy and erratic, his hands fluttering at his sides like restless birds. "I saw you back at the hospital."

Shit. "The hospital?" I repeated, stalling. "Dude, we weren't—"

"No, you're right," Holiday interrupted, elbowing me hard in the rib cage. "We were just there, visiting our friend Greg up in the ICU. He had an accident a few days ago."

"And then you just happened to wind up parked outside my motel?" Topher shook his head. "How fucking dumb do you think I am?"

He had a point—as far as logical explanations went, it was pretty damn thin—but all at once I saw Holiday's spine straighten the way it always did when she was preparing for a performance. "Dude," she said to Topher, lowering her voice like she was leveling with him. "Do you have any idea how hard it is to find a place to be alone on this island?" She jerked her head in my direction. "He's staying with friends who might as well be running a boardinghouse, I live with my *extremely* overprotective parents, and every single parking lot on the Vineyard is—your tax dollars at work—lit up like Times freaking Square. And I mean sure, you're less likely to be carjacked outside the Stop and Shop, but at what cost? We were just looking for a little privacy." Then, as if perhaps she was worried he wouldn't take her point: "You know, to—"

"Jesus Christ, *enough.*" Topher held a hand up to stop her, blowing a breath out through his nose as he weighed the plausibility of her story—or, possibly, just trying to figure out the fastest way to get her to shut up. "Of course you're friends with Holliman," he muttered finally, rolling his eyes like he should have guessed as much. "All of you Vineyard kids have the same look."

It was ridiculous—okay, it was borderline *pathological*—but the truth is that even in the moment there was a tiny part of me that felt pride at that, the idea that at some point in the last few years I'd managed to disguise myself well enough that this kid couldn't smell the Eastie on me. That as far as he was concerned, I fit in.

Topher looked around, like he was making sure there was no one else with us. Then he waved us off. "Get the fuck out of here," he ordered, rubbing hard at the back of his long, skinny neck. "I don't know what the fuck you think you're after, but if I see either one of you again, I'm going to fucking kill you."

And—yeah. It definitely didn't sound like he meant it in the metaphorical sense. Holiday and I scrambled back into the car, neither one of us saying anything as Holiday wrenched the key in the ignition and peeled off down the road.

"Is he following us?" she asked, glancing in the rearview; she was doing at least twice the speed limit, the engine working hard behind my knees. "Is that insane to ask?"

It wasn't. I craned my neck, squinting out the back window, but all I could see was darkness. "I think we're okay?" I reported uncertainly.

Holiday didn't answer. Her hands were steady on the wheel, but the rest of her definitely wasn't, her whole body shaking in the driver's seat beside me. "It's fine," she managed through clenched teeth when she noticed me watching. "It's an adrenaline rush, that's all." I wasn't sure which one of us she was trying to reassure.

Still, she kept her foot on the gas as we whipped down the road in the direction of August House; we might have made it all the way home like that if not for the raccoon that darted out into the road as we passed through town, its silvery back gleaming in the headlights. Holiday swore, swerving hard, and I gasped.

"Sorry," she said once we'd cleared it, her eyes glued to the road. A car whooshed past us in the opposite direction, its horn blaring in protest. "Sorry."

I thought of the night of the accident: the flashing lights, my shattered ankle. This wasn't that, I reminded myself, fighting off a shiver of my own. It *wasn't*. But still: "Pull over," I said finally, reaching out and putting my hand on hers. "Holiday. You gotta pull over."

"Okay." Holiday took a deep breath. "Yeah." She slowed to a stop in the empty parking lot of a grocery store. She'd been right, I thought vaguely: it was bright as a carnival, the neon lights winking cheerful yellows and reds across the blacktop. Neither one of us said anything for a moment. Holiday kept her hands on the wheel. It felt like the middle of the night, but in reality there were still plenty of people out and about on this part of the island, finishing up late dinners and spilling out of the bars. There was a group of kids about our age horsing around outside an arcade across the street, and I suddenly remembered that when Greer and I had finally gotten back to campus the night of the accident, there had been a bunch of underclassmen playing midnight Ultimate on the green outside the dining hall. *How is it possible that your lives are just proceeding as normal?* I'd wondered. *How is it possible the world is proceeding at all?*

I waited a moment for my heart to stop pounding, eventually realized that wasn't going to happen anytime soon, then turned to face her. "We need to stop," I decided. "For real this time. You didn't sign up for this. Shit, Holiday, *I* didn't sign up for this. At the very least, we need to go to the cops."

"What? No way!" Holiday exclaimed. "Fuck that." She'd been nakedly terrified a moment ago, but now she looked energized— exhilarated, even. Her cheeks and mouth were both bright red. "What would we even tell them?"

I gaped at her. "That a drug dealer just threatened to kill us?" I posited. "Just, like, as a jumping-off point."

But Holiday shook her head. "If we send the police after Topher now, all he's going to do is disappear," she reasoned. "We still don't have anything concrete to give them."

I hesitated. Holiday made sense, but I knew her well enough to know what she wasn't saying: She didn't want to give up the investigation yet, to step back or hand it over or admit we might be in over our heads here. Not after everything we'd been through.

And if I was being honest, neither did I.

As if she could sense she almost had me, she pressed her lips together, shook her head. "We're on the right track, Michael. I can feel it. Can't you feel it?"

I looked at her then, hair wild and eyes shining. I glanced down at her full, bright mouth. "Yeah," I said softly. "I can feel it."

We stared at each other, neither one of us saying anything; both of us were still breathing hard. I could see her chest rising and falling inside her hoodie. Just for a second, I imagined leaning across the gearshift and—

"Michael," Holiday said, and the sound of her voice pulled me back to myself.

"Yeah," I said, way too loudly. My whole body was hot and unpleasantly prickly; I was sure she could see what I'd been thinking scrawled all over my face. "It's late," I blurted, nodding at the clock on the dashboard to avoid meeting her gaze. "I should get back. We can figure this out in the morning."

Holiday nodded back, clearing her throat. "Absolutely," she said. "We don't have to decide anything right this minute."

We didn't talk all the way home.

I stood in the driveway for a long time after Holiday dropped me off, gazing up at the splendid, glowing facade of August House. This place had seemed so deeply glamorous to me just a few days ago, an avatar for everything I thought I wanted, and while it was still incredible—all gable and balcony and turret, shadows looming in the deep purple night—now it looked like a haunted house out of a little kids' storybook: beautiful but sinister, swollen with secrets. For a second I couldn't get over the urge to run. The ferry ran until late, I remembered suddenly. Theoretically I could be back in Boston by morning—safe at my mom's scratched, scarred kitchen table, far away from whatever twisted picture was starting to come into focus here on the Vineyard.

The screen door creaked open just then, a noise like something out of a horror movie; I jumped about three feet in the air, but it was only Jasper poking his head out, frowning at me in the glow of the porch light. "Yo, is that you?" he called across the lawn. "What the fuck are you doing out here?"

I looked from him back up to the house again, watching as a figure passed by the window in one of the upstairs bedrooms. "Being a creep," I told him, then shoved my hands into my pockets and trotted across the damp, dewy grass to follow him back inside.

16

IF THERE WAS, IN FACT, A HUGE STORM BEARING DOWN on the Vineyard, there was no way to know it from the weather the following morning. When I woke up, the sky was a clear, brilliant blue, the heat dry and an occasional breeze rustling the leaves on the trees that ringed the house. Meredith was waiting in the second-floor hallway when I got downstairs, a towel slung over her arm. "Jasper's been in there for forty-five minutes," she informed me with a grimace, nodding at the closed bathroom door. "I swear he's waxing his chest in there just to fuck with me."

"Nah," I said with a smile, "he pays to have that done professionally." I nodded up the narrow staircase. "You can use mine," I offered, then immediately frowned, trying to remember if I'd left my dirty boxers on the floor next to the shower. "Just be sure to hold down the handle on the toilet if you need to . . ." I cleared my throat. "Anyway. Um, how's Greg doing?"

Meredith shook her head. "Mostly the same," she admitted. "They had him on some medicine to keep him in the coma while they waited for the swelling in his brain to go down, but now they weaned him off it and were thinking he'd wake up on his own, but . . ." She trailed off. "It's just a waiting game, is all."

That . . . did not sound good. "I'm really sorry, Meredith."

"Yeah," she said, rubbing at her temple, "it isn't great."

I hesitated for a moment, both of us standing there in awkward silence. "Meredith," I said—thinking suddenly of my mom back at home and how she'd made a million different kinds of soups when our neighbor Mrs. Le was in the hospital for a knee replacement, all of them stacked neatly in our crowded freezer in flattened-out Ziploc bags. "Is there, like . . . anything you need?"

Meredith seemed surprised by the question. "You know something, Linden?" she told me quietly, raking a hand through her knotty red hair. "You're actually the only person who's asked me that."

I thought she might have been about to say something else, but the bathroom door swung open just then—Jasper emerging wrapped in a towel, surrounded by a cloud of steam. "Shit, sorry," he said, smiling faux-cheerily at Meredith as he sauntered down the hallway toward his bedroom. "Were you waiting?" She lifted her middle finger at his receding back before disappearing inside.

Holiday showed up after breakfast, bearing fancy iced teas and a laundry list of reasons she didn't think we should give up on the investigation just yet; in fact, what she really wanted to do was double down. "If we learned anything useful last night, it's that Topher Leal is more than capable of hurting somebody," she pointed out. We'd gone into Birdie's lush green vegetable garden for privacy, nobody around to hear us but the peppers and eggplants. "I think it's probably worth it to at least try and see if he's got an alibi for the night of the party."

"Are you kidding me?" I almost choked on my iced tea. "I don't want to get anywhere near that guy ever again. And I don't want *you* to get anywhere near him either."

"That's very chivalrous of you," Holiday said with a smile, "but you can relax. I'm not suggesting we knock on his door in a couple of rakish fedoras and start asking questions."

"Then what are you going to do, exactly?" I asked. We seemed to have tacitly agreed not to talk about whatever weirdness might or might not have occurred in the car last night—actually, Holiday seemed so exquisitely normal and unflustered that I found myself wondering if maybe I'd imagined the whole thing. "Call up some ferrety IT friend of yours that you've conveniently forgotten to mention until now and hack into the motel's security mainframe?"

Holiday shot me a look. "No, smartass," she said patiently. "I'm going to go over there, offer the manager a hundred bucks, and see if they've got camera footage they'll let me look at."

"I—oh," I said, feeling myself blush at the utter obviousness of it. I ran my thumb over the lid of my cup, which was still mostly full; the iced tea was the herbal kind, and tasted more like dirt than anything I might actually want to consume. "I mean, sure. That's an option too."

"I thought so." Holiday smiled, pleased with herself. Her own cup was empty except for the ice, the tip of the straw bright red from her lipstick; I looked at it for a moment, then looked away. "We shouldn't take my car, though," she continued thoughtfully. "Just in case Topher is looking out for it."

I hesitated. I knew Jasper wouldn't care if I dipped into the August House motor pool, but couldn't exactly tell him why I suddenly needed a set of wheels. *Hey, dude, you mind if I borrow the middle car for a little bit of attempted murder recon? Totally chill.* And if I lied and told him I was going out for food or shopping or even just to dick around, there was always the chance he'd want to tag along.

I went to Mrs. Kendrick instead. She was sitting on the patio in a lounge chair, reading a fat pastel hardback with a sticker on the cover bearing the logo of a celebrity book club. I'd been trying to give her a wide berth since the other night in the dining room, but this morning she seemed totally lucid as she nodded in the direction of the house. "Keys are on the hook in the mudroom," she told me, not even bothering to ask what I needed a car for. "Just be sure to get back before the rain starts—okay, Linden? The radio says it's going to be ghastly later."

The hurricane, I remembered suddenly. Birdie had been watching ominous weather coverage on the TV in the kitchen this morning during breakfast, though right now the sky was still mostly clear. "Of course," I promised. "I'll be back in plenty of time."

Holiday and I cruised by the motel parking lot a few times to make doubly sure there was no sign of the red Honda, then pulled up to the curb right in front of the office. "Should one of us stay outside?" I asked as I put the car in park. "To like, be a lookout?"

"He's not going to come into the office," Holiday said reasonably. "But if for some reason he does, I'd rather we were together." Then, as if perhaps she was worried I somehow wasn't picking up her underlying point: "Like. In front of a witness."

I tried not to gulp. "Right," I said, trying to keep my voice neutral. "Totally."

We found the manager watching YouTube videos on his phone and drinking a Diet Dr Pepper; he was probably in his late twenties, with a spray of painful-looking acne across his jawline and the general air of a person who definitely thought he was destined for greater things than standing behind the desk in a low-end motel all day. "I really shouldn't," he said when Holiday explained what we needed and offered him the cash.

"Probably not," she agreed with a smile that said they were in on this together. She leaned on the counter, tilted her head to the side, and slid the money in his direction. "But who's going to know?"

In the end he let us look at the tape, the three of us crowded into a small, windowless office off the lobby. The desk was littered with the remains of what I assumed had been his lunch, confetti of shredded lettuce and a half-eaten bag of Funyuns. It smelled like someone had unleashed a cloud of Axe body spray behind the counter at a Subway.

"We'd be looking for late last Friday night or early Saturday morning," Holiday instructed as the clerk scanned through the grainy footage. Judging by the condition of the property, I'd been half expecting an actual VCR hooked up in some dusty utility closet—or for the clerk to inform us there wasn't actually any footage at all—but instead the three of us were hunched around a computer in the corner, albeit one that looked nearly as old as Holiday and me.

"Sure thing," the clerk said distractedly, swearing under his breath as he struggled with the ancient rollerball mouse. Then he frowned. "Sorry—why did you say you were interested, exactly?"

I froze—somehow I had not anticipated this, the most obvious of questions—but Holiday was prepared. "We didn't," she said sweetly, "but my boyfriend is staying here, and I'm pretty sure he's cheating on me." She rolled her eyes with the forbearance of a long-suffering woman wronged. "He was supposed to meet me at a party the other night, and never showed. He said he fell asleep in his room and his phone was on silent, but a friend of mine says she saw him at some dive bar in Vineyard Haven doing body shots with his ex."

The clerk let out a low whistle. "My last girlfriend cheated on me," he said mournfully. "It feels like you can't trust anyone these days. In fact, I saw on this Subreddit that the government—"

"Seriously," Holiday interrupted, then dug her nails into my arm, nodding at the screen: Sure enough, there was Topher getting out of his car and heading into his hotel room. The time stamp on the screen read a little after 1:30, when Jasper and I had still been cleaning up the yard back at August House. Holiday and I watched in silence as he got himself a soda and some chips from the vending machine, then dug a key out of the back pocket of his jeans and climbed the exterior stairs to the second floor of the building, letting himself into a room at the far end before shutting the door neatly behind him.

"Maybe he comes out again?" I asked hopefully, nodding at the clerk to scan ahead. But the door to Topher's room stayed resolutely shut until well after Reyes and O'Neal had come and gone down the road at August House the following morning. By the time he emerged, bleary-eyed and bed-headed, it was almost eleven a.m.

"There's just the one door on those rooms, right?" Holiday asked finally. I could see the wheels in her brain turning as she tried to work out anything she might be missing. "No back entrances?"

"Not unless he climbed out the bathroom window and scaled the building," the clerk said. "We had a guy do that one time, trying to get away from his ex-wife. She was after him for monetary support for their French bulldog, who had sleep apnea? Fell right into a pile of trash next to the dumpsters and then tried to sue us for his back pain." He shook his head solemnly. "We live in a very litigious society."

"His car didn't move either," I reminded Holiday quietly, pointing to the Honda. "It definitely looks like he stayed in all night."

"Yeah," Holiday said, rubbing a hand over her face. For the first time since I'd met her at the coffee shop the morning after the party, she looked visibly disheartened. "I guess so."

The clerk peered back and forth between us, confusion written all over his greasy face. "Well, that's good news, isn't it?" he asked. "It means your boyfriend was where he says he was."

"That's good news," Holiday agreed quickly, mustering a game, cheerful smile. "It's *great* news, even. I really appreciate the help."

The clerk preened at her attention, clicking out of the security program and opening up his billing software. "What was that," he asked after a moment, "Room 212? Looks like he ordered some porn." He looked at us hopefully, clearly wanting to secure his place as a valuable member of the investigative team. "Like, if that's helpful?"

"What, like on the *television*?" I asked, unable to keep the surprise out of my voice.

"Looks that way," the guy said with a twisty grin. "*World's Naughtiest Nurses,* Part Six."

I shook my head. "Who pays to order porn on TV?"

"You'd be surprised, actually," the clerk replied thoughtfully. "We do a pretty decent business."

I could tell by the expression on Holiday's face that she'd had quite enough of this conversation, and sure enough: "Well, thanks again for your help," she said brightly. "This was really useful." Then turned back to me. "We should probably—"

I nodded. "Yep."

The weather had changed while we were inside the motel office: dark clouds beginning to gather at the eastern horizon, the humidity thick as a sodden beach towel pressed firmly against my face. The air around us seemed to snap with electricity as I peeled out of the parking lot, checking over my shoulder one last time for any sign of the Honda. Neither of us said anything, and I could feel my bad mood gathering density the longer we sat there in silence. I felt dopey and young and foolish; most of all, I felt like a person who'd wasted what was probably the nicest vacation he was going to have in quite some time playing cops and robbers with his old pal from nursery school. "So," I said unnecessarily as we idled at a red light in Vineyard Haven, "it wasn't Topher either."

Holiday sighed, leaning her dark head back against the passenger seat. "Doesn't seem that way," she agreed.

I took a deep breath. "Look," I said, "I heard you the other night when you said that I was the one who dragged you into this in the first place. But I kind of feel like at this point we need to face the possibility that Greg really did just get drunk and trip."

"Maybe," Holiday agreed, sounding utterly unconvinced.

"Maybe?" I repeated, gritting my teeth to keep from scowling. The light turned green, and I hit the gas harder than I necessarily meant. "You don't think so?"

"No, I'm not saying he didn't." Holiday shrugged like I was a wild-eyed door-to-door salesman with a briefcase full of herbal supplements or a little kid trying to sell her on the Easter Bunny. "It's just a lot of coincidences, that's all."

"I mean, it's *also* a lot of coincidences that every single one of our leads so far has led nowhere, wouldn't you agree?"

Holiday huffed a little laugh at that, indulgent. "Fair enough," was all she said.

The two of us were quiet, the afternoon light taking on an eerie purple quality out the windshield as the heavy gray clouds thickened like pudding in the sky. I glanced at Holiday out of the corner of my eye, my own irritation flaring at the sight of her sanguine expression. I was tired of her theories. I was tired of her plans. It had been a mistake to bring her into this in the first place,

I thought sullenly; I'd forgotten how tenacious she could be when she wanted something, the way she gnawed at unanswered questions like a dog with a bone.

I was planning to say goodbye for real when I dropped her back at her parents' house—I was going home to Boston tomorrow, and I didn't want to burn my last night here trying to solve a mystery that by all accounts wasn't one—but as we pulled into the driveway, Holiday turned to look at me, curious. "See you later?" she asked.

I cringed a little—I couldn't help it. I'd forgotten that I'd mentioned Jasper and Eliza's hurricane party to her a couple of days ago; I knew I was being an asshole, but even as I nodded, I wondered if there was some way for me to subtly convince her not to come. I wanted a fun, normal night, free from thoughts of drug dealers and bloody sweatshirts and people secretly hooking up with other people's moms. More to the point, I wanted to be with Eliza, and—though I couldn't articulate to myself exactly why—I knew having Holiday around was going to put a serious kink in that plan. It occurred to me, not for the first time, that maybe there was a reason she and I hadn't talked all these years.

"Yeah," I said, mustering what I hoped was a convincing smile, "totally. Eight o'clock?"

Holiday smiled back. "I'll be there," she promised.

17

BY THE TIME I GOT BACK TO THE KENDRICKS', THE EN-
ergy at August House had taken on a buzzing, frenetic quality.
Birdie was in the kitchen fixing a dinner that could be eaten
at room temperature in case the power went out, while Dean
screwed the galvanized hurricane shutters closed with an electric
drill. Mrs. Kendrick had gone into town for last-minute supplies:
"By which I mean, more wine," Jasper said with a grin as he hap-
hazardly let the air out of the pool floats so they wouldn't fly away
in the storm. Only Wells seemed completely undisturbed by the
low-grade chaos: he swung slowly in the hammock, his face inscrutable behind his sunglasses.

"Meredith still at the hospital?" I asked Jasper. The two of us
were dragging the lounge chairs into the shed at the back of the
pool house, the shrill screech of metal on stone grating against my
nerves.

Jasper nodded. "Hopefully she'll stay there," he said, tossing
me an outdoor pillow to add to the pile. "Could be the apocalypse,
right? Gotta hoard those resources."

"Uh-huh," I said with a smirk. His apparent concern for the end of the world hadn't stopped him from inviting Aidy or Doc, not to mention the half-dozen people that Wells had told to come by if they wanted. I tried to imagine my mom opening our house to a bunch of strangers on the night of a hurricane a week after a teenager had wound up floating unconscious in our pool, then immediately decided that there were so many completely impossible clauses in that sentence that it was a useless mental exercise. Better, I reminded myself, to go with the August House flow.

Eliza got back a couple of hours after I did, strolling into the house with the unhurried confidence of a girl who expected bad weather to wait for her go-ahead. "Hey," I said, a slow, involuntary grin spreading over my face at the sight of her. We'd texted a little bit—okay, we'd texted a *lot*—but it was different to see her in person, her sharp collarbones and graceful wrists and perpetual expression of faint amusement. I'd *missed* her, I realized; even as I had the thought, it occurred to me that I didn't want to say goodbye to her at the end of this weekend. Shit, I didn't want to say goodbye to her at all. "You're back."

"I'm back," Eliza agreed. She tilted her face up, expectant; when I kissed her, I could feel the curve of her own lazy smile against my mouth. "Were you worried about me?"

"Nah," I said, straightening up again. "Just didn't want to wind up marooned alone in a storm with the rest of these degenerates, that's all. Could be a real *Lord of the Flies* situation."

"I mean"—Eliza handed me her overnight bag—"when is it not?"

The rain had already started by the time Birdie and Dean took off in the late afternoon, the drum of it audible even through the thick metal shutters. I felt a pang of guilt as I watched them go, remembering that they still had their own house to secure down the road. It occurred to me to run after them, to see if they needed a hand, but before I could decide either way, Jasper was calling my name from across the kitchen. "Should we make party punch?" he wanted to know, his sandy head buried in the glowing depths of the fridge. "Like, some play on a dark and stormy? Or is that too fucking corny?"

"It's corny as shit!" Eliza called from the other room, to which Jasper flipped her a bird she couldn't see.

"I didn't ask you!"

A noisy roll of thunder rumbled just then, the growl of it palpable right through the soles of my sneakers; Whimsy whimpered from her post near the pantry, and I flinched. I thought of the long line of cars I'd seen at the ferry port earlier, all of them lined up to get the hell off the island. "Look," I said to Jasper, dropping my voice so that Eliza wouldn't hear me, "I'm fully aware that this is going to make me sound like a giant pussy, but like . . . this is safe, right? Us all being here?"

Jasper laughed. "Yeah, dude," he said, "it's safe." Then he shrugged. "I mean, I think so, anyway. What the fuck do I know?" He handed me a bottle of tequila from the freezer, then— apparently having decided on his own that party punch was indeed in order—fished out some pineapple juice to go with it. "And if it's not, it's a pretty metal way to go, right? Blown to kingdom come during a hurricane?"

I laughed, though nothing about it seemed particularly funny to me. I'd ignored half a dozen texts from my own mom urging me to try to get a standby ticket for the ferry back to the mainland this morning; now that it was too late to bail out, I found myself unable to ignore the distinct possibility I'd made a serious mistake. I felt weird and unsettled, my nerves jangly and on edge in the same way they'd been that day at the pool when Wells and I had played Orange. I was relieved in spite of myself when Holiday showed up a few minutes later, the tightness in my chest easing a bit at the sight of her round, familiar face.

"It's *miserable* out there," she announced, pulling two bags of Pirate's Booty out of her tote bag and handing them to Jasper. "Here," she said, "I brought supplies."

Jasper grinned. "I knew you were the kind of girl to have around in an emergency." He took the snacks and headed for the kitchen, but I grabbed Holiday's arm before she could follow.

"Your parents were seriously cool with you coming over here?" I asked.

Holiday looked at me a little strangely. ". . . Yes?" she said. "Why wouldn't they be?"

"I mean," I pointed out, feeling more than a little foolish, "it's a *hurricane.*"

That made her smile. "No, I know it is," she promised. "But that's just what happens out here in the summer. Staying on-island and like, making a casual bad-weather cheese plate while listening to Miles Davis is what separates us from the tourists. It's fine."

"Right." I frowned. "Wouldn't want anyone to confuse you for a tourist."

Holiday made a face. "Don't be like that," she chided gently. "You know what I mean."

"No, I do," I said, and I *did;* still, I couldn't help brushing up against the unpleasant reminder that at Holiday's core she had a lot more in common with the Kendricks than she did with me—her indomitable rich-girl nonchalance, the certainty deep in her bones that nothing truly bad was ever going to happen. It was the same bulletproof confidence that had her strolling into the Mandarin Oriental to spy on her favorite boy band. It was the same hard-headed recklessness that had her dragging me after Topher Leal.

We made camp in the den, sprawling out on the enormous sectional and sitting cross-legged in nests of pillows on the thick, fluffy rug. Aidy helped Jasper set out the snacks that Birdie had made before she left, a giant pitcher of something bright and boozy appearing on the table beside them. Wells connected a play-list to the speakers. Eliza and Doc laid out a hand of Spit. The storm grew in intensity outside the window, the rain a deluge and the wind screaming like some tortured creature out of a folktale; the overhead lights flickered as thunder shook the house. Eliza was right; it *was* cozy, in an old-fashioned, New England, boarding-school common room sort of way.

So why couldn't I shake this deep, ceaseless dread?

I wasn't the only one in a weird mood tonight. It was barely noticeable—as far as any of the Kendricks were concerned, she was the same as she ever was—but there was definitely something going on with Holiday. It was strange to think that she and I were somehow back in a place where I knew her well enough to know when she was hiding something; it was stranger still that maybe I'd known her that well all along, even when we weren't really talking to each other, like there was some invisible tether connecting us. I wasn't sure it was something I actually liked.

"Hey," I said finally, pulling her into the library and shutting the glass-paneled door behind us. "What's going on with you tonight?"

"What?" Right away Holiday shook her head, all innocence. "Nothing." She made a show of looking around at the bookshelves and the artwork, the grand piano with its framed family photos on top. "This place is really very tasteful," she observed.

"Okay," I said, making a face. "Do you want to do a song and dance, or do you want to talk to me?"

"I want to do a song and dance," Holiday said immediately, but before I could reply, her shoulders dropped. She took a deep breath, crossing the room and sitting down on the edge of the green velvet couch. "I have to tell you something, and you're not going to like it." Then, without so much as a pause for me to brace myself: "I've been doing a little research on Eliza."

I felt my skin go cold inside my hoodie. "What?" I asked. *"Why?"*

"Easy," Holiday said immediately. "I just, something about her alibi didn't sit right—"

"Her alibi?" My eyes widened. "Her alibi is literally me, Holiday. I told you she was with me the night of the party."

"For the entire night?"

"For enough of it," I insisted stubbornly. "She didn't have anything to do with this."

"I mean, okay, Michael." Holiday huffed like I was an unruly child. "Do you want to hear what I found, or not?"

I didn't, not really. Still, I shrugged, sitting down in a delicate antique chair that was almost certainly not built to hold me, or anyone else; it creaked in protest as I leaned all the way backward, crossing my arms in front of my chest. "I mean, you're going to tell me either way, aren't you?"

In fact, for a second Holiday looked like she was considering keeping the information to herself after all; then she sighed. "Remember how we figured out that first night I came over here that Eliza and I had a couple of friends in common?" she asked. "I messaged one of them a few days ago, just to see if anything pinged."

I snorted. "What, to spy on her?"

"Oh, please, Michael, we've been spying on everybody!" Holiday rolled her eyes. "I hadn't heard back, and I figured it was a dead end, but she wrote to me this afternoon."

"And said what?" I asked. "That Eliza is a seasoned assassin who secretly walks around with a dozen knives tucked into her bra?"

"I mean, you'd know a lot more about what's in her bra than I would," Holiday shot back immediately, then blushed. "That's not what I—" She broke off, blowing out a noisy breath. "Whatever," she continued a moment later, straightening her shoulders. "Look. This is a rumor, that's all. I haven't had a chance to look into it for real yet, and I'm not even saying it's anything we should act on. But Eliza told you she used to board at Walden, right?"

"Yeah," I said cautiously, "for a little while."

"Did she tell you why she left?"

I was silent, the chair squealing as I slouched backward and stretched my legs out like some slacker in detention back at Bartley. I wanted to be a little intimidating, all of a sudden. I wanted to take up space.

"I'll take that as a no," Holiday decided. "Well, supposedly there was a girl that she used to ride with at school who she had some kind of extremely dramatic rivalry with, and this other girl was the favorite to win the USEF medal, which is, I guess, the big national tournament?" She shrugged. "I don't know, I'm emphatically not a horse person; I think they're weird and unnatural creatures. But anyway, last year, two days before the qualifying meet . . . apparently, this girl had like, a catastrophic fall."

I laughed out loud, darkly tickled by the utter absurdity of it. "Oh my god," I said. "I was right—this *is* a knives-in-the-bra situation. Are you actually going to sit here right now and tell me you think Eliza somehow pushed this girl off her horse and magically nobody noticed? Who the fuck do you think she is, Matilda?"

Holiday looked at me like I was being stupid on purpose. "Of course not," she said. "But first of all, nice reference, and second of all, I *do* think it's possible Eliza might have had something to do with the horse getting spooked to begin with. And it sounds like the disciplinary board at Walden thought so too, because she got called into the headmaster's office for a meeting right after it happened, and two days after *that,* she was gone."

Well. I had to admit that as far as circumstantial evidence went, it didn't sound great. But there had to be some benign explanation. After all, hadn't all our other supposedly solid leads turned out to be nothing but delusional conjecture? I shook my head, though in truth my brain was firing in a million different directions. "You're reaching," I insisted, setting my jaw. "You haven't liked Eliza from the very beginning—"

Holiday's eyes widened, visibly stung. "Are you kidding me?" she asked, jumping to her feet. "I've been nothing but totally cool with Eliza!"

"Okay," I said, as obnoxiously as I possibly could. "I mean, if you say so."

"Are you seriously—I mean, are you honestly about to—" Holiday sputtered, then stopped herself and took a deep breath. "Look," she tried, sitting back down on the arm of the sofa. "All I'm saying is that we can't rule out the possibility that she's capable of violence. And we can't rule out the possibility that she had something to do with what happened to Greg."

"We also can't rule out the possibility that nothing even happened to Greg in the first place!" I hissed. "I never asked you to go digging into Eliza's private business, Holiday. I never asked you to do any of the crazy shit you've done."

"Are you *kidding* me?" Holiday countered, her lipsticked mouth dropping open. "You're the one who asked me to get involved in the first place! Literally this whole entire investigation was your idea!"

"Yeah, I know, you love to keep reminding me, except for the part where I *actually* came to you so that you could talk me out of it!" I exploded. "And instead you just completely took over and dragged me down a million different rabbit holes, and now, when it's become abundantly clear that whatever happened to Greg was just an unfortunate fucking accident, you're grasping at straws trying to—what, even? Sabotage things between Eliza and me?"

"*Sabotage* you?" Holiday repeated. "Michael, whatever is or is not happening between you and Eliza is so far down on the list of things I give two shits about that I—I—" She broke off, apparently at a loss for an appropriate conclusion.

I took advantage of the opening. "Is it really?" I asked. "Because you realize it sounds like you're jealous."

Right away, I knew it was the wrong thing to say to her. Holiday's eyes narrowed; she stood up slowly, drawing herself to her full height. She looked like Joan of Arc about to ride into battle. She looked like a queen about to declare a total war. But under that she mostly just looked . . . hurt.

"You know what, Michael?" she said to me. "Enough. You think I'm in *love* with you, or something? I don't even like you that much anymore! You're obsessed with money and prestige and power and this idea that the universe owes you something that you haven't gotten. You've spent the last week projecting every weird Daisy Buchanan fantasy you have onto this girl and now you can't even consider the fact that you might be wrong about her, because your entire worldview will come crashing down like some sad house of cards and you'll have to shoot yourself in the head to cope with it. I've read that book already, in ninth-grade Honors English. It was boring then too."

I stared at her for a moment, neatly annihilated. The worst part was how readily the words had come to her, like she'd been sitting on them for a lot longer than right this minute. The second-worst part was that already there was a part of me that knew she was probably right. "Fuck you, Holiday," I managed, which admittedly wasn't stellar as far as biting comebacks but was the best I could do under the circumstances.

"Fuck you, Michael!"

We stood there for a moment, facing off across the expensive Persian carpet. "I shouldn't have come here," she said finally—her voice quiet now, almost like she was talking to herself. "I should go."

That was when the lights went out.

"Shit," we said in unison, our inflections identical. Our scowls were a matching set. It was the kind of thing we would have laughed at fifteen minutes earlier: the mind meld that she and I seemed to have sometimes, both of us thinking the same thought at the same time. Now it just made me hate her even more. It was like she was in my head, like she knew all my secrets and could clock the way my brain worked. She was too close, and I wanted space.

Still: "Where the hell are you going to go, Holiday?" I asked crankily, motioning at the boarded-up windows. "We're both stuck here, at least for right now."

"Fine," Holiday said, the set of her jaw so sharp you could have used it as a bottle opener. "Then let's just go back to pretending we're strangers, shall we? That seemed to suit you fine all these years."

"It did, actually."

"Great."

"Perfect."

Both of us stood there for a moment, the whole situation vaguely farcical in its awkwardness. The argument demanded that one of us storm off, except for the part where there was nowhere for either one of us to go. Instead we made our way clumsily back into the den, where Jasper was lighting enough candles to create a fire hazard: warm light flickered across the walls, casting the whole room in an old-fashioned glow. "What's up with you guys?" he asked, blowing out a match in the direction of our stony faces.

"Nothing," Holiday and I said at once.

Jasper was just starting to reply when Mrs. Kendrick appeared in the doorway with a handful of flashlights, passing them out like full-size Hershey bars to lucky trick-or-treaters at Halloween. "You kids doing all right in here?" she asked, glancing nervously in the direction of the boarded-up window. "I have to say, I honestly didn't think it would be this bad."

"We're fine," Wells promised, not bothering to hide his cocktail. "This house is two hundred years old, right? It's survived a lot worse." He nodded at his brother. "Jasper's burrito farts, for example."

Mrs. Kendrick smiled wanly. "Dad and I are going to head upstairs, then. Be careful, will you?" She jumped as thunder cracked with such ferocity I could feel it in my teeth. "And give me a shout if the house blows away."

Once she was gone, Jasper lifted an eyebrow. "Off to sleep the peaceful sleep of the deeply medicated," he observed coolly. "And on that note: Who wants more punch?"

I stayed as far away from Holiday as humanly possible for the rest of the night, trying not to brood too visibly while she played some complicated variation of the Celebrity game with Jasper and Doc across the room. I couldn't tell if she was laughing extra loud for my benefit or not; when I glanced in her direction, she was murmuring something to Doc, the two of them presumably commiserating about what a complete and utter douchebag I was. Let them, I thought sullenly, shuffling into the kitchen to grab a beer out of the refrigerator. They deserved each other.

"Now who hates parties?" asked a singsong voice behind me. I turned around and there was Eliza barefoot in the doorway, leaning against the jamb with a knowing smile.

I grinned back at her, my own personal dark cloud lifting at least a little. "I don't *hate* them," I corrected. "I'm just . . ."

"In a mood?"

"Maybe."

"Hmm," Eliza said, taking a speculative sip of her vodka and soda. She was wearing denim shorts and a cropped white tank top, a flat, tan strip of her stomach just visible in between. "Wonder what we could do to get you out of it."

I gazed at her across the kitchen for a moment, desire and trepidation and uncertainty tangled up inside me like an undoable sailor's knot. *Capable of violence,* Holiday had said. *A Daisy Buchanan fantasy.* I pushed her words out of my head. "You tell me," I replied.

Eliza set her glass down on the kitchen counter. Held out her hand for mine.

18

I DIDN'T LOOK BACK AS I FOLLOWED ELIZA THROUGH the den and up the darkened staircase, though I could feel Holiday's eyes on my back from her station on the couch. There was a part of me that hoped she really *was* jealous, even though I knew that made me an asshole. There was a part of me that hoped this hurt her.

Eliza put a finger to her lips as we crept down the hall past her parents' room. The click of her bedroom door sounded very loud. I wondered if she could hear my heart beating; it felt like my chest was moving visibly, like I was some kind of romance-novel heroine in a dress with a lacy bodice. If I had to guess, I was definitely the more nervous party here; still, I felt like I had to at least ask. "Have you ever—" I broke off, feeling myself blush. "I mean—"

"Done this before?" Eliza smiled. "Yes, Linden. I have done this before." Then, looking at me carefully: "Have *you* done this before?"

I nodded, thinking for a moment of Greer's narrow single room before I pushed her out of my mind once and for all. I didn't want to be thinking about Greer. I didn't want to be thinking about Holiday. I didn't want to think about anything but Eliza and how soft her skin was, the smell of the hollow at the base of her neck.

Once it was over, we stayed in her bed for a long time, listening to the storm rage on outside. The wind was shrieking like an animal being tortured and the rain was lashing against the windows, but it was cozy being cocooned in the soft sheets and fluffy duvet, Eliza's head heavy against my shoulder. Our bare ankles brushed underneath the covers, one of her long legs tangling around mine.

I trailed my fingers up and down her arm, waiting to relax, but no matter how hard I tried to ignore it, I couldn't deny that there was a part of me that felt . . . not right. As much as I tried to push it out of my mind, I kept thinking about what Holiday had said back downstairs in the library: *a super-dramatic rivalry. An accident. Gone from school two days later.*

Holy shit, what was *wrong* with me? I was suddenly suspicious of Eliza now that we'd *slept* together? That was gross, and probably misogynist. Either way, it made me basically the worst person in the world.

So why couldn't I chill the fuck out?

Eliza, for her part, seemed completely unconcerned, propping herself up on one elbow to look at me. "Serious face," she observed, reaching out to run a finger along my brow.

I nodded at the window as the wind let out a particularly hair-raising yowl. "Just hoping I don't go flying naked into the Atlantic when the roof of your house blows off, that's all."

Eliza grinned. "Pretty dark talk for a guy who just got hurricane-laid."

That made me smile. "You know," I said, reaching out and lacing my fingers through hers, "you're not wrong."

"Cheer up, Linden," she instructed, flopping backward into the pillows. "It's not so bad. Actually, for the first time all summer, I have to say it kind of feels like everything's working out the way it was meant to."

"Oh yeah?" I raised an eyebrow. "What, like you and me?"

Eliza laughed. "Don't flatter yourself, bro," she said, but then she shrugged. "Yeah, us, maybe. But other stuff too." She held her elegant hands up, counting on her fingers. "My family being back together after what was, frankly, a huge boner of a year. Getting this amazing chance to go to Paris. And even everything that happened with Greg, like . . ." She trailed off. "I don't know."

I felt myself get very, very still. "What about him?" I asked quietly.

Eliza wrinkled her nose. "I mean, don't think I'm a terrible person for saying this, but he kind of got what he deserved, right?"

"I—" My voice cracked. I cleared my throat, trying for all the world to sound normal and not like a person whose heart was suddenly flinging itself against his rib cage like something out of an Edgar Allan Poe story. "What do you mean?"

Eliza shook her head. "I don't know," she said again. "I've just been reading a lot about the law of attraction, right? If you're a good person, and you put good out into the world, good will come back to you. And if you're a piece of shit, eventually that catches up with you too."

She could have just been talking generally, I reminded myself. And it's not like her having a bone to pick with Greg was news to me. Still, I couldn't get Holiday's warning out of my mind. Every time I remembered the smug expression on her face back in the library, I felt a fresh surge of anger rise up inside me like a riptide. What did she think she was doing, trying to poison me against Eliza? And what was *I* doing, letting it work?

Except Holiday *hadn't* looked smug, actually. She'd mostly just looked . . . sorry.

Eliza reached out and picked up her phone, glancing at the screen for a moment before setting it facedown on the nightstand and smiling at me. "I'll be right back," she said, shimmying back into her shorts and tank top and padding off in the direction of the bathroom. "Don't, you know. Get blown naked into the Atlantic Ocean."

"I'll try."

Once she was gone, I glanced at the phone. Glanced away again.

Glanced back.

It was a massive invasion of her privacy, I reminded myself. And as far as I was concerned, she wasn't even a suspect.

I literally dug through Wells's underwear drawer with my bare hands, reminded a voice in my head that sounded suspiciously like Holiday's. *And you're telling me you're going to get squeamish* now?

I reached for the phone, then hesitated, casting a furtive glance in the direction of the bathroom. In another second the screen was going to lock and I wouldn't be able to get in without a password. "Fuck me," I muttered, and plucked it off the nightstand.

Eliza's background was a photo of all the Kendricks on the beach—from earlier this summer, I guessed: the sun setting behind them, all of them showing off their healthful-looking tans and impressive orthodontic work. I tapped the icon for messages and scrolled through her texts as fast as I could, looking for—what? A detailed confession? A quick selfie she'd snapped with Greg's unconscious body on the steps of the August House pool? I paused with my thumb on Doc's name, then stopped myself before clicking through to read whatever messages the two of them had sent to each other lately. That *definitely* wasn't what I was after, I told myself firmly. I wasn't a total douchebag, the kind of guy who would invade her privacy just for shits.

I was a goddamn detective, and I was going to get to the bottom of this fucking thing once and for all.

Even as I had the thought, I felt myself blush, the absurdity of this entire situation hitting me with as much force as the angry waves crashing outside. There was nothing here to see, obviously. I was acting exactly like the weird, anxious outsider I didn't want to be, looking for a problem where there was none and screwing things up with the most beautiful girl—

All at once I stopped scrolling. My thumb twitched over the screen.

There they were just sitting in her message history, three short texts from Eliza to Greg from the night of the party:

> What the fuck did you think you were doing tonight, asshole?

> Stay away from my fucking family

> Or I'll make you regret it.

My head swam. Holiday had been right. Fuck, of *course* Holiday had been right; Holiday was always right. I felt like an idiot. I *was* an idiot. I'd let my infatuation with Eliza blind me to what was right in front of my face this whole time.

I scrubbed a hand over my face, dread seeping up through my body like seawater filling a hole in the sand. Was that why Eliza had brought me up here in the first place, because she knew Holiday was onto her and she wanted to throw me off? I felt sick at the idea. I might have tried to sound sure of myself when I was talking to Holiday, but I had no idea what Eliza had done after I'd stumbled back to my room on the night of the party. There was plenty of time for her and Greg to have had some kind of argument. There was plenty of time for things to have gone wrong. What exactly had she said, about getting up to let Whimsy out early that morning? All at once I was sure it had been a lie.

I heard the bathroom door open just then and quickly set the phone back on the nightstand where I'd found it. "We should get back downstairs," I announced when Eliza came back in. "People are going to wonder where we went."

"I hate to tell you this, Linden, but I think people probably know where we went," Eliza said with a smile. Then, as she looked at me more closely: "Everything okay?" She raised her eyebrows. "Is this the part where you tell me you've been thinking of entering the seminary?"

I tried to muster a laugh, but couldn't exactly get there. "Yeah," I joked, not quite meeting her eyes, "totally." I forced myself to take a deep breath as I climbed out of bed and scooped my clothes off the floor—after all, I reminded myself, it wasn't like she was going to hit me over the head with a table lamp or pull a pearl-handled revolver out of her nightstand drawer—but still, I wanted to get out of this room as soon as humanly possible. I wanted to get as far away from her as I could. I yanked my shirt over my head so fast I almost ripped my own ear off. "You ready?" I asked, my voice rough.

Eliza was still peering at me from the doorway, her gaze a little uncertain. "Um, yup," she said, moving to the mirror and running a hand through her hair. All at once everything about her seemed practiced to me, theatrical—after all, wouldn't she have just looked at herself in the bathroom? What was she playing at here? "Let's go."

Back downstairs the party had gotten rowdier, the music cranked so it was audible over the wind and the pitcher of party punch empty on the coffee table. Jasper was lying upside down on the couch, feet swung up over the cushions and his sandy hair just brushing the rug. Holiday was still talking to Doc, the two of them tucked cozily into the window seat like the oldest and dearest of friends; I caught her eye and jerked my head in the direction of the library, which I was pretty sure was the international sign for *I need to talk to you about our erstwhile murder investigation immediately, please and thank you,* but she turned her gaze away as if she hadn't seen.

Fine, I thought snottily. *Fuck her, then.* I would handle this one on my own. I grabbed a bottle of Jameson off the bookshelf and took a swig to settle my nerves, wincing at the sudden burn in my chest. Then I did another.

"Look who's finally ready to party," Wells said with a smirk. He was lounging on the chaise with his ankles crossed, a mostly empty glass dangling from his fingers.

"Something like that," I agreed, heading for the kitchen. "Who needs a beer?"

Jasper somersaulted off the couch and followed me inside, digging a bag of pretzels out of the pantry and peering skeptically at a wedge of expensive-looking cheese. "Dude," he said when he noticed me draining the better part of a Sam Summer in roughly thirty seconds, "you okay?"

"I'm fine." I finished the beer, set the empty bottle in the recycling. "Making up for lost time, is all." I glanced across the kitchen, where Whimsy was lying on her bed with her head on her paws, her amber eyes half-lidded. "Can I ask you something?" I said, a sudden thought occurring to me. "Does Whimsy ever randomly wake up and bark to go out in the middle of the night?"

Jasper snorted. "No way," he said, handing me the cheese and a box of spicy crackers before reaching down to scratch her behind the ears. "This dog would sleep through the rapture." He frowned. "Why?"

I felt my heart sink. "No reason," I said, knowing it was stupid to feel freshly disappointed. I guess I'd just been hoping, that was all.

Wells was lifting his glass just as we came back into the living room, getting somewhat unsteadily to his feet. "I'd like to propose a toast," he announced grandly. "To Greg."

"Oh, Jesus," Jasper said, but he was smirking. "Here we go." He leaned against the bookshelf, arms and ankles crossed. "Let's hear it."

"To Greg," Wells repeated, standing up straight and tall and proud like the best man at a wedding. "New money, lifter of free weights, wearer of unironic Croakies."

"And general piece of shit," Eliza chimed in, settling herself neatly on the bottom step. She motioned for me to come sit next to her, but suddenly I felt rooted in place.

"And general piece of shit," Wells echoed, bowing slightly in her direction. "Now, some of you might say to me, 'Wells, isn't it low-end to relish the bad fortune of one's enemies?' And to you I might reply, so they say! But in the words of Senator William Learned Marcy of New York: To the victor go the spoils. And in the words of anyone who ever had the unfortunate luck to meet Greg Holliman: Who fucking cares, bro? That guy sucks."

Jasper and Eliza burst out laughing, Aidy covering her mouth to hide a giggle. Even Doc couldn't hold back a grin. I staggered a bit, head starting to swim as the alcohol caught up with me; the overall effect was like being in a fun house full of monsters who wouldn't stop talking. It was ghoulish. It was fucked up. I looked over at Holiday, desperate, but she was still steadfastly ignoring me, her expression inscrutable as she watched the proceedings unfold.

"Of course, Greg wasn't *all* bad," Wells continued; he was clearly enjoying the attention, a little-known comedian randomly called upon to deliver the opening monologue on *SNL*. "It is undeniable that he did occasionally come through in times of pharmaceutical trouble. And if you ever find yourself in the position of needing to cast the Judd Nelson role in your remake of *The Breakfast Club*—"

"Enough," said a ragged voice, hoarse and cracking. It took me a second to realize it was my own. "Just stop!"

All at once the room got very, very quiet; even the wind seemed to still. "Aw, Linden," Jasper said easily, "he doesn't mean anything by it. We're just kidding around."

"Kidding around about *what*?" I demanded. "The guy is in a fucking coma. Like, whatever the hell else you think about him, what part of that is funny to you?" I shook my head. "All of you walk around treating life like one of your weird, fucked-up family games, only apparently, there are no rules and none of you care who loses." I turned back to Wells. "Is having an affair with his mom part of the joke too, PS? Or do you guys have a real connection?"

The words were out before I could think better of them. Wells's face went purple as an end-of-summer eggplant; Jasper opened and shut his mouth like a fish. "Um, I'm sorry," he managed finally, turning to his older brother, *"what now?"*

"Fuck you, Linden." Wells's expression was nasty. "You don't know what you're talking about."

"You and Helene Holliman?" Eliza asked, sounding sincerely caught off guard for maybe the very first time since I'd met her. "Seriously?"

I expected Wells to deny it, but he only set his jaw. "It's not like that," he insisted. "It's—"

"Holy shit," Jasper interrupted. "Holy *shit*, I didn't actually believe it until right this second, but not only is he fucking Greg's *mom*, he's going to try to convince us it's love and I'm going to have to go fling myself into the fucking sea." He shook his head, rasping out a brittle smoker's laugh. "You've got some nerve, bro. All year long all I've heard from you is how you're the only one with any loyalty to this family, and the whole time—the whole fucking time!—you're dicking around with—with—"

"Helene!" Eliza was laughing now, like she was tickled by the dark absurdity of it. *"Helene."* She looked at Jasper. "Remember that one summer she thought she had, like, invented mojitos? And every night at cocktail hour it was like, 'Who wants—'" She broke off, popping up from her perch on the step and doing an exaggerated mom-shimmy.

I stared at her for a moment, unable to keep my lip from curling in disgust, and Eliza dropped her arms. "I'm sorry," she tried—looking a little bit wounded, reaching for my hand. "I know it's not actually funny. I just—"

"Don't," I ordered. It felt like her touch might scald me, and I jerked away. "Honestly, you're even worse than the rest of them. How can you stand there and act all innocent when you're the one who—who—"

"Michael." Holiday had been silent up until now, but all at once she was on her feet, crossing the room in my direction and shaking her head. "Don't do this."

But Eliza held her hand up. "No," she said, regal and imperious as a house cat, "let him talk." She looked at me curiously. "When I'm the one who what, exactly?"

Even through the haze in my head, there was something about the tone in her voice and the way that Holiday was looking at me that made me think something was deeply, deeply wrong here. But it was too late now. I'd come this far. "When you're the one who pushed him in the pool in the first place."

Wells laughed out loud at that, the sound of it halfway between a bark and a chuckle. Aidy's mouth dropped open; a scoff escaped the back of Doc's throat. "What the fuck, dude?" Jasper said softly. Eliza wasn't smirking anymore.

"Michael," Holiday said again, but I shook my head and pressed on. "It all fits," I insisted, turning back to Eliza. "I know you sent those texts to Greg the night of the party. You told me yourself you're an insomniac—after I went back to my room, you must have found him lurking around in the yard. Maybe he came back here to talk to Meredith, maybe he was looking for a fight with one of your brothers, I don't know, but whatever happened, he wound up in the pool with a giant gash in his head. That's why you were the one to find him. You didn't get up to let Whimsy out. You were already there."

Nobody said anything for a moment after I was finished. I was breathing hard. The room was spinning, though I wasn't sure if it was the adrenaline or the liquor. It was possible I was drunker than I thought. The rain had stopped, I realized belatedly; someone had turned the music off, the only sound my own heart thudding wildly in my ears.

Doc was the one who spoke first. "Bro," he said. "She was at my house, you fucking idiot."

Eliza shook her head, an expression on her face like she'd already decided it wasn't worth it. "Don't," she said faintly.

"I'm not going to just sit here and listen to him shit all over you," Doc countered. He was looking at me like I was something he'd stepped in in a darkened parking lot and was now going to have to clean off the bottom of his shoe. "She woke up and you had bounced and she needed someone to talk to, so she came over. That's where she was. With me. Talking."

I blinked. "About what?" I asked dumbly.

"None of your fucking business, Linden!" Doc was almost laughing.

"No," Eliza said, "it's fine. You know what? I'm not actually going to sit here and let him shit all over me either." She raised her chin, defiant. "We were talking about my family, Linden. We were talking about the fight, and Wells's preternatural inability to control himself for five seconds, not to mention my dad's PTSD and my mom being real cute with her meds and the fact that half the time I can barely will myself to get out of bed in the morning. You know, the kind of shit you might ideally want to talk about with the person you're fooling around with, except for the part where most people don't want to hear it. God knows you didn't." Her eyes flashed as she nodded at Doc. "At least I have one friend in the world who's actually interested in who I am and not whatever fantasy they can hang on me."

"That's not—" I started reflexively, then broke off as I choked on the shame. "I mean, I didn't—"

"Didn't you?" Eliza fired back. "How many times did I leave the door open for you to walk through? And how many times did you run in the opposite direction?" She shook her head. "I left Doc's right before the sun came up," she told me. "I walked up the beach, let myself in through the gate—and that's when I found

Greg in the pool. I didn't want to tell you where I'd been because you were already being such a fucking weirdo about Doc that I didn't want to accidentally push you away."

"But—you broke your brother's arm," I insisted helplessly, looking around for anyone who might help me shore up the ground I was rapidly losing. "You left Walden because that girl got hurt."

"I left Walden because I was depressed, you absolute dipshit!" Eliza was laughing now, a disbelieving shriek. "I was one uncontrollable crying jag from the funny farm, so they sent me home to the warm bosom of my family, for all the good it fucking did me." Her whole body was suddenly sharp and angular as a crane's. "Nice to know you've been digging into the boarding-school gossip circuit for my sake, though. Makes a girl feel all warm and fuzzy inside."

"You're trash, Linden," Wells said, arms folded in front of him. "Truly."

I looked around the room then: from Doc, who was clearly enjoying the spectacle of me getting my comeuppance, to Jasper, who looked faintly sick, to Eliza, whose eyes were bright with fury and tears. *I'm sorry,* Holiday mouthed when I got to her.

"The whole time we've been hanging out, you've been tallying up some imaginary score against me," Eliza accused. "You're so obsessed with whether or not everyone else is playing by some arbitrary set of rules you made up in your head—who's winning, who's losing, who's got how many points. But the only one treating anyone's life like a game is *you.*"

I opened my mouth, then closed it again, at an utter loss for how to respond. But in the end I didn't have to: The front door of August House swung open just then, all of us startling at the interruption. Meredith appeared in the front hall a moment later, wet and bedraggled in a bright yellow slicker, her red hair dark with rain and plastered to her pale forehead.

Jasper found his voice first. "Shit," he said, more sincere than I'd heard him sound toward her since the day I'd gotten to the island, "are you okay?"

Meredith shook her head. "He died," she announced, then turned around and disappeared up the stairs.

19

A FEW HOURS LATER I STOOD IN THE STANDBY LINE for the first ferry out of Oak Bluffs, hands jammed into my pockets and my duffel slung across my back. The sky was bright white, the ground strewn with broken branches; the whole island had that dazed, post-storm feeling, sandblasted and raw.

The party had broken up more or less immediately after Meredith's appearance, Eliza jumping to her feet and following Meredith up the front staircase, Holiday and Doc slipping out as quickly and unobtrusively as they could. "Hey," I said to Doc as he was headed out onto the porch. "Listen. I just want to say—"

But Doc cut me off. "You're a dumbass, Linden," he announced, then turned, letting the screen door clatter shut behind him.

"Well," I said to no one in particular once he was gone. "I have to say, I do appreciate his lack of bullshit."

"Yeah." Jasper offered me a half smile, then jammed his hands awkwardly into his pockets. "Look, bro," he started, but now it was my turn to interrupt.

"I'm going," I promised. "First ferry out."

Jasper nodded, the relief written all over his face. "Yeah," he said again. "I think that's probably a good idea."

Clearly, I'd worn out my welcome at August House, on top of which I was more than ready to collapse face-first back into my bed at home and sleep until school started. Still, I couldn't deny it stung that Jas was so ready to see the last of me. I'd spent the last three years trying to fit in with him and the rest of our friends at Bartley. And in the end I'd thrown it all away—for what, exactly?

I'd packed my stuff as quickly and quietly as I could manage, hesitating for a moment outside Eliza's closed bedroom door. I lifted my hand to knock, then thought better of it. I told myself it was because she was probably too busy with Meredith to listen to my sorry excuses, but the truth was I knew there was nothing I could possibly say to make up for the way I'd treated her. She—and Holiday—had been right. I'd invented an imaginary version of Eliza for myself to fall for, swiftly and elegantly sidestepping every indication she'd tried to give me that that person didn't actually exist. I'd been so focused on the idea of her as some beautiful, unattainable icon of the good life that I'd never stopped to consider the possibility that she actually cared about me and what I thought about her. And the minute she'd let her guard down, I'd turned around and punished her for it. I *was* a dumbass. Eliza deserved better.

Not that it mattered at this point. I would probably never see her again.

I shifted my weight on the sidewalk, trying not to shiver inside my hoodie. There was a damp, chilly post-hurricane breeze blowing in off the water, ruffling my hair and lifting goose bumps on the back of my neck—a reminder, as if I needed one, that the summer was just about over.

I was just about to show the attendant the ticket on my phone when I heard someone call my name; when I turned, I was surprised by the familiar sight of Holiday's car idling in the parking lot. "Michael!" she called again, leaning out the driver's side window, her mane of dark, curly hair blowing wildly around her face. "Wait!"

A handful of people turned to stare at the sound of the commotion, and even after everything, I felt my cheeks get red with the attention. "Sorry," I said to the attendant. "I'll, um, be right back."

"Ferry's leaving in five minutes," she warned me.

I nodded, hitching my duffel up on my shoulder and jogging over to Holiday's window. "Sneaking out without saying goodbye?" she asked.

I shrugged. "I mean, I kind of assumed that you, like everyone else on this island, were tired of looking at my fucking face."

"Well, that's a fact." Holiday's lips twisted. "But we're friends, right? Besides," she said, her expression keen as the eye of a hurricane, "I know who pushed Greg into the pool."

Right away, I shook my head. "Enough," I said. "It's over, Holiday."

"It's not," she insisted, and something about the look in her eyes made me think this time was different. "Get in the car."

I glanced over my shoulder at the ferry. Every instinct in my body was screaming at me to say goodbye and climb aboard—to go back to my mom's house, to try to figure out what the hell I was going to do about the rest of my life.

Then I looked at Holiday, and I got in the car.

"Okay," I said a few minutes later, snapping out of the dazed, obedient silence that had enveloped me since I slid into the passenger seat of the messy sedan. It felt like everything that was happening had taken on a hazy, inevitable quality—that all roads led to wherever we were headed, even though I still had no idea where that was. "Enough. Where are we going?"

Holiday grinned a Cheshire grin. "That's a good question," she allowed, "but the better one is: What do we know for sure?" She lifted one hand off the steering wheel, counting on her fingers. "One: Topher Leal, midlevel drug dealer from the not-so-mean streets of Southie, is hanging around the Vineyard looking for his money. Two: clearly, Greg didn't pay him back before the party at August House. Three: it must have been a pretty big debt if Topher thought it was worth it to stay put—or was too scared to go home—even after Greg wound up in the hospital. And four: Topher's the kind of guy who's more than willing to apply a little pressure if need be. So—assuming he didn't have a sudden attack of conscience and flush all the drugs down the toilet before vowing to live life on the straight and narrow, which I think is a *pretty* safe supposition at this point—why didn't Greg just pay Topher what he owed and get it over with?"

"I . . . have no idea." I was barely following. "He was secretly an addict and put it all up his nose instead of selling it? Gave the money to the Greater Boston Food Bank? Lost it all playing Skee-Ball at the penny arcade?"

"Maybe," Holiday allowed. "Or: someone stole it."

That got my attention. I turned to look at her, the pieces still not quite locking together in my mind. "Who?" I asked, and that was the moment I suddenly realized where we were heading. "Holiday—"

"I'm glad you asked," Holiday interrupted, turning onto the long, winding road that led back to August House. "We're about to find out."

Meredith was waiting on the front porch when we pulled into the driveway. She was perched on a massive, monogrammed suitcase, flicking through her phone way too fast to actually be reading anything on the screen. She stood up when she saw us, then narrowed her eyes: "What are you doing back here?" she asked suspiciously. "I thought you were my Uber."

"I've been thinking about picking up a side hustle, actually." Holiday nodded at the suitcase as she climbed the rickety steps. "Are you taking off too?"

Meredith nodded. "I can't wait to get out of here," she confessed, sinking back down onto the suitcase and rubbing a hand over her puffy, tear-streaked face. "I just want to go home."

"That makes sense." Holiday smiled sympathetically. "It's been a brutal week. And I guess there's nothing to be gained at this point by hanging around the scene of the crime."

I sucked in a jagged breath even as Meredith looked at her blankly. "What's that supposed to mean?" she asked.

Holiday looked slightly disappointed, like she'd been hoping for something a little more clever. "I mean, we can obviously go through this whole one-act play about how I'm a crazy lunatic if you want to," she offered agreeably, "but like you said, you're waiting for an Uber, so it seems like a waste of everyone's time." She grinned. "I've gotta tell you, one gifted fake-crier to another? That's a really impressive performance you've been putting on."

Meredith's expression was icy. "I have no idea what the hell you think you're talking about," she announced, then looked back at me with open contempt. "Although, speaking of performances, Eliza told me about the little show you put on last night. Really classy, taking advantage of your rich friends' hospitality and then turning around and accusing them of all kinds of crazy, hateful shit."

The screen door creaked open just then, Wells stepping barefoot out onto the porch looking decidedly hungover, his hair sticking up in a million different directions. "Why the fuck are you talking so loud right now?" he asked Meredith beseechingly, then noticed Holiday and me. "And why the fuck are you two carnies still here?"

I sputtered for a moment, caught up short by the same hot rush of humiliation that I'd felt last night after I'd delivered my little address to everyone at August House. Still, I couldn't help but notice that Meredith wasn't making a move to go anywhere. Instead she was watching Holiday carefully: one lion considering another from across the savanna, trying to decide if it was dangerous or not.

Holiday ignored both of them for a moment. "You asked me earlier who would have had access to Greg's cash," she reminded me. "We know Wells did—in *fact*," she said, turning to look at him with one eyebrow arched, "we know that Wells had access to a lot more than that over at the Hollimans'. But we also know that he left August House after the party and didn't come back again until right before Greg's body was found. So who does that leave?" She turned back to Meredith then, her tone almost conversational. "Your parents used to have a place out here, right? But they sold it?"

"Thank god," Meredith replied, her sharp jaw set. "This island is so basic."

"I tend to agree with you," Holiday admitted with a wink, "but I don't think that's why they sold the house. Your mom was a big investor in that women's coworking start-up, wasn't she? The one that imploded when it came out that the founder was a total perv?"

I whipped my head around to look at her, surprised. "How did you know that?" I asked.

Holiday smiled. *"Perfunctory,"* she reminded me, *"Google."* She turned back to Meredith, looking at her with something like compassion. "Your parents lost everything last year," she said quietly. "That's why they sold the Vineyard house, and the one in Westport."

"Your parents sold the Westport house?" Eliza asked, stepping out onto the porch. "You didn't tell me anything about that." She looked from Wells to me to Holiday, her eyes darkening with confusion and displeasure at the sight of us. "What's going on?"

"It needed a total gut job," Meredith explained hastily. "They're just renting until they find something they like better."

"The Georgette McKeown being yours made sense to me," Holiday continued thoughtfully. "Those necklaces are expensive, but the anchor was part of a line that came out a couple of years ago. That Oak and Thunder raincoat you were wearing when you came home last night, though—that's brand-new this season." She glanced at me. "We saw it the other day at the boutique in town—do you remember, Michael? And it retails for close to seven hundred dollars."

"Yeah," I said slowly, "I remember."

"It was a *gift*," Meredith protested, her eyes cutting from Holiday to Eliza to the raincoat itself, which was draped over the porch railing like a forgotten beach towel at the end of the season. "Not that it's any of your business."

But Holiday shook her head. "Nice try," she said. "I went over there this morning when they opened and talked to the salesgirl. I said you were my sister, that you'd jumped on the raincoat before I had a chance to and I wanted something similar. Lucky for me, she remembered you." Holiday nodded at the slicker. "You only bought it a couple of weeks ago. And you paid cash."

"First of all, who in the fuck would ever believe *you* were my sister?" Meredith exploded, looking outraged by the very notion of it. "Second of all, what does it even matter how I paid?" Her expression was haughty, but I didn't have to be rolling in money myself to understand what Holiday was getting at. People like Meredith and the Kendricks—people like Holiday herself— always used plastic. There was no way Meredith was just randomly taking seven hundred dollars in cash out of the ATM for a day of retail therapy.

Which meant there was only one logical place for her to have gotten it.

"I actually think it's a pretty easy case to make to say that Meredith killed Greg," Holiday continued thoughtfully. "You stole the money after you guys got back together—either because you sincerely needed it or because you were trying to jam him up with Topher to get back at him for cheating on you, or some combination of both. He confronted you the night of the party, things got out of hand, and you pushed him. It's neat, right? It's tidy. But I don't actually think that's what happened."

"What *do* you think happened?" That was Jasper, stepping cautiously outside with Aidy following closely at his heels. We were all gathered on the porch by this point, drawn to the careful unfolding of Holiday's story like moths flinging themselves helplessly at a screen door in the middle of the night.

"Why are you all standing around listening to this bullshit?" Meredith demanded. She'd gotten up and was pacing across the creaking floorboards like a zoo animal; so far there was no sign of the Uber, though I couldn't help but wonder what would happen when it finally showed up. "It's absurd. It's insane! It's like, the deranged rambling of a lonely person who listens to too many true crime podcasts instead of having an active social life."

"My social life is pretty full, actually," Holiday said mildly. She was *enjoying* herself, I realized with a start. She'd worked it all out in her mind and was glad to finally be sharing the information, like a physicist who'd made some exciting discovery in the world of quantum mechanics. There was a part of me that wondered if it wasn't a tiny bit cold-blooded—after all, was Holiday taking pleasure in solving the puzzle of Greg's murder really that much different from the Kendricks yukking it up at the thought of his bad fortune?—but the rest of me was too transfixed by her reasoning to care.

"I kept thinking about those scratches on your neck," she told Meredith now, tugging speculatively on one dark strand of hair. "You told Linden and me that you and Aidy got into a fight the night of the party, and she pulled off your necklace and scratched you." She paused. "But Aidy bites her nails."

Well, shit. I turned to Aidy—all of us did, like something out of a cartoon—and sure enough, she was gnawing away at her thumbnail as she listened, the rest of them all chewed down to the bloody quicks. She took a startled step back at our sudden scrutiny, jamming her hands into her pockets; Holiday shot me a look like, *See what I mean?*

"I noticed the other day when we were getting lunch at Red's," she explained quietly. "They're way too short to cause that kind of damage."

"I never said *she* scratched me," Meredith snapped. "The necklace scratched me when she pulled it off."

"In three different spots?" Wells asked, leaning over and peering at the faint pink marks still visible on the side of Meredith's throat. "Fat chance."

"Oh, now you're a detective too?" Meredith demanded. "I don't have to listen to this." She reached for the handle of her suitcase, but Wells stuck one foot in front of the wheels.

"Hold on a second," he said in the same cool, detached, impossible-to-argue-with tone he'd used to invite me to play Orange what felt like an entire lifetime ago. "I want to hear this."

Meredith stayed where she was.

"*Somebody* definitely scratched you when they pulled that necklace off," Holiday asserted, "but it wasn't Aidy. Which means the story you told us about the two of you guys getting in an argument at the party was bullshit, which means that her corroborating it was *also* bullshit, which means that for some reason you guys are covering for each oth—"

"It was an accident," Aidy blurted suddenly. It was the first time she'd spoken since she'd followed Jasper out here; her blue surfer-girl eyes were wide and terrified. "We never meant to—"

Meredith whirled on her. "Oh, do *not*," she snapped with an animal ferocity. Then, to the rest us: "I have no idea what she's talking about."

Aidy looked terrible, now that I was gazing at her more closely, with dark rings under her eyes and a hastily covered breakout visible along her jaw. Her normally tan face was pale and gaunt. "I'm not like you," she said to Meredith softly. "I can't do this anymore. Not after everything that happened. Not when he's—"

"I said shut up!"

"You shut up, Meredith!" Aidy's voice rose. "You've been making my life a living hell in one way or another for the whole entire summer, and I'm fucking sick of it. All I was trying to do was help you."

"How did any of this help me?" Meredith fired back. "All you did was make everything a million times worse."

"Should I have just let him hit you, then?" Aidy demanded. "Or who knows what else?"

"Whoa whoa whoa," Eliza said, holding her hands up, "Greg was going to *hit* you?"

"Of course not!" Meredith insisted, then, more quietly: "I don't know. I was handling it."

"You were *not* handling it!" Aidy insisted, then looked at the rest of us. "The night of the party—" she started, but Meredith cut her off.

"Stop," she said, her voice urgent. "I swear to god, Aidy, I will make you regret—"

"I don't care anymore." Aidy sank down onto the floor of the porch, pulling her knees up and burying her face in her hands. "I don't *care.*" I thought she might be crying, but when she lifted her head a moment later, her expression was resigned. "I'm so tired. I just want it to be done."

None of us said anything for a moment. When Holiday spoke, her voice was soft. "Aidy," she said, squatting down on the floor beside her, "what happened?"

Aidy sighed. "The night of the party," she said again, shooting a look at Jasper, "after you fell asleep, I was heading out—not because I like, *regretted* anything, I just didn't want it to be weird in the morning—when I heard Greg and Meredith arguing out on the patio. I guess he'd showed up at the party earlier to have it out with her, but then when you guys"—she gestured at Jasper and Wells—"whatever. He knew she'd taken the cash he had squirrelled away, and he couldn't pay what he owed that Topher guy, and he was pissed. And whatever, none of that was my problem—no matter what Meredith likes to tell people, I didn't actually give half a crap about Greg—but then he shoved her."

"None of this happened," Meredith informed us shrilly. She'd toggled back to bald-faced denial, yanking at her hair as she paced across the porch. "I have no idea what she's talking about. *She* has no idea what she's talking about."

"I just . . . reacted," Aidy said. "I have a sister who had a bad boyfriend situation a couple of years back, and I just . . . yeah. I ran at him and pushed him as hard as I could. And he was so fucked up." She raised her chin then, looking searchingly at the rest of us. "That's the thing you have to understand about Greg—like, he's this big guy, there was no way I could ever hurt him even if I was trying to, but he just . . . crumpled. He hit his head on the edge of the pool—you know how the lip of it kind of goes up at the edge? And then he was just . . . in."

She rubbed her face again, like she was trying to scrub away the memory. "I panicked," she recalled. "I jumped in and tried to fish him out, but I could only get him as far as the staircase. I was soaking wet, and Meredith was hissing at me to get the fuck out of the water before someone saw us; we were trying to be as quiet as we could. We didn't know if he was dead or alive."

"Why didn't you call for help?" I couldn't help but ask.

"And say what, exactly?" Aidy's voice was sharp. "That I'd accidentally brain-damaged the rich vacationer who'd tossed me over to go back to his private-school girlfriend? I know the cops around here love to just bend over backward for summer folks, but please believe me when I tell you they're not like that with everyone. I already have an arrest on my record from last summer—for being drunk and disorderly," she clarified, "not that it's anyone's business. And I would like to get off this fucking island and have a future at some point."

"And Meredith knew that if the police got involved, eventually they'd figure out that she'd taken the money." Holiday straightened up. "You planted the necklace," she said to Meredith, sounding almost admiring. "And you scratched your own neck to make it look like you'd gotten into a fight with Aidy."

"You're cracked," Meredith insisted, but Aidy nodded.

"She knew that someone would find it the next morning," Aidy explained. "We were obvious suspects anyway, because of how we'd both been romantic with him. But if we made it even more obvious, and then we were each other's alibis, then . . ."

"Then nobody would look at either one of you twice," Holiday finished. *Tidy,* she'd said earlier, and it had been. Except for one variable.

"What was your plan if Greg woke up?" I asked.

Meredith and Aidy looked at each other, then quickly away, as if the eye contact was blinding. Neither one of them answered, but the implication was clear.

They'd been hoping he wouldn't.

And—at least until Holiday and I came along—they'd lucked out.

We were silent then, all of us trying to figure out what on earth we were going to do now. A lone seagull screamed overhead. "Meredith," Eliza said finally, her voice barely above a whisper, "probably you should cancel that ride."

20

REYES AND O'NEAL SHOWED UP AT AUGUST HOUSE twenty minutes later, taking us into the library and interviewing each one of us in turn—or trying to, anyway. The Kendricks called their lawyer more or less immediately. Meredith refused to say anything until her parents, both corporate litigators, made their way out to the Vineyard from Connecticut. The police put her in the back of their squad car anyway, a flash of red hair and a haughty expression; Aidy was already sitting in the backseat, eyes trained resolutely forward.

"You ready?" Holiday asked once they were gone, nodding at her sedan in the driveway. It felt like lifetimes since she'd scooped me up at the ferry this morning, like it had happened to someone else altogether.

"Yeah," I agreed slowly; then, at the last possible second, I shook my head. "Actually," I said, "two minutes? There's something I should do first."

Holiday raised her eyebrows with an expression that pretty clearly indicated she didn't want to stick around this place for any longer than we had to, but all she did was gesture up at the house. "You know what, Michael?" she said. "Be my guest."

I grimaced, remembering that we'd never actually made up after our fight in the library. "Thanks," I said, knowing the word was wholly insufficient for the circumstances. "Two minutes."

I found Eliza reading in the hammock, which had somehow survived last night's storm. Even after everything that had happened, she still looked like all I'd ever wanted, lying with an arm tucked behind her head, in shorts and a Fleetwood Mac T-shirt. I had to remind myself that I didn't actually know her at all. I hovered at the edge of the yard for a moment, gathering my courage. Then I cleared my throat.

"I should have known you still weren't actually gone," she said, barely bothering to look up at me. "You're like a possum or something. Some animal that lives in someone's alley and eats their garbage. Who's always on the lookout for something rotten."

"Yeah," I admitted, forcing myself not to fidget. "That . . . pretty much sums it up."

Eliza was quiet for a moment, running the corner of her book cover back and forth underneath her thumbnail. "None of us wanted this to happen, you know," she said softly. "I mean, you've made it pretty clear that you think we're a bunch of remorseless country-club monsters, but we were real friends, once upon a time. All of us were—my brothers, Meredith, Greg." She shook her head. "Haven't you ever hated your friends a little?" she asked. "Haven't they ever said or done something that made you think you'd be better off without them?"

I swallowed hard, trying not to glance in the direction of the driveway. "Yeah," I said again, then: "Eliza." I ran a hand over my jaw. "We both know I owe you one hell of an apology."

Eliza let out a sharp, brittle laugh. "Oh, Linden," she said, looking at me with some pity. "Please don't."

"No," I said, "I mean it. For last night, obviously. I was drunk, and I was amped, and I had no idea what I was talking about, but that's no excuse."

"No," she agreed coolly. "It's really not."

I could feel myself shriveling under the weight of her obvious contempt, but I made myself keep going anyway. It had been more than just small behavior, the way I'd treated her. Whatever fucked-up stuff had happened in this house the last couple of weeks, I didn't want to be someone who added to it. "That's not all I want to say, though. I wanted to apologize for just . . . how I've acted with you in general. For being so distracted by the person you were in my head that I couldn't see the person you actually were. The person you were trying to show me. You deserved better, and I'm sorry."

I saw surprise flicker over her face at that. For a moment I thought it might have gotten through, that we'd be able to part ways as, if not exactly friends, then at least not as enemies.

"Well!" she said, her voice taking on that bright, cheerful cruise-director quality that I knew meant I was headed for danger. "Whatever image of me you've got in your head now, you should try to forget about her." She smiled, and it looked like a razor blade. "I'm going to forget about you the minute you leave."

I nodded. "I deserved that," I told her. "But I hope we see each other again."

"I don't." Eliza's tone was final. "Goodbye, Linden."

I looked at her for another minute, then turned to go, skirting back around the side of the house to avoid the Kendricks and the police. I was just making my way through the garden, which was bursting with end-of-summer produce the Kendricks wouldn't be here to eat, when I heard the sound of someone sucking in a ragged breath. I turned and there was Jasper on one of the wicker couches on the side porch, his head dropped so I couldn't see his face. "Hey," I said. "You good?"

"What?" Jasper snapped upright, like a soldier being unexpectedly called to attention. There was an expression on his face I didn't recognize, vulnerable and half-wild. In fact, it almost looked like he'd been . . . crying? "Dude," he said, clearing something phlegmy from his throat, "how the fuck are you still here?"

He was smiling as he said it; he'd pulled himself together just like he always did, forever an illusionist. But this time, I didn't believe the trick. "I don't actually know," I admitted sheepishly, "and I swear I'm going to get out of your face for real in a hot second, but . . . seriously. Are you okay?"

I watched as he drew himself up, his mouth opening to launch into what I knew would be assurances about how fine and okay he was. But then he just sort of . . . sagged. "You know," he said, his voice so quiet I almost didn't hear him, "he wasn't always such a bad guy."

For a moment I truly had no idea who he was talking about. Then it clicked. "Greg?" I asked, surprised.

"Yeah." Jasper wiped his face roughly with the back of his hand. "Look, I know everybody thinks he was a total shithead. And don't get me wrong, I hated his fucking guts this last year. But we were kids together, you know? Like, my literal first fucking memory is us catching hermit crabs together down on the beach." He shook his head. "I don't know what happens to someone," he told me. "When they're just . . . gone like that."

I nodded slowly, wanting to say the right thing to comfort him and not sure exactly what that might be. I thought again of them all growing up side by side, the Kendricks and Greg and Meredith— all of them born into these long, golden dynasties, none of them having any reason to think it would ever end. Jasper was nothing if not a prince of privilege, and in a lot of ways it was hard to feel sorry for him. Still, at the end of the day his best friend from when he was a little kid was lying dead in a morgue somewhere. Mine was waiting for me out in the car. "I'm really sorry, Jas."

"Yeah, well." He shrugged, lifting his chin in a way that was almost defiant. "Shit happens, right?"

"Shit does." I smiled a little, half-hearted. "Can I ask you something?" I said. It had been eating at me since the first night I'd gotten to the Vineyard, an unanswered question at the back of my mind. "All last year, back at the dorms . . . why didn't you tell me about what was going on with your dad?"

"I'm not embarrassed," Jasper said immediately, his voice fierce. "Whatever my brother might think, I'm loyal to this family. But there's some shit in life you don't really want to talk about, you know? Not even with the people you're close to." He glanced at me sidelong, smirking a little. "Not that it made a difference to you and Ms. Singh. You guys dug up the dirt on everybody, whether they wanted you to have it or not."

I cringed at that, a prickly heat creeping up the back of my neck. I wanted to explain to him that it wasn't what Holiday and I had been trying to do, that we'd only wanted to help, but even as the excuse formed in my head, I knew it wasn't entirely true. There was a part of me that had resented the Kendricks, whether or not I'd admitted it to myself. A part of me that had wanted to prove they weren't as perfect as they seemed.

We stood there in silence for a moment, both of us deep in our own heads. I'd spent a lot of time over the last few days wondering what other secrets Jasper might be keeping from me, if he was really the kind of person I'd thought. But if anyone here had spent his vacation—hell, his entire life—playing a long, complicated game of Lies, it wasn't him.

I took a deep breath. "Listen," I said, "in the spirit of putting it all out there: there's some stuff I haven't been honest with you about."

Jasper cleared his throat one more time, looking at me with some interest. "Oh no?"

I shook my head. "I'm at Bartley on a full scholarship," I confessed. "Back in Boston, I live with my mom in a two-bedroom apartment above our landlady. I didn't even have an internship this summer—I needed to bank as much money as I could, so I worked doubles at Star Market six days a week. I'm not like the rest of you guys—I never have been. I'm completely broke."

Jasper gazed at me for another moment. Then he nodded. "Dude," he said, "I know."

I gaped at him. "You—what?"

Jasper sat back down on the edge of the porch. "Relax, Linden," he said with a smile. "You talk a good game and everything, but it's kind of obvious."

"It is?" I opened my mouth to ask him how I'd given myself away, how I could possibly keep it from happening again, if other people knew. Then I realized it was beside the point.

Jasper rolled his eyes. "This isn't a Brat Pack movie, dude. Nobody cares about that shit but you."

I didn't think that was true, not really. But just for a moment, I wondered what might have happened if I'd given him the chance to prove me wrong.

I glanced over my shoulder in the direction of the driveway. "I should go," I said finally.

Jasper nodded. "Sure," he said, flattening his palms against the floor of the porch and leaning backward. He was already turning into himself again: easygoing, casually bulletproof. "I'll see you back at school, yeah?"

"Yeah," I said, "totally"—though in truth I had no idea if he would or not. My scholarship wasn't a sure thing. If I didn't head back to Bartley, I doubted our friendship would survive. It was entirely possible we'd never see each other again.

I didn't say anything like that, though—just lifted my hand in a wave before I headed around the front of the house. Holiday was waiting in the driveway, sitting on the hood of the sedan with her feet up on the bumper. She looked tired, a little bit ragged. But she also looked satisfied as all hell.

"So," she said brightly, hopping down and sliding behind the wheel. "How was your vacation?"

I snorted. "Wasn't all bad," I said, collapsing into the passenger seat.

Holiday glanced behind her as she put the car into gear, pulling down the long, winding driveway. "Oh no?" she asked with a grin. "Which parts made it especially worth it to you? The capital crime or the public humiliation?"

"The fried clams," I deadpanned, and Holiday laughed. The sun broke through the clouds just as we pulled out onto the main road, the damp pavement gleaming in front of us. I rolled my window down, the cool breeze on my face helping to clear my head. "I owe you an apology," I told her.

Holiday nodded. "I mean, yes," she said with a smile, "you do. By all means, please proceed."

"Not just for what happened last night, though make no mistake, I was a giant douchebag and I'm really fucking sorry. But also for just kind of . . . disappearing off the face of the planet for the last few years."

Holiday shrugged. "We both disappeared," she pointed out. "Lucky for us, the universe has a way of course-correcting." She grinned. "You know. With like, a casual murder."

"I think that was probably their real motive," I agreed.

"Oh, for sure."

"I couldn't have figured any of this out without you," I told her. "I mean, I *didn't* figure any of this out. You did. I feel like I was wrong about everyone and everything from the first second I got off the ferry."

Holiday shrugged. "You were right about one thing," she admitted, "as profoundly as it pains me to admit it. I *was* jealous, honestly. Not because I'm desperate to bone you," she clarified quickly, even as my heart did a funny thing inside my chest. "But the truth is I missed you, all those years we weren't really talking. And I liked hanging out with you again. I guess there was a part of me that was worried that if you got in deep with Eliza, that would be over." She grinned. "Lucky for me, Eliza hates your fucking guts now."

"Fuck you!" I said, but I was laughing. "She definitely does, though."

"Oh, for sure." We were approaching the ferry dock now; Holiday turned into the parking lot and pulled to a stop. "Good luck at Bartley," she said. "Don't wait until somebody else gets killed before you text me again, yeah?"

"I won't," I promised, leaning over the gearshift to give her a hug. Her hair smelled like tea and like salt water, soft against the side of my face. "Grand larceny next time, how about?"

"Arson, maybe." She smiled. "Take care, Michael."

"You too."

I was one of the last people to make it onto the ferry, and it was already crowded when I climbed on board. I made my way onto the uppermost deck, the sun warm on the back of my neck. Most of the benches were occupied, but I found a place to stand by the railing, the engine humming through the soles of my sneakers. I watched as Holiday pulled out of the parking lot, her hand thrust through the window in a wave like she knew I'd be looking. It occurred to me that, all things considered, I probably should have felt a lot worse than I did.

We'd barely left the port when I felt the familiar buzz of my phone in my back pocket. I dug it out, fully expecting a text from my mom about where she should meet me back in Boston; my heart tripped in my chest when I saw the name on the screen.

Greer.

I know I'm probably the last person you want to hear from, she'd written, *but we need to talk.*

The ferry pitched underneath me, or at least that's what it felt like; I gripped the railing with my free hand to keep from stumbling, though the sea was resolutely calm. I hit the icon to dial Greer's number like a reflex, and she picked up almost before it rang. "I didn't know if you'd call," she said, instead of hello.

"Of course I called," I said, trying to ignore both the twist in my gut at the sound of her voice and the knowledge that she wasn't actually surprised at all. That was how our relationship had always worked: I came when she beckoned. She wanted me, I showed up.

She asked me to do something, and I did it.

No matter the consequences.

I glanced back in the direction of the Vineyard, the lush green island receding in the distance. "Greer," I said, trying to keep my voice even. "What's going on?"

ACKNOWLEDGMENTS

Liar's Beach is brand-new territory for me in many ways, and I am deeply grateful to everyone who not only believed in my ability to do it but actively helped me get it done. Thank you to my editor, Wendy Loggia, and the entire team at Delacorte Press, especially Alison Romig, Emily Harburg, Alison Impey, Casey Moses, Megan Shortt, Colleen Fellingham, Tamar Schwartz, Tracy Heydweiller, and incredible cover artist Ewelina Dymek. To everyone at Alloy Entertainment, always, but especially Viana Siniscalchi and Sara Shandler and particularly Josh Bank, who liked my weird idea from the beginning. Love and endless gratitude to the friends and colleagues whose texts and emails and DMs have made the last couple of years significantly less lonely, and especially to my family, without whom none of the rest of it would matter at all. I am so enormously lucky.

THEY'LL DO ANYTHING
TO KEEP A SECRET.

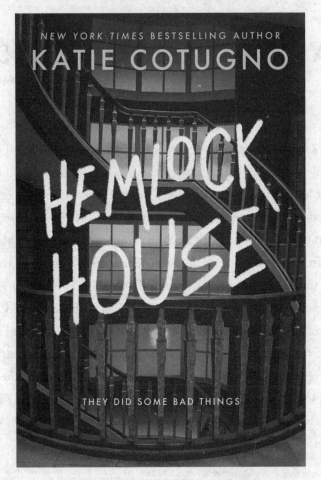

NEW YORK TIMES BESTSELLING AUTHOR

KATIE COTUGNO

HEMLOCK HOUSE

THEY DID SOME BAD THINGS

KEEP READING FOR A PREVIEW!

1

Thursday, 10/17/24

A FACT THAT SEEMS RELEVANT TO MENTION BEFORE we begin, though of course it didn't occur to me to look it up until much later: statistically, it's actually very unlikely for a person to fall victim to a violent crime in the city of Cambridge, Massachusetts.

The rate of robbery is remarkably low, at just 52.6 annually per 100,000 residents, compared to 135.5 throughout the United States and 118 just across the Charles River in Boston. Rates of assault are admittedly higher, though occurrences still clock in well below the national average, with a rate of 224.3 per 100,000 residents.

And murder? Well, murder is rarest of all, with a rate of just 0.8 per 100,000 residents, compared to a national average of 6.1. "Even if you were *trying* to get murdered in Cambridge," Holiday mused later, eyes narrowed behind the metal rims of her giant glasses, "you'd really have to, like, apply yourself."

At least, that's what we'd always thought.

Anyway, like I said, I didn't know any of that the fall of my first year at Harvard, and I probably wouldn't have cared about it even if I did. Anyone trying to tell me would have had to shout over the sound of my teammates egging me on as I stood on a metal folding chair and shotgunned a hard seltzer in the dining room of the lax house, the sweet, fizzy dregs of it trickling down the side of my neck and into the collar of my hoodie.

"He's got style, he's got grace!" Cam declared as I finished, clapping me hard between my shoulder blades. Every first-year lacrosse player was paired with an upperclassman mentor, and he was mine; in the weeks since I'd arrived on campus he'd not only set my daily workout plan and invited me over to watch the Pats on Sundays but had also imparted such valuable information as which dining halls had the best cereal selection and never to use the shower stall next to Ryan Jakes, a junior defenseman who was notorious for pissing into the communal drain. "He's Miss United States."

"Thank you, thank you." I wiped my mouth with the back of my hand, fully aware that this was absolutely not, under any circumstances, an achievement for which to feel proud of myself, but feeling a tiny bit proud of myself anyway. It's always kind of a high-wire act, trying to figure out where and how to fit in on a new team. If *cheerful drunk* wasn't quite what I wanted to be known as over the next four years, it was a better position to start from than *whiny little bitch who can't hang*. "As always, I appreciate your love and support."

"Let's see him go again," suggested Dex Rutland, a sophomore midfielder. The grin on his pale, freckled face just missed being friendly. "What do you say, Linden?"

of the upperclassmen on the lacrosse team had moved off campus a few years back, when Harvard randomized their housing selection process and made it harder for teams to self-sort into particular dorms. Since then, the lease on this place had been passed from one lax captain to the next, the walls and floors and carpets bearing the not-inconsiderable scars of hundreds of parties way wilder than this one. "Come on," I shouted over the noise, jerking my thumb in the direction of the kitchen. "I'll get you a drink."

Greer let me take her hand as we weaved through the crush of bodies in the narrow center hallway, past the once-grand front staircase that led up to the bedrooms and the tiny little telephone nook tucked underneath. "That's cute," she said when she noticed it, and she sounded sincere, which I took to mean she hadn't looked closely enough to see the giant, erupting cock and balls carved into the woodwork of the antique bench.

The kitchen was mercifully empty, the heavy door swinging shut behind us and muffling the clatter of the party. Greer hopped up onto the scarred Formica counter as I pulled a beer from one of the picnic coolers lined up beside the door to the cluttered mudroom, handing it over before grabbing one for myself and perching against the edge of the wobbly wooden table. "So," I said, reaching out and clinking my can against hers, "what's up?"

Cam looked at me, the question clear in the wrinkle of his smooth brown forehead. I was just about to oblige—one thing about me, for better or for worse, is that I will basically never back down from a dare—when I felt a slice of cold air from the direction of the foyer and caught sight of a familiar cardinal-red peacoat slipping in through the front door.

"Hey!" I called a beat too quickly, hopping down off the chair so fast my bad ankle nearly gave out and left me sprawled on the dingy Persian rug. I ignored the goading jeers of my teammates as I threaded my eager way through the crowd. "You came."

"I came," Greer agreed with a forbearing smile, tucking her hands into her pockets and popping up onto the toes of her boots, pressing her cold cheek against mine. She wore a pair of round tortoiseshell glasses and an oversized L.L.Bean pullover, a vintage Tiffany bean around her neck. "I like old things," she'd told me once, the two of us sprawled on my bed back at the Western Massachusetts boarding school we'd attended together. Now, two years later, I couldn't help but hope that included boyfriends. "Hi."

"Hi yourself," I said, my heart vibrating dorkily in my chest. "I didn't think you were going to show."

"I almost didn't," she confessed, "but Bri is already here somewhere, so I figured—" She broke off, eyes narrowing as she looked across the warm, crowded living room, where Dex had graciously taken over in my stead and was already halfway through a twenty-four-ounce can of White Claw. "I thought you said this was going to be, like, a chill, low-key kind of thing."

"Is this not low-key?" I asked sheepishly, my voice getting lost as the rest of the guys erupted into cheers over my shoulder. Most